SYNTHETIC IDENTITY

A TYLER NETWORK THRILLER

THE TYLER NETWORK

SCOTT TISCH

SCOTT TISCH BOOKS

Published by Scott Tisch Books

Cover design by Greg Hoffman

Edited by Beth Dorward

First edition: May 2026

❀ Formatted with Vellum

For Judi and Paul - We all miss you!

1

STEAK 954

It was no surprise that he called the meeting at Steak 954 in The W Hotel; it had been my favorite restaurant before I moved away from Fort Lauderdale. I had no idea why my father would ask me to a business meeting when I'd left the family business on no uncertain terms four years ago. I took a deep breath as I pulled up to the valet.

This place looks the same.

The beach looked amazing, the palm trees swaying in the light ocean breeze. There were lots of spring-breakers and that meant lots to look at. *Not now.*

I entered and approached the table and saw the empty chair between my older brother Randy and my father Tommy.

Four years is a long time. Long enough that the man sitting at the head of the table didn't quite match the version I'd been carrying around in my head. Tommy Tyler had always been a big man, broad through the chest and shoulders, the kind of frame that made a room feel smaller when he walked into it. That was still there. But the edges had softened. His dark hair, slicked back the way he'd worn it my entire life, had gone gray at the temples. The skin around his eyes looked thinner, slightly hollowed, and there was a roughness to his face that hadn't been there before. He'd aged ten years in four. The gold chain still caught the light. The linen shirt was still unbuttoned one button too many. But underneath the old swagger, something was wearing down, and he either didn't know it or didn't care.

He spotted me and his whole face changed. That was the thing about Tommy. When he turned on the charm, you forgot everything else. You forgot the hollowed eyes and the rough skin and the fact that he hadn't called you in six months. You just saw your father, glad to see you, and for about ten seconds it felt real.

Randy stood and waved me over.

My brother had always been the bigger one. Four years older, two inches taller, thirty pounds heavier, and not an ounce of it wasted. Where I could disappear into a room if I wanted to, Randy filled every corner of one. He was wearing a patterned shirt that probably cost more than my rent, sleeves pushed up to show the Rolex he'd bought himself the year I left. His dark hair was styled with the kind of effort that's supposed to look effortless but never does when you know the person. We had the same coloring, the same brown eyes, the same jaw. People used to say we looked like the same guy drawn by two different artists. Randy was the bolder version. Louder lines, more contrast, everything turned up.

"There he is." Randy motioned to the nearest waiter. "Get this man a drink."

"Some things never change." I nodded at my brother.

"Look at you." Randy shook his head, grinning. "Same

haircut, same jeans, same nothing. Four years in Maryland and you still dress like you're trying not to be noticed."

"Maybe I'm not."

"That's the problem, Danny. You're not bad looking. You clean up fine. But you walk around like you're auditioning for the role of guy in the background. Meanwhile I'm out here carrying the family's reputation." He straightened his shirt collar for emphasis.

"Welcome back, it's good to see you. It's been a long time." My father stood to embrace me.

I broke away and spent a few minutes making my way around the table, saying hello to the group, some of whom I hadn't seen in ages.

Anthony Jr. was there; he always was when Tommy called a meeting. We'd grown up together, two kids running deliveries for our fathers before we could legally drive. Where Randy was my brother by blood, Anthony was my brother by choice.

He looked good. Better than good, actually. Anthony had always been handsome in a way that snuck up on you. Not loud about it like Randy. He was my height, maybe an inch shorter, with his father's olive complexion and dark eyes that moved fast and missed nothing. His black hair was cut shorter than I remembered, cleaner, pushed back off his forehead in a way that reminded me of old photos of Uncle Tony in his thirties. He'd filled out since I'd seen him last. Still lean, but there was a solidity to him now, like someone who'd grown into his frame. He was wearing a fitted black shirt, no logo, nice watch that wasn't a Rolex but wasn't cheap either. The kind of thing you'd notice only if you knew what to look for. That was Anthony. He could sit at this table full of guys dripping gold and designer labels and somehow look like the most put-together person in the room without trying. He still had the neighborhood in him, though. You could see it in the way he sat; one arm draped over the back of the empty chair next to him, legs spread wide, taking up space the way guys from Queens do without thinking about it. Half wiseguy, half something else. Something his father was turning him into, whether Anthony realized it yet or not.

We'd been partners for years, handling logistics and money laundering while our fathers moved product.

He stood up and pulled me into a hug. "Danny. Been too long, man."

"Four years. You look good."

"Clean living." He grinned. We both knew that was bullshit.

Adam Freeman sat near the end of the table, quiet as always. I'd known Adam since I was a kid; he'd been around Tommy's operation for as long as I could remember, though his exact role was always unclear. Problem solver, maybe. Or fixer. The guy you called when normal solutions didn't work.

Where Tommy was fading, Adam had only gotten sharper. He was lean and trim, the kind of fit that came from discipline rather than any gym. His silver hair was neatly combed, not a strand out of place. Clean-shaven. Angular face. Pale blue eyes that gave you absolutely nothing unless he decided otherwise. He wore a navy sport coat over an open-collared shirt, and I'd have bet everything in my checking account that both cost more than anything else at this table, including Randy's Rolex. But where Randy wore money like a billboard, Adam wore it like a uniform. Quiet. Precise. Every detail intentional.

"Adam," I said, nodding.

"Danny. Good to have you back." He stood, shook my

hand. His grip was firm but brief. Everything about Adam was economical. No wasted words. No unnecessary gestures.

"Didn't expect to see you here."

"Your father asked me to sit in." He said it the way you'd mention the weather. Nobody asked why. He had a reputation for making problems disappear. How he did it, nobody knew.

"Things are good?"

"Keeping busy, you know how it is." He had a way of being present without revealing anything about himself.

"Good to see you." I moved on to the next person, filing away the fact that Adam was here. Tommy didn't bring Adam to meetings unless he was expecting complications. Which meant this pitch, whatever it was, was bigger than I'd thought.

I moved around the rest of the table. A couple of Tommy's old partners whose names I'd never bothered to learn. No new faces; that wasn't surprising. My father liked to keep his group small and tight because any one of them could probably get him sent up for five to ten.

As I sat down, I noticed Anthony watching me with that look he got when he was trying to figure something out.

"What?" I asked.

"Just wondering if you're really as miserable up there as Randy says you are."

"Randy talks too much."

"Randy's usually right." Anthony took a sip of his drink. "Maryland's not you, Danny. Never was."

"Maybe I'm trying to be someone different."

"Maybe. Or maybe you're just postponing the inevitable." He raised his glass. "Either way, good to see you."

I clinked glasses with him, wondering if he already knew

what Tommy and Randy were planning. Probably. Anthony always knew.

Woody the waiter came to the table; I hadn't seen him in a while so we bullshitted for a few minutes. I ordered the surf and turf, mid-rare. While we were waiting for our food, we made small talk. The tension was palpable. I didn't have to wait long to find out why.

Randy took a sip of his Stoli and grapefruit, turned to me. "So. Look, Dad and I, now that you came back." He set down his drink. "We need to talk."

"I'm not back."

"That's what we need to talk about." Tommy did his impression of The Godfather. "It's time you came back to the family." It had been said to make me laugh, but I knew he wasn't joking.

"Do we have to get into this again? I'm not interested. I'm engaged to a very sweet girl and I live in Maryland!"

"Come on. Don't." Randy laughed. "Danny. We talk every couple months. I know you're miserable." He leaned closer. "The white picket fence thing? How long before you snap?"

"Danny. Danny." Tommy rubbed his face. "Who raised you? Remember the…" He looked at the ceiling. "Larceny in your blood. It's in there." He tapped his own chest. "Loyalty, Danny. Where's your loyalty?"

Loyalty. Right. This from the man who'd chosen getting high over my safety more times than I could count. The man who'd missed my high school graduation because he was on a three-day bender. The man who'd left twelve-year-old me alone in a car outside a crack house for four hours while he "handled business."

But that was the thing about Tommy. He could say the word "loyalty" with a straight face because he'd rewritten history in his head. In his version, he was father of the year. And somehow, even knowing better, part of me still wanted to believe him.

"This is bullshit. I told you a long time ago, I'm done with the drug thing."

"This one isn't about drugs, but it's a hell of a game," said Randy.

"I don't care."

"Yeah you do. I can see it in your eyes. You're dying to know what we're into, otherwise you wouldn't be here." Tommy had a big smile on his face, as if this was a tennis match and he had just won a point.

"Besides," said Randy, "we need your particular skills for this one."

"That means there's lots of cash and computers involved."

"This honest life. The. What is it, five hundred a week? Something like that?" Tommy laughed too loud. "Right?"

I put my head down, ashamed. "$650." My voice was low. I missed the things good money could buy. I was miserable. My fiancée could never truly understand where I came from; she could never understand the mentality behind this kind of operation.

Tommy laughed. "Really? You were making more than that when you were twelve."

"How long you gonna..." Randy shook his head. "The straight-edge thing. The boring bullshit." He gestured vaguely north. "Before you lose it? Before you..." He stopped. "Just be yourself, Danny."

I was battling internally, knowing they were right. I wanted to be where the action was. Diana couldn't give me what I needed. There was no action in Maryland, and eventually the little façade of a life I'd built there would drive me crazy. This was about resisting the danger of my family, but the truth was, no matter how dangerous that life was, I missed it.

"Let's talk about this later. I just got here. I'd like to catch up with everyone." I watched Woody heading toward the table.

Woody always took care of us. "Hey Danny, you haven't been around in a while. You wanna make a bet?"

"Not today, man. I'm just here for the food and the scenery." A group of bikini-clad college girls walked by.

"Did you rent a car?" asked Randy.

"Yeah, Mustang convertible."

Woody placed our food on the table.

"Good. Be at my place at nine-thirty tonight. I got a surprise for you. Meanwhile, let's eat."

"Oh shit, I'm in trouble now," I said.

After the meal, Dad left the restaurant. "You boys have fun tonight."

LATER, as I was driving across town to Randy's, I knew they were going to take me out and show me how much fun it would be if I moved back.

When I pulled the Mustang into Randy's driveway, the white stretch limo was waiting. Randy was standing by the open door with a bottle of Veuve Clicquot. I took a deep breath and took the bottle from his hand.

"Took you long enough. Come on, get in," said Randy.

Seated inside the limo were my stepbrothers Jake and Colin, Chester and Vick (Randy's crew), and our longtime family friend Alex. Randy waited while I got into the limo, jumping in after me. Cliff, our regular driver, closed the door.

"Here..." Alex passed me a joint of high-grade exotics.

"I heard you were moving back." Chester passed me the mirror.

"Don't get ahead of yourself." I passed the mirror to Colin without sampling its contents. "I haven't decided anything."

"You know you're gonna move down. Why you fighting it so hard?" Randy smiled.

"Give the guy a break," said Jake. "It's his first night in town. You've got all weekend to convince him."

"Seriously Randy, you're way too intense for this early," said Alex.

"What's our first stop anyway?" I asked.

"I thought we'd have a drink at Pier 66," said Randy.

We got out of the limo and headed to the revolving restaurant at the top of Pier 66 on 17th Street, with its panoramic view of Fort Lauderdale's famous waterways. In a past life, we boys often came here to talk business. Randy and I went to the bar while the rest of the group checked out the girls on the dance floor.

"Give me a shot of Louis Tres," said Randy. "Actually, give him one too."

"Moving up in the world, are we?" We clinked glasses.

"Danny. Listen. Bigger than..." He whistled. "Biggest we've ever had."

"That's a bold statement coming from you. We've made a shitload of cash together."

"This is bigger," said Randy.

"No drugs, right?"

"Dad and I both promised you that we wouldn't involve you in that. We'll stick to that."

"Okay, you've got my attention," I said. "Tell me."

"It's white collar. Clean. Smart." Randy paused, watching my face. "Uses your particular skill set."

I kept my expression neutral, but my mind was already working. White collar. My skill set. That meant data, systems, something technical. Credit, maybe. Or identity.

Randy grinned. "There it is."

"There's what?"

"That look. You're already running scenarios in your head. I can practically hear the gears turning." He took another sip. "What are you up to, three possibilities? Four?"

"I don't know what you're talking about."

"Bullshit. You've got that look you used to get when we were kids and Dad would describe a job. Half the time you'd figured out the angle before he finished explaining it." Randy leaned back, enjoying himself. "So what do you think we're into?"

"I'm not playing this game."

"You're already playing it. You just don't want to admit it." He raised his glass. "Your piece could be as big as twenty-five grand a week."

I nearly choked on my $300 shot of cognac. "You're kidding, right?"

"Nope."

"So what is it? What's the play? You need something hacked?"

Randy shook his head. "Not here. Tomorrow. Dad's place. Dinner." He raised his glass. "Then we talk."

"Come on, Randy. You drag me down here, dangle

twenty-five K a week in front of me, and you're not gonna tell me what the hell this is?"

"Exactly right." He set his glass down, turning to face me fully. "This is...look, it's not street-level, five-minute explanation over drinks. No." He shook his head. "Sophisticated. Technical. Your wheelhouse." He paused. "Dad wants to lay it out right."

"Why the mystery?"

"Because we need to know you're serious first. Tomorrow night. Dad's place. Eight o'clock. You show up, we'll lay it all out. But Danny." He grabbed my shoulder. "If you're not interested, just fly back to Maryland tomorrow. We'll never mention it again."

"That's an ultimatum."

"That's a choice." Randy released my shoulder. "Tonight, enjoy yourself. Think about what you really want. Tomorrow night, we'll show you how to get it."

I could see Jake and the rest of the group heading in our direction.

"Okay, I want to know more. Let's talk details tomorrow."

"Are you assholes done talking business yet? We want to go out," said Vick.

"Damien confirmed for eleven. His new venue. Capacity's around eight hundred, VIP section holds twelve to fifteen." Colin looked excited, which was kinda off brand for him.

Randy dropped a two-hundred-dollar tip on the bar and called Cliff on his phone. "We're on our way down."

~

WE COULD SEE the line wrapped around the building,

waiting to get into the club as the limo pulled up to the velvet ropes.

"Showtime," said Randy.

"Let the games begin," I said.

As far as the club owners were concerned, we were members of a famous band, complete with an entourage. We had done this before. Everyone had a part to play. Alex was security. As the limo door opened, he was the first one out, a pro. Alex knew exactly how to play his role. He stepped out, did a quick scan of the crowd to make sure it was safe for the rest of us, then a discreet wave letting us know it was okay.

Next out of the limo was Colin, Randy's personal assistant. The first thing he did was walk over to the bouncer with a $200 handshake. The bouncer spoke into the microphone on his lapel. Before we knew it, the club owner was at the door greeting Colin with a hug.

"Hey, there he is. What's up, my brother?" asked Damien.

"It's been a while. Whatcha been up to?" Colin asked as Damien headed toward the car.

"This place is keeping me on my toes, man. It's nuts, but I wouldn't have it any other way. Come on, get the rest of the gang. Just wait until you see the room I got set up for you guys."

The rest of us got out of the limo. Randy, the lead singer, dressed in a loud red and yellow Versace shirt and dark sunglasses. He walked like the rock star he was portraying. Randy was followed by Jake, Chester, and Vick, all members of the band, all dressed in Bernini shirts and jeans, also with the requisite sunglasses. I was the last out of the limo, dressed in my blue Hugo Boss suit with white silk tee shirt. I was the tour manager.

The entranceway to the club was wall-to-wall auto-graphed pictures of famous people. The last time we were at one of Damien's clubs we had all signed one; I saw it on the wall as we passed through. We were led, with bouncers front and rear, and Damien beside us, through the main level of the club. The thumping bass was intense as I noticed the bodies crowded on the dance floor. The lighting seemed to be moving to the music as we turned left and headed up the stairs that led to the club's second level, alternative music playing, mellower than downstairs. Once we reached the second level, Damien took out a set of keys.

"Here we go, best VIP room on the planet." Damien called the bouncer over. "Mike, you are on this door for the rest of the night. No one in unless they're with one of these guys. I set up the basics for a bar. Let me know if you need anything else."

We entered the room. Huge sliding glass windows looked down on the main dance floor. The room was furnished with long soft velvet couches. Two very attractive waitresses were assigned to us for the rest of the evening.

"This is amazing," said Chester. "Can we bring some of those girls up here?"

"Which ones?" asked Damien. Chester pointed. "No problem. I'll be back in a few minutes."

I got myself a Grey Goose and cranberry and sat down to take in the scene. Randy was sitting back on one of the couches. He had this thing he did when he wanted to project an image that had an almost hypnotizing effect on everyone within range of his mojo. In this case, he decided to be a rock star and everything around him transformed to fit that narrative, almost as if he were projecting the image in his mind out onto the world.

Jake settled onto the couch next to me, watching Randy work the room.

"You know what I love about Randy?" Jake's voice was flat. "He actually believes it. Every time. He's not pretending to be a rock star. In his head, he is one. The rest of us are just living in his reality."

"That's either impressive or insane," I said.

"Little of both." Colin appeared with drinks. "The truly scary part is that it works. Watch those waitresses. They're not faking it. They genuinely think he's somebody."

"He is somebody," I said. "Just not who they think."

"Story of this whole family," Jake said.

"You love this crap, don't you?" I asked Randy as he came over.

"So do you. That's why you're here." Randy leaned back, surveying his kingdom. "Look, it's gonna be different this time. I'm just using the game as a means to go legit."

"You, legit. That's funny."

"Ha ha," he said. "Seriously, I'm using the money from this to finance a record. I'm gonna make this real. I want you to produce it. You know about music, you know about business. I need you. The four brothers united once again, and we just use the game to get us there."

Damien arrived with four models, some of the most beautiful women I'd ever seen. One of them, a blonde about five-eight with an amazing figure and deep blue eyes, came over and sat on my lap.

"I know you're not getting this up in Maryland," Randy said as he gestured to the room.

"True that!"

I SPENT the rest of the night dancing and hanging out with Danni, the model who'd been sitting on my lap. We danced and drank and snorted cocaine and disappeared into the limo for several hours. The seduction was at full force now. Randy knew that I was thoroughly bored at home, and broke. For someone with a background like mine, this is a dangerous combination.

I woke up the next afternoon with searing pain inside my head, and a beautiful blonde lying with her head on my chest. It had been at least five years since I'd partied like that. I swallowed four aspirin with a large glass of Gatorade. I stumbled out of the bed trying to figure out where I was. A boat. A nice one, docked at one of the fancy marinas off 17th Street. And I had no idea how I'd come to be here. No crew around, no captain. Clearly Randy had arranged for privacy.

I found my clothes and made my way out of the cabin and stood alone in the beautiful Florida sunshine, dark glasses protecting my eyes. I heard footsteps on the deck behind me before a pair of soft arms encircled my waist as lips kissed the nape of my neck.

"Good morning," said Danni, in a sexy morning-after voice.

"Good morning." I turned to face her. Her arms still encircled my waist, our bodies pressed closely together. I took off my sunglasses, gently took her face in my hands, and kissed her passionately.

"I was hoping you were a morning person." She broke the embrace, took me by the hand, and led me back into the cabin.

"Morning, noon, night. You are absolutely beautiful, how could I resist?"

I stood with my back facing the bed. I grabbed Danni and kissed her with intensity and passion. I slowly moved my lips to the back of her neck. I could feel the goose bumps appearing on her skin, the pace of her breathing increasing as she let out a soft moan. We found ourselves back in bed doing what came naturally.

I KISSED Danni goodbye and called Jake to pick me up. I was waiting in the marina office, nursing a bottle of water and trying not to die from my hangover when my phone rang.

Diana.

Shit.

I stared at the screen for three rings, debating whether to answer. If I didn't, she'd just call back. If I did, I'd have to lie to her. Again.

I answered. "Hey."

"Hey yourself." Her voice was warm, relieved. "I was getting worried. You didn't call me back last night."

"Sorry, it got late. Family stuff ran long."

"How's it going down there? How's your dad?"

"He's good. Same as always." I watched a boat pull into the marina, its wake gently rocking the other vessels. "How are you? How was school?"

"Exhausting. Twenty-four second graders on a Friday is basically controlled chaos." She laughed. That laugh I used to love. Still loved, in a way that made everything more complicated. "I'm just grading papers. Missing you."

I could still smell Danni's perfume on my clothes.

"Miss you too."

"When's your flight back?"

"Sunday night. Late."

"Danny, is everything okay? You sound weird."

"Just hungover. Randy took us out last night."

"Of course he did." She sighed. "Did you at least have fun?"

"It was fine. You know Randy. Always has to make everything into a production."

"Well, try to behave yourself today. And don't let them talk you into anything crazy."

If she only knew.

"I won't," I lied.

"Promise?"

"Yeah, promise."

Another pause. Longer this time. When she spoke again, her voice was quieter. "Danny, I know your family can be... intense. But you're coming back, right? I mean, you're not, you wouldn't..."

"Diana, I'm coming back. Sunday, I promise."

"Okay. Good." The relief in her voice made it worse. "I love you."

The words stuck in my throat. I'd said them a thousand times. Meant them, even. But sitting here in a marina office, smelling like another woman's perfume, wearing sunglasses to hide my hangover, they felt like ash in my mouth.

"Love you too," I said anyway.

"See you tomorrow night. Safe flight."

"See you tomorrow."

I hung up and stared at the phone in my hand.

Tomorrow night I'd be in Maryland. Eating chicken parmesan. Listening to Diana talk about her students. Pretending to be the man she thought I was.

The man I'd tried to be for four years.

The man I wasn't sure I could be anymore.

My phone buzzed with a text from Jake: *Outside.*

I stood, grabbed my things, took one last look at the boats in the marina. Somewhere out there, Danni was probably still asleep on that yacht; Randy had arranged it through one of his contacts. Tomorrow she'd be a memory. A story Randy would tell at parties. A mistake I'd never mention to Diana.

If I went back to Maryland.

If I could go back.

~

"Hey," I said as I got in Jake's car.

"How was your night with what's her name?"

"Danni. It was amazing, what I can remember anyway. Waking up with her was nice."

"Diana. What's the plan there?" he asked.

"I don't even want to think about it yet. I've got other things on my mind."

"Speaking of which, the old man called looking for you. I told him you were indisposed."

"Thanks."

"Don't thank me yet. You're expected at his place for dinner tonight at eight."

"So I guess tonight is the big pitch. He's gonna do everything in his power to get me to move down here."

"Why don't you just move down?" asked Jake.

"It sounds so simple when you put it like that."

Jake smiled. "You want it to be hard?"

"This is not as simple as it sounds. We're talking serious money. It's a big risk."

"I know. He approached me last week. Same pitch, different packaging."

"Dad is making some big moves, getting all four of us into it. If we go down, it's the whole family."

Jake tilted his head with a sly grin. "The family that plays together stays together."

"Yeah, but with this family we're likely to stay together in prison."

"So...more family time?" We laughed harder than I had in a long time.

"At least it'll make a good story for the book."

"That's one way to look at it."

JAKE and I arrived at Dad's house around 8:15. Randy and Colin were already there. Randy was lighting the grill because Dad was terrified to do it. Colin was playing bartender. Rachel was screaming at Dad about something or other. In other words, it was the typical family dinner at the Tyler residence.

"Hey bro, how you feeling?" asked Randy.

"I've got the hangover from hell, but aside from that, not too bad."

"What's up, Danny?" asked Colin.

"Chillin," I said.

"What happened to you last night? I saw you leave with that model chick, and then we didn't see you again." Randy showed his mischievous grin.

"Hey, you can talk while you work. Grab a knife," said Tommy.

"I picked him up at some fancy marina this afternoon," said Jake.

I started on the appetizer, sesame-seared tuna over arugula salad with citrus balsamic vinaigrette. I turned to Randy. "I woke up with Danni on some yacht. To be honest, I'm not even sure how we got there."

"Awesome. She was hot," said Colin.

"Yeah, she was," said Jake.

Randy was scoring the Porterhouse steaks and pushing some garlic into them. "I told you life is more fun down here." He started putting crumbled blue cheese onto portabella mushroom caps. "Where else are you going to party like a rock star and eat like a king?"

"Besides," Rachel said as she sat at the kitchen table rolling a joint, "it would be nice to have you in town. You need to get rid of that bitch you call a fiancée and move down."

"Don't hold back, Rachel. Tell me what you really think," I said. "Subtle as always."

"Like a brick through a plate glass window," said Jake. We both laughed.

"Let's talk about this after dinner," said Tommy. "Hey Danny, open that bottle of wine."

"Sure, what'd ya get?" I asked.

"Jordan, Cab."

"Nice."

Randy came in from putting the steaks on the grill. "Five minutes on each side and we're done."

"Make sure they're mid-rare," said Rachel, "and close the goddamned door."

"Let's smoke that before we eat," said Tommy.

Rachel lit the joint, took a hit, and passed it to me. I inhaled deeply and walked it over to my father. "Here."

"Thanks. You know, it's really nice to see you. We're family. We should be doing this more often. I've missed you." He had that look on his face, the one he got when he was working someone. The same look he used on marks, on cops, on women. The same look he probably used on my mother before she wised up and left.

The difference was, I could see it. And he knew I could see it. And he did it anyway because that's who Tommy was. He couldn't turn it off even if he wanted to.

"Me too," I said, rolling my eyes.

"Hey. Hey." He pointed at me suddenly. "Airplane. Jumping out of one. You and me." He looked around the table. "None of these..." He waved dismissively. "None of them will do it."

"Why the hell would you jump out of a perfectly good plane?" asked Randy, who was training to be a pilot.

"Because I'll have a perfectly good parachute," I answered. "I'm in. When?"

"When you move down," Dad said.

"Again with the subtlety," I said.

"Don't you love how he just sneaks those in there?" asked Jake.

"Symbolic. You know? Jumping into..." Tommy made a gesture with both hands. "New life. New everything. It'll be..." He nodded to himself. "It'll be something."

"I haven't made any decisions. Hell, I still don't know the details."

"You will," said Randy. "You will."

"Steaks have been on for six minutes per side. Should be at optimal temperature now," said Colin.

"Let's eat," said Rachel.

AFTER DINNER, Dad came up to me. "Hey, let's go into my office. I want to talk to you for a few minutes." He turned to Randy, Jake, and Colin. "Give us ten minutes, then come in."

"You got any good cigars?" I asked.

"Yeah."

We went into the office. Dad sat down behind his mahogany desk and put his feet up. He reached for the humidor on his desk and tossed me a Monte Cristo torpedo. I clipped the cigar, lit it, and sat down on the rust-colored couch across from his desk.

"Okay," he said. "What do you know?"

"Not much, just what Randy told me. White collar, something about credit, needs my computer skills."

"And what do you think about that?"

"I think I don't have enough information to think anything."

Dad leaned back, studying me. "Randy says. You know what Randy says." He waved his hand. "Smartest with computers. The system you built, you were what, fifteen? Fourteen?" He didn't wait for an answer. "The thing about computers, Daniel..."

He paused, and I could see him choosing his angle. This was Tommy in sales mode. Every word calculated, every pause strategic. I'd watched him do it my whole life. The only question was whether I'd let it work on me.

"Computers, they're only as good as..." He snapped his fingers, looking for the word. "The data. What you feed them. Garbage in." He pointed at me. "But the right data? The right data can make anything look..." He stopped, smiled. "You know what I mean."

"The right data can make anything look real."

"Exactly." He took a long pull on his cigar. "Randy tells me you understand databases. Credit bureaus, financial records, that kind of thing."

"I understand how they work, yeah."

"And if someone wanted to create...let's call them profiles. Digital profiles that looked real enough to pass veri-fication. Could you do that?"

I felt my mind start working on the problem automatically. "Depends on what kind of verification. Basic checks? Easy. If you're talking about fooling credit bureaus, that's more complicated. You'd need social security numbers that weren't flagged, addresses that checked out, employment history that matched up with..."

I stopped myself too late.

Tommy was grinning. "See? This is..." He slapped the desk. "Three steps ahead. Already. That's why we..." He stood up, paced. "That's why."

"I haven't said yes to anything."

"You don't have to say yes. You already did. Just now. The way your mind went straight to the solution instead of the problem." He came around the desk, sat on the edge closer to me. "Danny, I'm not asking you to do something you can't do. I'm asking you to do something you're built for. Something that's been in you since you were a kid taking apart my computers to see how they worked."

"That's not the same thing."

"It's exactly the same thing. Curiosity. Systems. Finding the gaps." He put a hand on my shoulder. The same gesture he'd used a thousand times. Warmth and pressure, comfort and control. "I'm not going to give you the full picture tonight. You're not back in the fold yet. But I will tell you this: it's white collar. It's technical. It plays to your strengths. And it's the kind of thing that requires someone who can see patterns, who understands systems."

"And it's illegal."

"Very." He didn't even pretend otherwise. "But it's not drugs. I promised you that. This is cleaner. Smarter. The kind of thing where if you're careful, if you're smart about it, the risk is minimal."

"There's always risk."

"True. But the reward makes it worthwhile." He opened the door. "That's all you get tonight. You want to know more? Come back. For real. Not for a visit. Come back and be part of this family again."

Randy, Jake, and Colin came in and lit cigars. Dad poured everyone a shot of Grand Marnier 150.

"So?" Randy asked, looking at me. "You interested?"

"I'm listening."

"That's not an answer."

"It's the only answer you're getting tonight."

Randy grinned. "Fair enough." He raised his glass. "To possibilities."

"To family," said Dad.

"To execution within acceptable risk parameters," said Colin, always the pragmatist. "To not screwing this up."

We drank.

"One more thing," I said. "This thing with credit. You said it needs someone who understands systems. What kind of scale are we talking about? Small operation? Or something bigger?"

Randy and Tommy exchanged a look.

"If we do this right," Randy said carefully, "it could be very big. That's why we need you to build something that can scale up. Something automated. Something that can handle volume."

"Volume means databases," I said. "Multiple data sources. Real-time verification. You'd need to pull from different systems, cross-reference, make sure everything matches up."

"Could you build that?" Tommy asked.

I thought about it. "Theoretically? Yeah. I could build something. But I'd need to know more about what you're actually trying to accomplish."

"Come back to Florida," Randy said. "Come back for real, and we'll tell you everything. But Danny," he leaned forward, "if you come back, you're all in. No halfway. We're not going to lay out the whole operation just so you can say no."

"So I'm supposed to commit without knowing what I'm committing to?"

"You know enough," said Tommy. "White collar. Technical. Needs your database skills. Involves credit systems. Could make you very, very wealthy. That's all you need to know."

He was right. It was enough. My mind was already working on it, puzzle pieces fitting together. Credit systems. Databases. Profiles that look real. Volume operation that could scale.

I was pretty sure I knew what they were doing. Or at least the general shape of it.

"I need to think about it."

"That's all we're asking," said Tommy. "Think about it. Then decide."

We finished our cigars and drinks. Randy drove me back to my hotel.

"You're going to say yes," he said as I got out of the car.

"You seem pretty confident about that."

"I know you. That look." He pointed at my face. "You're already building it in your head. The system, the architecture, the whole thing." He grinned. "You couldn't stop yourself if you tried."

He wasn't wrong.

"Get some sleep," Randy said. "We hit the beach tomorrow. Have a few drinks and...just a little bit of push to get you to move back to Florida."

"Only a little," I rolled my eyes. "Can't wait."

"You say that now. But by the time you get on that plane Sunday, you're going to be one of us again."

I watched him drive away.

Then I went up to my room and lay awake for hours, my mind running through possibilities.

Credit systems. Databases. Digital profiles. Volume operations.

By the time I finally fell asleep, I had a pretty good idea what they were planning.

And I was pretty sure I could build it.

The question was: should I?

The rest of the weekend was much of the same; beach time Saturday afternoon, another night out Saturday, lazy Sunday morning before my afternoon flight. It was a lot of fun, a lot of not-so-subtle pressure. The whole family wanted me to jump in.

2

———

THE FLIGHT HOME

"I'll see you next week," said Randy as I left his place Sunday morning.

"Don't push it. I'll talk to you later." I got into the Mustang and headed for the airport.

I boarded the plane, sat down in my seat, and tried to relax. The flight attendant must have seen anxiety on my face and assumed it was fear of flying.

"Don't worry sir, it's a short flight and I'll make sure you're okay."

"Thanks." I didn't see the point in explaining that it wasn't flying that was making me anxious. I was out of sorts because I knew I had a huge decision to make. I was on my way back to Maryland contemplating a choice that would not only change the course of my life, but Diana's as well.

But first, I needed to figure out exactly what I was getting into.

I pulled out the cocktail napkin where I'd been sketching during the beach days. Randy and Tommy had been careful not to say too much, but they'd given me enough.

Credit systems. Digital profiles. Volume operations. Databases that need to scale.

I started connecting the dots.

If you wanted to exploit credit systems at volume, you'd need identities. Not stolen ones; those get flagged immediately when the real person notices fraudulent charges. You'd need identities that no one was watching.

Identities that looked real but weren't.

Synthetic identities.

My pen moved across the napkin, sketching out the architecture. You'd start with social security numbers, the foundation of any credit identity in America. But where would you get clean SSNs? Stolen ones get flagged.

Random ones don't pass verification.

Unless...

Unless you used SSNs from people who'd died recently. Recent enough that the death certificate was filed but not yet processed into the system. A window of opportunity where the number existed but wasn't being watched.

I wrote: *SSN source: deceased, recent, unprocessed*

Then you'd build profiles around those numbers. Names pulled from census data. Addresses from public records. Employment histories that looked legitimate. Feed all that data into the credit bureaus, create a credit history going back months or years.

The bureaus wouldn't flag it because every individual piece would check out. The SSN would verify. The address would exist. The employment would match public records. It would all look real because the components were real, just assembled into someone who didn't exist.

By the time I crossed into Georgia airspace, I'd worked out the entire system architecture.

Database layer: social security death records, census data, public records, employment databases.

Processing layer: automated profile generation, credit report filing, verification checking.

Output layer: complete synthetic identities ready for credit applications.

And if you automated the whole thing? If you built it right? You could generate identities faster than the credit bureaus could flag them. By the time they realized "John Smith" didn't exist, you'd already maxed out his credit cards and moved on to the next hundred identities.

It was elegant.

It was brilliant.

It was absolutely illegal.

And I could build it.

I'd been building systems like this since I was sixteen. The inventory tracker for Tommy that could show two sets of books. The evidence-wiping tools for Randy's crew. The fake ID generator that pulled real photos and data to create documents that would pass any scan.

This was just the next evolution. Bigger scale, higher stakes, but the same principle: find the gap between what's supposed to happen and what actually happens, then exploit it.

The flight attendant came by. "Can I get you anything?"

"Whiskey. Neat."

She brought it back, and I stared at my napkin covered in notes and diagrams.

What the hell am I going to say to Diana?

~

I took another sip of my whiskey and tried to think about something other than my criminal family.

Diana. I should think about Diana. She'd be waiting for me at the apartment, probably with that nervous smile she got when she was worried about me. I wondered what the hell I was going to tell her.

I thought back to the day we met. Two and a half years ago, a bookstore in Annapolis. I was in the self-help section, reaching for some book about starting over, when another hand reached for the same book.

"Oh, sorry," she said.

She had freckles across her nose. A good laugh, genuine. She taught second grade and felt ridiculous looking at self-help books too.

"Want to go get coffee instead?" she asked.

I should have said no. But she was smiling at me like I was just a regular guy, and I wanted so badly to be just a regular guy.

We sat in that coffee shop for three hours. She told me about her family, parents married thirty years, childhood in suburban Maryland where the most exciting thing that happened was the annual church carnival. I gave her the sanitized version of mine. Family was complicated. Came to Maryland for a fresh start. Not exactly lies, but not exactly truth either.

"I do want that someday," she said. "The husband, the kids, the house with the backyard. I know it's not very modern of me, but I like the idea of building something stable, you know? Something that lasts."

I knew, even then, that I couldn't give her that. That stability wasn't in my DNA. But I didn't run. Instead I said, "That sounds nice."

A YEAR LATER I PROPOSED. I didn't have much money, but I scraped together enough for a small diamond ring. She cried when I gave it to her.

"It's perfect," she said.

We set a date for June. Started planning a life I wasn't sure I could live.

DIANA CAME FROM A CLOSE-KNIT FAMILY. She had a support system I'd never experienced. She'd be okay. When Randy called about the Florida trip, I knew what it meant. The excuse to stop pretending. Diana had encouraged me to go. Said family was important, that life was too short to hold grudges.

RANDY AND TOMMY needed what I could do. My skills. The ability to see systems and break them.

That was my value. That was what I brought to the world.

THE PILOT'S voice came over the intercom. "Ladies and gentlemen, we're beginning our descent into Baltimore. Please return your seats to the upright position."

I sat up, my heart pounding. I pulled out my phone, looked at Diana's last text from this morning: *Have a safe flight! Can't wait to see you tonight. Love you.*

I typed out a response, deleted it. Typed another, deleted that too.

Finally I just wrote: *Landing soon.*

I hit send and turned off my phone.

Whatever was about to happen, I couldn't avoid it any longer.

I was jolted back to the present when the landing gear of the plane came down.

Shit.

Now I had to face Diana.

3

THE EDUCATION OF DANNY TYLER

I got home from the airport after midnight. The apartment was dark except for the glow of the TV. Diana was asleep on the couch, still in her work clothes, khaki pants and a cardigan with an apple embroidered on it. One of her students' mothers had made it for her last Christmas. She wore it at least once a week.

There was a pizza box on the coffee table, half-eaten. It was late but she made sure I had food. The thought made my chest tight.

The summer of 2005 was one I'd never forget. I'd just turned seven. Dad rented a house on Little Shinnecock Bay in the Hamptons. Randy and I were spending our summer vacation there.

The house was situated on the bay about 500 feet away from the locks that separated Little Shinnecock Bay from Great Shinnecock Bay. Anthony Jr. was there too; Anthony Sr. and Tommy were partners, so we spent a lot of time together. While our fathers did business, Anthony and I built sandcastles and caught crabs off the dock.

"Are we going to Flying Point today?" Randy asked Rachel.

"We're going in about half an hour."

Randy turned to me. "You know that means at least two hours. You wanna take a walk to the store?"

"Okay."

At the store, Randy and I loaded up on the candy we'd need for our day at the beach. There was always money lying around the house here and there. Randy and I helped ourselves. I don't think the adults ever noticed.

"Think they're ready yet?" I asked on our way back from the store.

"Probably not."

"Are we gonna get in trouble for going to the store?"

"I doubt if they even noticed we were gone. They're kind of stoned."

"What's it like?" I asked.

"Being stoned?"

"Uh-huh."

"It makes your body feel good all over, and your mind feels like you live in the clouds," he said, with all the wisdom of a ten-year-old. "Sometimes it makes you hungry too."

"Is that why Dad and Rachel always forget stuff and yell at each other?"

"I don't know," Randy hesitated. "Probably."

We got back to the house and sat down on the front porch. An hour later, Dad and Rachel finally came out.

"Aren't you guys ready yet?" asked Dad sarcastically. "We've been waiting forever." He laughed and got into the car.

WE GOT to Flying Point and some of Dad's business partners and their kids were already there. Anthony Sr. was there with Anthony Jr. We called him Uncle Tony, even though he wasn't really our uncle, just Tommy's closest friend and partner. The adults set up chairs and umbrellas while we kids headed straight for the water.

"Hey, you want to help me?" asked Anthony, holding up a plastic shovel.

"Sure."

We spent the next hour building an elaborate sandcastle, complete with a moat and towers. Other kids joined in. For a while, I forgot about the strangeness of my family. I was just a kid at the beach.

Later on, Dad and his friends set up the barbecue and started cooking. The aroma of sausages and hamburgers and hot dogs filled the air. The smell of pot was in the air as well. I was used to it, it had been smoked around me since I was born, but I'd never tried it.

"Hey Danny, come here," said Dad. "Sit down, let's BS for a while."

"Um...okay."

Anthony Sr. was playing sixties music on guitar, and a circle was forming around him as everyone came to sit down and watch the sunset. There were several joints being passed around the circle. Randy was sitting to my left.

One of the joints reached my father. He took a hit, held his breath, and looked at me.

"Here, you wanna try this?" He extended his cupped hand, holding the joint.

"What's it like?"

"Just try it. It's kinda cool," said Randy.

I took the joint in my hand. My father and Randy were studying me intently. Now when I look back on it, this was a rite of passage in my family.

"Don't you think he's a little young for that?" said one of Dad's friends.

"I don't think there's anything wrong with it. Why should I hide it?" asked Dad.

"You're kinda liberal with your kids, huh?"

"Yeah, I guess."

"Okay, what do I do?" I asked.

"Just suck on it, then swallow the smoke, like this." Randy demonstrated.

I followed his lead. At first I didn't feel anything. Then about ten minutes later, I found myself enjoying everything around me. The music. The smell of the food. The sunset. I felt like my problems weren't that bad.

I was a seven-year-old who had to deal with things most kids never thought about. This was a great escape, and it was right there on that beach that I fell in love with smoking pot.

I didn't consider the philosophical question of my father giving drugs to a young child until I was much older. All I knew, there and then, was that I was now part of a group I'd always felt separated from.

Maybe now I would have something in common with my father.

I was seven.

The Business, Age 8

Now that I was smoking, once I'd passed the test, it was about a year before Dad approached me with an offer.

"Hey, I have a job I want you to do for me," my father said.

"What's up?" I responded.

He walked me into the bedroom that substituted for an office. Sitting there in the middle of the floor on top of a blue tarp was a huge mound of marijuana and three triple-beam scales.

"I'm going to show you how to use the scale, then I want you to weigh out one-pound piles and put them into zip-lock bags," said Dad.

"Do I get paid?"

"You can keep what's left over. It should be a pound or two. You can either keep it or sell it to your friends."

"I don't know, it seems kinda weird," I said.

"Don't be silly. It'll be really cool. I've been waiting to bring you into the family business for a while, not everyone gets this. If you do well, then we can give you other stuff to do where you can make some real money."

I'd just turned eight. I had no idea what "real money" was.

"Come with me," Dad said. "I have something else to show you."

I followed my father into another bedroom. What I saw changed me for life.

Piled three feet high on top of the queen-size bed, taking up the entire surface, were stacks of hundred-dollar bills wrapped in plastic packages.

"Whoa, how much is that?" I asked.

"About five million. There's five thousand in each package."

"Is it ours?"

"Some of it is mine. Some of it belongs to my business partners."

"Why not put it in the bank?"

"Daniel, do you know what illegal means?"

"I'm not stupid, Dad. It means it's against the law."

"What I do is against the law."

"I know." I'd figured that out years ago.

"So what does this have to do with the money?"

"Can't put illegal money in a bank. Not until it's been cleaned."

"Cleaned how?"

"Made to look as though it comes from a legitimate or legal business."

"So why don't you just pretend it came from a pizza place or something like that? Everyone pays cash for that stuff."

Dad laughed. "Very good, Daniel. That's exactly what we're doing with this money. But it takes a long time, because pizza places don't make that much money in a short time, so you can only clean a little money at a time."

"Oh, then just have lots of them."

"You're going to be very rich one day, Daniel," said Dad.

I smiled at the thought, and then I got worried. "What happens to us if you go to jail?"

"I don't want you to worry about that," said Dad. "You will be taken care of. But there is something I want to teach you, and it's very, very important."

"What?"

"If you ever get into trouble with the police, ever in your life, I want you to remember this."

"Okay. Tell me."

"If the police ever want to ask you questions, no matter what it's about, you say: 'I'll be happy to answer your questions, officer, just as soon as I speak with my attorney.' Always be polite."

"Okay."

"Daniel, this is very important. I want you to memorize it. Repeat it."

"Now?"

"Yes, now."

"Okay. I would be happy to answer your questions, officer, just as soon as I speak with my attorney."

"Very good. Don't forget. Now get to work."

I went back into the other bedroom and started breaking the bale down into one-pound packages. I was in now. Part of the family. It had been my introduction to the glorious side of crime.

I started making money. Suddenly I was able to buy things my friends couldn't afford.

I was eight years old, memorizing how to invoke my Fifth Amendment rights.

Truman, **Age 9**

It wasn't all fun and glamour. There were times when I saw the true nature of the drug culture, and it scared the shit out of me.

"Can we go eat now? I'm hungry," I asked.

"I know," said Tommy. "I just have one more stop to make."

"Can't we eat first?"

"No, but it will only take five minutes."

"That's what you always say. That means at least an hour."

"Don't piss me off, Daniel. We'll go eat when I say so."

We found a parking spot outside a tenement in Astoria. It was the first time I'd been to this place, although I'd been to many like it.

"Here, carry this," Dad said as he handed me a duffel bag.

"It's your business. Why do I have to carry it?"

"Shut up, Daniel. Do as I say."

We took an elevator to the third floor. The building was a typical New York City housing project. Shady characters waved to my father as though they knew him.

We knocked on the door. I heard the clicking of at least five locks. The door opened and we were admitted to a living room furnished with a couch that looked like it had been picked up from the street and a folding table with one chair. The smell was a combination of urine and baking soda.

A large brown and black Doberman Pinscher was barking furiously at us.

"Truman, shut up and go lie down," said Mike.

Mike was a friend of my father's. Six feet tall and rail thin. His hair was long and bushy and looked like it had never been washed. The smell, when he got close to me, made me gag.

Truman did as he was told but didn't take his eyes off me.

"Hey Tom, how you doin'?" asked Mike.

"Not bad. My kid is being a pain in the ass, though," responded Tommy.

I gave him a dirty look, crossed my arms, and sat down on the nasty couch with a huff.

"Let's go in the other room and take care of business then, shall we?" said Mike.

"You're not gonna leave me alone with that dog, right?" I was terrified.

"You're being silly as usual. The dog is not going to hurt you," my father said.

Mike and my father went into the other room and slammed the door.

Truman was on his feet again. He walked slowly toward me, growling and baring his teeth. He jumped up on the couch where I was sitting and stared me down. Teeth bared. Still growling.

He stayed like that until my father and Mike came out forty-five minutes later.

My father was in a much better mood now. He must have gotten high while he was in the other room.

"You ready to go eat now?"

"I'm not hungry. Just take me home."

That was the day I learned that my father would choose getting high over my safety. Every single time.

I was nine years old.

The Ghost, Ages 12-16

By the time I was twelve, I'd moved beyond just handling cash and weighing product. I'd discovered computers.

It started with a stolen laptop, one of Randy's friends had boosted it from a car in Manhattan and couldn't figure out how to bypass the password. He was going to wipe it and sell it for parts.

"Let me try something first," I said.

Two hours later, I was in. Not because I was some genius, but because I was persistent and curious. I'd found some hacker forums online, learned about password-cracking tools, taught myself the basics.

Randy was impressed. "The hell did you learn that?"

"Internet. It's not that hard if you know where to look."

"Think you could do that again? With other computers?"

I could. And I did.

Within a year, I was the go-to guy for anything digital. Need to wipe a phone? Danny can do it. Need to crack into someone's email? Danny's your guy. Need to make a fake ID that scans properly? Danny knows how.

It wasn't just about being useful to the family, though that was part of it. I genuinely loved it. The logic. The problem-solving. The feeling of breaking through barriers that were supposed to be unbreakable. Though now I was juggling the computer stuff and breaking up bales.

Computers made sense in a way people never did. They followed rules. If you understood the rules, you could make them do anything.

When I was fourteen, Tommy brought me a challenge.

"I need an inventory system," he said. "Something that tracks product coming in and going out. But it needs to show two different sets of books, one real, another for if anyone comes looking."

"You mean like cooking the books?"

"Exactly like that. Can you build it?"

I thought about it. "Yeah. I can build it."

It took me three months, working on it after school in Anthony Jr's back room. I taught myself database programming, figured out how to create parallel tracking systems, built in a kill switch that would wipe the real data if someone unauthorized tried to access it.

When I showed it to Tommy, he actually looked proud. Maybe for the first time in my life.

"This is good, Daniel. Really good. How much did this save us?"

"In shrinkage? Probably ten grand a month. In security? Can't put a price on it."

"Shrinkage." He smiled. "That's a nice word for theft."

That's when I realized: I was better at this than I was at anything else. Better at computers than I was at school. Better at systems than I was at people. Better at being a criminal than I'd ever be at being normal.

I was sixteen years old, and I'd just built my first money-laundering tool.

The system worked so well that Anthony Sr. wanted one too. Then some of their other partners. By the time I was seventeen, I was building custom software for half the mid-level dealers in Queens, making more money than most adults with real jobs.

Randy started calling me "the ghost." Because I could make digital evidence disappear. I could move through systems without leaving traces. I understood that the real power wasn't in the streets anymore, it was in the databases, the networks, the invisible infrastructure that everyone depended on but nobody understood.

That's what I brought to the family. Not muscle. Not charm. Not street smarts. Technical expertise. The ability to exploit systems that other criminals didn't even know existed.

THE PARTNERSHIP, Ages 18-24

Even though the computer stuff was my true passion, I became a courier. Our fathers thought it would be a good idea for Anthony Jr. and me to team up. They were right. The two of us made deliveries all over Queens. Nobody looked twice at us because we were kids.

Anthony held the product, I handled the cash.

When we graduated, we were promoted and started bringing large amounts of cash to Florida two or three times a month, carrying trunks full of product on the return trip.

The two of us spent years learning how the business operated, but we each developed our own specialties.

Anthony focused on logistics, moving product, managing routes, coordinating drivers. He was the people guy. He could read someone in thirty seconds, tell you if they were solid or likely to flip.

I focused on the technical side.

By eighteen, I was building entire digital infrastructures. Encrypted communication systems so the crew could talk without leaving phone records. GPS tracking for shipments that couldn't be traced. Software that scrubbed metadata from documents before they were shared.

I became the guy who made the operation invisible.

The FBI could raid a location and find product, but they'd find no records. No communications. No evidence of the network. Just drugs and whoever happened to be there, never enough to roll up the organization.

That was my value. Making sure that even if one part got caught, the rest stayed hidden.

The Breaking Point, Age 24

Thinking about those years made me recall the night I decided to leave, four years ago.

Anthony and I were supposed to pick up $500,000 from a storage unit in Flushing. When we pulled up, I spotted the unmarked cars immediately.

"FBI," I said. "They're everywhere."

We drove around the block. More surveillance. Back entrance covered. This was a trap.

I called Tommy from a payphone. "The storage place is hot. We had to bail."

"You go get my fucking money!" he screamed.

"Are you crazy? There are cops everywhere…"

"If you don't show up with that money, there's going to be hell to pay."

I hung up on him and turned to Anthony. "He wants us to walk into an FBI trap rather than lose his money."

We found another way. A friend of ours had rented a storage unit that backed up to Tommy's, just a cinderblock wall between them. An hour later, we drilled through the wall, grabbed the cash, sealed it back up. The FBI never saw us.

That night I dropped the money at Tommy's feet.

"Here's your goddamned money. I'm done. I can't believe you were willing to let us get busted."

"Don't be stupid, Daniel. You didn't get caught."

"Fuck you. I'm out."

In the car afterward, Anthony was quiet for a long time. Finally: "You really leaving?"

"I have to. Before he gets me killed."

"Where will you go?"

"Do you remember that pick up we made in Maryland? I kinda liked it there. Maybe I'll check it out for a while."

"That's not you, man. That's not your world."

"Maybe I can make it my world."

"Be good," he said when he dropped me off.

"Or be good at it."

Three days later, I was in Maryland, trying to become someone I wasn't.

DIANA'S soft breathing was the only audible sound, though my heart hammering in my ears tried to drown it out. Sweet Diana, peaceful, innocent, and good.

I set my bag down as quietly as I could, but she stirred anyway. Years of teaching second grade had given her mom-level awareness of any sound in her space.

"Danny?" Her voice was thick with sleep. She sat up, brushing hair from her face. It was out of its usual ponytail, falling around her shoulders. "What time is it?"

"Late. You should go to bed."

She rubbed her eyes, looked at me properly. "Your flight was supposed to get in at nine."

"I know. I missed it. Caught a later one."

"You didn't call."

"My phone died." The lie came so easily. Too easily.

She stood up, and I could see her brain waking up, starting to process. "You didn't call from the airport?"

"I just wanted to get home."

"You've been weird all week, Danny. Then you miss your flight and don't call me for four hours?" She crossed her arms. Not angry yet, but getting there. "What's going on?"

"Nothing. I'm just tired."

"Don't do that. Don't shut me out." She walked closer. "Did something happen in Florida?"

Everything. Everything happened in Florida.

"We need to talk."

The words hung in the air between us. Three words that never meant anything good. I watched her face change as she understood.

"Okay." Her voice was very quiet. "Let me make coffee."

"Diana, it's almost one in the morning."

"I'm not having this conversation half-asleep." She went to the kitchen, and I heard her filling the coffee maker with water. Her hands would be shaking slightly, they always did when she was nervous, but she'd keep them busy so I wouldn't notice.

I sat down at our kitchen table. Our table. The one we'd picked out together at IKEA six months ago, arguing about whether to get the round one or the rectangular. She'd wanted round, "better for conversation," and I'd caved because that's what I always did. Let her believe we were building something together.

She brought two mugs over, sitting down across from me. Wrapped her hands around her mug even though the coffee was too hot to drink yet. Steadying herself.

"So," she said. "Talk."

Where to even start? How do you tell someone their entire relationship has been built on a foundation of lies?

"I saw my father," I began.

"I know. You said you were going to."

"He wanted to offer me a job."

Her eyebrows went up slightly. "A job? Doing what?"

"Working with him. And Randy. It's a family business thing."

"I thought you weren't part of that anymore. I thought that's why you left."

"I did leave. I have left. But they want me to come back."

She took a sip of coffee, winced at the heat. Set the mug down carefully. "And what did you tell them?"

This was the moment. The moment I should tell her everything. About the credit fraud, about the money, about who I really was. But I looked at her sitting there in her teacher cardigan with her freckled face and her wholesome goodness, and I couldn't do it. Couldn't stain her with the truth of my life.

"I told them I'd think about it."

The words landed like stones.

"You told them you'd think about it." She repeated it slowly, like she was translating from another language.

"About going back to work for your father. The father you haven't spoken to in four years. The father you said was involved in shady business."

"Diana..."

"What kind of job is it, Danny?" Her voice was still calm, but I could hear the steel underneath. Teacher voice. The one she used when a student was lying about who started the fight.

"It's complicated."

"Uncomplicate it for me."

"I can't."

"Can't or won't?"

"Both."

She stood up abruptly, walked to the window. Our apartment overlooked a parking lot, nothing scenic, but she stared at it like it was the most interesting thing in the world. "I've been patient, you know. For months now. Watching you pull away. Watching you check your phone every five minutes. Watching you stare at the walls at three in the morning like you're in prison."

"I didn't think you noticed."

"Of course I noticed!" She turned around, and there were tears in her eyes now. "I notice everything, Danny. That's the problem. I notice and I wait for you to talk to me and you never do. And I tell myself to be patient. That you're working through something. You'll come to me when you're ready." She wiped her eyes angrily. "But you're never ready, are you? You never let me in."

"I'm trying to protect you."

"From what?" She walked back to the table, leaned her hands on it. "From your family? From your past? Or from you?"

All of it. All of the above.

"This job they're offering," I said slowly. "It's good money. Really good money."

"I don't care about money."

"I know you don't. But I do. I care that I'm making $650 a week selling electronics to people who don't need them. I care that I can't afford to take you to a nice restaurant without checking my bank account. I care that the ring I gave you is so small I'm embarrassed every time you wear it."

"I love this ring." She touched it instinctively, protective.

"You deserve better."

"I deserve honesty!" Her voice cracked. "I deserve a partner who doesn't lie to me about where he's been and what he's thinking and who he really is!"

"You want honesty?" Something snapped inside me. All the months of pretending, of trying to be someone I wasn't, just broke. "Fine. You want to know what this job is? It's not legal, Diana. It's not a nice office job with a 401k and health insurance. It's the kind of job that could get me sent to federal prison if I get caught."

She stood very still. "What?"

"My family. The shady business I mentioned? It's not shady, it's criminal. My father is a criminal. My brother is a criminal. And for most of my life, so was I."

"You're lying." But I could see in her eyes that she knew I wasn't.

"I'm not. I came to Maryland to get away from it. To try to be normal. To try to be the kind of person who could have the life you want. But I can't, Diana. I've been trying for two years and I can't do it."

"What did you do?" Her voice was barely a whisper. "Before. What kind of criminal stuff?"

"Does it matter?"

"Yes, it matters!"

"Drugs, mostly. My father was a dealer. A big one. I grew up around it. Started working for him when I was a kid. By the time I was sixteen I was making more money in a month than you make now in a year."

She sat back down heavily. "Oh my God."

"I left because I was scared. Because I saw what it did to people. Because I didn't want to end up dead or in prison. But I was never rehabilitated, Diana. I was just hiding."

"And now you want to go back."

"I don't know what I want."

"Yes you do." She looked at me, really looked at me, and I saw the exact moment she figured it out. "You already decided. That's why you're telling me. You're not asking for permission or advice. You're telling me goodbye."

I couldn't deny it. We both knew it was true.

"Diana..."

"How long?" she asked. "How long have you been lying to me?"

"Since the beginning."

She flinched like I'd slapped her. "The beginning."

"Not about my feelings. Those were real. But about who I was, about my past, about what I was running from. I should have told you before we got serious. I should have told you before I proposed. I'm sorry."

"You're sorry." She laughed, but there was no humor in it. "You let me fall in love with someone who doesn't exist. You let me plan a wedding. You met my parents, my siblings, my friends. You came to church with me, for God's sake. And the whole time you were lying."

"I wanted to be that person. The person you thought I was. I really tried."

"But you couldn't do it." She was crying now, but her

voice stayed steady. "Because what? Living a normal life with me was too boring? Too hard? Not exciting enough?"

"Because it's not who I am!" I stood up, frustrated. "I tried, Diana. I really fucking tried. But I can't spend the rest of my life pretending. I can't go to your family's church picnics and chat with your coworkers about lesson plans and smile through another dinner where your father asks me when I'm going to get a real job. I'm dying here. Slowly suffocating. And I know that's not your fault, you're perfect, you're everything anyone could want, but I can't be what you need me to be."

"All I needed was honesty."

"You needed a nice Catholic boy with a normal family and a normal job and a normal life. You said it yourself that first day in the coffee shop. That's what your parents wanted for you. That's what you wanted. And I'm not that guy. I never was."

She wiped her eyes with the heels of her hands. "So what now? You go back to Florida and become a criminal again? That's your plan?"

"I don't have a plan. I just know I can't stay here."

"Can't or won't?"

"Both."

We sat in silence for a long moment. The coffee was cold now, untouched. Outside, someone's car alarm went off, then stopped.

"I really loved you," she said finally. "The you I thought you were. I don't even know if the real you exists."

"He doesn't." It was the most honest thing I'd said all night. "I'm sorry, Diana. You deserved so much better than this."

"Yeah." She stood up, walked toward our bedroom, her bedroom now, then stopped at the doorway. "I need you to leave. Not right this second, but soon. By the end of the week."

"Okay."

"And Danny?" She looked back at me, and her eyes were red but dry now. "I hope whatever you're looking for in Florida, I hope it's worth it. I hope it's worth throwing away everything we had."

"We didn't have anything. That's the problem. It was all pretend."

"It wasn't pretend to me."

She went into the bedroom and closed the door. I heard the lock click.

I sat at the table for a long time, staring at the two cold cups of coffee. Then I pulled out my phone and texted Randy.

I'm in. I'll be there by Friday.

His response came immediately: *I knew you would be. Welcome home.*

But Florida wasn't home. Maryland wasn't home. I didn't have a home, just places I was running from and places I was running to.

I thought about Diana in the bedroom, probably crying into her pillow. I thought about how she'd told her mother just last week that I was "the one." I thought about the wedding invitations she'd been looking at, the house she'd bookmarked online, the life she'd imagined for us.

None of it had ever been real. Not really.

I grabbed my duffel bag, threw some clothes in it. I'd come back for the rest later, when she wasn't here. I'd leave my key on the counter. Make it easy for her.

Before I left, I walked to the bedroom door. I could hear her crying now, trying to be quiet about it. My hand hovered over the doorknob.

"Diana?" I said softly.

"Go away, Danny."

"I really am sorry."

"I know." Her voice was muffled. "But it doesn't change anything. You're still leaving."

"Yeah."

"Then just go. Please."

I took my hand off the doorknob. Set my key on the kitchen counter next to her coffee mug. The one that said "World's Best Teacher" that one of her students had given her.

I didn't sleep that night. Diana was in the bedroom with the door locked. I sat in the living room with my laptop, knowing I was about to do something I couldn't undo.

I'd been thinking about insurance. About what happens when things go wrong in the life I was about to rejoin. Tommy had been in the game for forty years, longer than most people lasted. But I'd seen what happened to his partners over the years. Some got arrested. Some disappeared. Some ended up dead.

I'd spent four years trying to be normal, and it hadn't worked. But that didn't mean I had to be stupid about going back.

I needed an exit. A real one.

It took me three hours to build the framework. Started with the Social Security Death Index, public records, no hacking required, completely legal to access. I filtered for recent deaths: people who died in the last 90 days, from states with slow bureaucratic processes.

Found him on page seventeen: David Raymond Marcus. Chicago, Illinois. Died at 28 from congenital heart failure. SSN issued in 1997. Clean record, no flags.

Perfect.

I pulled census data for common middle names. James was safe, unremarkable. David James Marcus. Born March 15, 1997, made me 28, close to my real age. Easier to remember, easier to maintain.

Address next. I needed somewhere real but anonymous. Large apartment complexes in cities with high turnover. Brooklyn worked, close enough to Maryland that I could claim familiarity, big enough to disappear in. Found a building on Flatbush Avenue with 200 units. Used unit 4H, which according to public records had changed tenants three times in the last two years.

Employment history. Nothing flashy. Database administrator for a medium-sized medical billing company in Manhattan. The kind of job that explained technical skills but wasn't memorable enough to verify. I back-dated it eighteen months, long enough to look stable, short enough that no one would dig too deep.

Credit history was trickier. I filed initial reports with all three bureaus. Store card from Target, $500 limit, twelve months of payment history. Gas card from Shell, eighteen months, all on-time payments. Small amounts, responsible behavior, the kind of profile that disappeared into the noise of millions of other unremarkable Americans.

By four a.m., David James Marcus existed in the system. Not perfectly, a real background check by someone who knew what they were looking for would find gaps. But for casual verification, for getting on a plane, for opening a bank account, he'd pass.

I encrypted the files, buried them three layers deep in my hard drive under innocuous folder names. Then I sat back and looked at what I'd created.

My escape hatch. My insurance policy. If Randy turned

on me, if the FBI came knocking, if I needed to disappear, David Marcus was waiting.

The irony wasn't lost on me. I was using the exact skills Tommy wanted me for to build an identity that would let me escape if everything went wrong. I was planning my exit before I'd even arrived.

After quickly stowing my laptop in my duffle,I closed the apartment door quietly behind me and walked to my car. It was four-thirty in the morning and the parking lot was empty except for a stray cat picking through garbage.

I sat in the driver's seat, engine running, watching the lights in our apartment. Her apartment now.

The light in the bedroom stayed on for a long time.

Finally, I put the car in drive and headed for the highway. South. Toward Florida. Toward Randy and Tommy and the life I'd always known I'd end up back in.

Behind me, Diana's light finally went off.

I didn't look back.

4

FIRST WEEK

I stood in the doorway of Jake's condo, my duffel bag at my feet, looking at what was supposed to be my new home.

Marina del Ray. Third floor. Water view. The kind of place that should have felt like a fresh start but instead felt like a storage unit where I'd be waiting for the next thing to happen.

The apartment was mostly empty. Jake had taken his furniture, leaving behind a couch that had seen better days, a kitchen table with two chairs, and a mattress on the floor in the bedroom. The walls were bare. The closets were empty. Even the refrigerator was unplugged, door hanging open like a mouth waiting to be fed.

I dropped my bag and walked to the sliding glass door that led to the balcony. The view was actually pretty nice. The Intracoastal stretched out below, boats moving lazily across the water, palm trees swaying in the breeze. Florida in all its tropical glory.

This should have felt like freedom. Like possibility. Like the start of something new.

Instead, it felt like I'd traded one empty apartment for another.

I thought about Diana. Probably packing up my stuff right now. Boxing up the life we'd pretended to build together. She'd keep the engagement ring, not because she wanted it, but because throwing it away would feel too final. Too much like admitting she'd wasted two years on someone who'd been lying the entire time.

I pulled out my phone. No messages. I'd turned off my location services. Deleted most of my social media. Made it harder for anyone from Maryland to track me down if they wanted to. Not that anyone would. Diana wasn't the type to show up demanding answers. She was the type to cry alone in her apartment and then move on with quiet dignity.

I was the asshole who'd left.

My phone buzzed. Text from Randy: *You settled in yet?*

Just got here.

Good. Office tomorrow morning. Nine a.m. Dad wants to show you something.

What?

You'll see. Don't be late.

I set the phone down and looked around the apartment again. I should unpack. Hang up clothes. Make this place look like someone actually lived here instead of just existing between one thing and the next.

But I didn't move. Just stood there looking at the empty space, wondering what the hell I was doing.

What am I doing? The thought bounced around my brain.

I was leaving behind a stable life. A good woman. A legitimate future. For what? To work with my criminal family? To commit fraud? To make money in ways that could send me to prison?

This was insane.

But the alternative was going back to Maryland. Back to selling electronics. Back to pretending to be someone I wasn't. Back to suffocating under the weight of normalcy.

I'd tried that. For two years, I'd tried to be the kind of person Diana deserved. The kind of person who went to church and had dinner with future in-laws and talked about buying a house with a backyard.

And I'd been miserable every single day.

So maybe this was insane. But at least it was honest insanity. At least I'd be doing something I was actually good at. At least I'd be around people who knew what I really was.

I finally opened my duffel bag. Started unpacking. Hung some clothes in the closet. Put toiletries in the bathroom. Set my laptop on the kitchen table.

The apartment still looked empty, but at least now it had evidence that someone lived here.

My phone rang. Randy.

"Hey," I answered.

"You okay? You sound weird."

"I'm fine. Just settling in."

"Good. Listen, about tomorrow. Dad's pretty excited. He's been working on this thing with me for a few weeks, and now that you're here, we can actually pull it off."

"What thing?"

"I told you. You'll see tomorrow. But Danny..." He paused. "It's good. It's really good. I think you're going to be impressed."

"Impressed by what?"

"By what we've been building. By what we can do now that you're here." I could hear the smile in his voice. "This is going to be big, bro. Bigger than anything Dad's done before. And you're the missing piece."

"No pressure."

"Hey, you came back for a reason. Might as well lean into it." He paused. "You hungry? I can bring over some food. Christen the new place."

I looked around the empty apartment. "Nah, I'm good. Need to get organized here."

"Alright. But nine a.m. tomorrow. Atlantic Business Solutions. It's in a strip mall on Commercial Boulevard. I'll text you the address."

"Strip mall? Real classy."

"It's perfect. Boring. Forgettable. The kind of place you drive past a thousand times and never remember." He laughed. "See you tomorrow. And Danny? Welcome home."

He hung up before I could tell him this didn't feel like home.

I SPENT the rest of the afternoon making the apartment marginally more livable. Went to Target, bought sheets and towels and basic kitchen supplies. Stopped at a grocery store, stocked the fridge with beer and sandwich supplies. Came back and set everything up.

By the time I was done, the apartment still looked mostly empty, but at least it was functional. A place where a person could sleep and eat and exist.

Around seven, I ordered pizza. Ate it standing at the kitchen counter, looking out at the water. The sun was setting, turning everything orange and pink. Beautiful. The kind of sunset that should have made me feel grateful to be in Florida instead of Maryland.

Instead, I just felt alone.

My phone buzzed. Text from an unknown number. I almost didn't open it, but curiosity got the better of me.

Hey Danny. It's Diana. I just wanted to make sure you got there safe. I'm not trying to start anything. I just needed to know you're okay.

I stared at the message for a long time.

She was checking on me. Even after everything. Even after I'd broken her heart and walked away. She was making sure I was safe.

I should have blocked her number. Should have made a clean break. But instead, I texted back: *I'm safe. Thank you for checking.*

Three dots appeared. Disappeared. Appeared again.

Good. I'm glad. Take care of yourself.

You too.

The three dots appeared one more time, then vanished. No more messages.

I deleted the thread. Blocked the number. Not because I was angry, but because I knew I'd be tempted to reach out. To tell her I was sorry. To tell her she deserved better. To tell her I was already regretting this choice.

And that wouldn't help either of us.

I finished my pizza and threw away the box. Cracked open a beer. Went out on the balcony.

The boats were still moving across the water. People heading somewhere. People with destinations and purposes and plans. I wondered what that felt like. To know where you were going. To be certain about your choices.

I pulled out my phone, looked at the last text from Randy. *Nine a.m. Don't be late.*

Tomorrow. Tomorrow I'd see what Randy and Tommy

had been building. Tomorrow I'd find out what they needed me for. Tomorrow I'd commit to this new life for real.

Tonight, I was just a guy in an empty apartment, drinking beer on a balcony, wondering if he'd made the biggest mistake of his life.

I woke up at seven without an alarm. Old habit from years of working with Tommy. You show up early or you don't show up at all.

I showered, got dressed, tried to make myself look like someone who had his shit together. Failed, but at least I looked awake.

The address Randy sent was easy to find. Commercial Boulevard, a strip mall between a nail salon and a tax prep office. The sign said "Atlantic Business Solutions" in boring corporate letters. Perfect camouflage.

I pulled into the parking lot at 8:45. Randy's Mercedes was already there. So was Jake's truck and Colin's sedan. And another car I recognized, Uncle Tony's black Cadillac.

I sat in my car for a few minutes, engine off, looking at the building. The whole crew was here. Except Tommy, weird.

I could still leave. Could text Randy some excuse. Could drive back to the apartment, pack up, head somewhere else. Somewhere new. Start over for real this time.

But I didn't.

I got out of the car and walked to the door.

It was unlocked. Inside, the office was buzzing with activity. Three high-end workstations networked together, all running. A server rack in the corner, lights blinking.

Multiple monitors displaying spreadsheets and data. This wasn't some amateur setup. This was professional.

Randy was at the main terminal, configuring something. Jake sat at another workstation, typing rapidly. Colin had paperwork spread across a desk in the corner, creating what looked like corporate documents.

And Uncle Tony sat in a chair near the window, watching quietly.

Anthony Russo Sr. had been part of my life for as long as I could remember. Tommy's oldest friend, his closest partner, the man we called Uncle even though there was no blood between us. He was in his early seventies now, though you wouldn't guess it unless you looked carefully. He was a compact man, not tall, maybe five-nine, but dense in a way that had nothing to do with muscle and everything to do with gravity. People leaned toward him without realizing it. He had thick silver hair combed straight back, a deep olive complexion weathered by decades of Florida sun, and dark eyes that stayed still when everything else in the room was moving. He dressed the way he did everything: carefully. Pressed slacks, a fitted polo, leather shoes that had been polished more than once. No gold. No flash. If Tommy wore his money on his sleeve and Randy wore his on his chest, Uncle Tony kept his in a vault and showed you the key only if he felt like it. He smelled like he always had, like cigars and something expensive that I could never place as a kid and now recognized as cologne that cost more per bottle than Tommy spent on a night out.

He had a coffee cup in his hand and that calm expression he always wore. The one that made you feel like he was three steps ahead of whatever you were thinking.

"There he is," Randy said, not looking up. "Right on time. Coffee's in the corner."

"Uncle Tony," I said. "Didn't expect to see you here. Where is Tommy?"

"Something came up," he said simply. "I wanted to make sure the technical side was properly set up. Your father's good at many things. Technology isn't one of them."

"That's what I'm here for," I said.

"Exactly." He took a sip of coffee. "Randy tells me you can automate the whole process."

"If it works the way they say it does, yeah."

"It works," Randy said. "I tested it. Uncle Tony verified the accounts. But it is very slow, we need you to automate it"

I looked at Uncle Tony. He nodded once. "The money's real. The credit lines are active. Your brother proved the concept. Now we need you to scale it."

Jake looked up from his terminal. "Hey Danny. Welcome to the operation. I've been testing the identities Randy created. Making sure the credit cards actually work, that the accounts are active, that nothing bounces back."

"And?" I asked.

"Ten for ten. Every identity he created passed verification. Every card works." Jake grinned. "This is actually happening, but its slow as fuck. That's where you come in."

Colin spoke up from his desk. "I've established seventeen shell entities across three jurisdictions. Caymans, Panama, Isle of Man. The routing structure has four layers of separation from any domestic account. Once we're generating at volume, I can process approximately $2.4 million monthly without triggering automated flags. Technically."

I poured myself a cup of coffee, trying to process what I was seeing. They'd already built half the operation. Everyone had their role. They were just waiting for me to provide the technical backbone.

"Show me what you've got," I said to Randy.

He pulled up a spreadsheet. "Three weeks ago, I generated ten synthetic identities. Manually. It took me days." He pointed at the screen. "Ten names. Ten social security numbers. Ten complete profiles with addresses, employment history, everything. I filed credit reports with all three bureaus."

"Where'd you get the SSNs?"

Randy glanced at Uncle Tony, who gave a slight nod.

"Social Security Death Index," Randy said. "Public records. People who died recently. Uncle Tony showed me how to filter for SSNs that aren't flagged yet. Recent enough that the death certificate is filed but not processed into the system. There's a window."

I nodded. "Sixty to ninety days, depending on the state's processing speed."

Randy's eyebrows went up. "Yeah. Exactly. How'd you..."

"I worked it out on the flight back from the recruitment weekend," I said. "It's the only way to get clean SSNs at scale. Stolen ones get flagged. Random ones don't verify. But recently deceased? There's a processing gap."

Uncle Tony was watching me with renewed interest. "You figured that out on your own?"

"It's basic logic. If you understand how the credit system works, you can see the vulnerabilities." I looked at the data on Randy's screen. "What I didn't know was that you'd already tested it. That's the impressive part. The theory's easy. Execution is what matters."

Randy laughed. "Of course you already figured it out. That's why we need you. I can test a concept. You can build a system." He pulled up another screen. "Look at this."

Ten accounts. All active. All with credit lines.

"Total available credit: $47,000. Average of $4,700 per identity."

I studied the numbers on the screen. Ten accounts. All active. All with real credit lines attached to people who didn't exist.

"This is real," I said.

"Very real," Colin said from his desk. "I've got the offshore accounts ready to receive. Once we start moving money, it flows through three jurisdictions before landing somewhere we can actually touch."

"Forty-seven thousand in credit lines," I said. "Walk me through the split."

Randy's expression flickered; just for a second, but I caught it. "Tommy takes twenty percent off the top. Standard. Then Uncle Tony gets his two hundred K back first, plus fifteen percent of everything after that until he's made whole on the investment. What's left, we split four ways."

I did the math. On forty-seven thousand, that meant almost ten grand to Tommy before anyone else saw a dime. Another seven or so to Tony. The four of us splitting what remained.

"Twenty percent," I said. "For doing what, exactly?"

"For being Dad." Randy's voice was carefully neutral, the tone he used when he'd already lost an argument and didn't want to lose it again. "For the connections. The protection. Forty years of knowing which cops to avoid and which palms to grease."

"Uncle Tony I understand. He put up the capital, he's taking the risk. But Tommy…"

"Danny." Randy cut me off, glancing toward the door like Tommy might walk through it. "I know. Believe me, I've had this conversation. Multiple times." He turned back to the monitors. "But that's the deal. You want to renegotiate, take it up with him directly. See how that goes."

Jake snorted from his workstation but didn't say anything.

"Besides," Randy added, "twenty percent of nothing is nothing. Twenty percent of a million a month still leaves us with plenty. Focus on the upside."

I let it drop. But I filed it away, Tommy Tyler, taking a fifth of everything his sons built while contributing nothing but his name and his blessing. The patriarch's tax. The price of being a Tyler.

It would matter later, when Tommy was gone and no one mourned the loss of his cut. But I didn't know that yet.

"So what do you need me for?" I asked.

"Scale," Randy said. "Danny, it took me *days* to create those ten identities. Manually pulling data, manually filing reports, manually checking each step. But if you automated it? If you built a system that could generate profiles, pull the right SSNs, file with the bureaus automatically?"

"Fifty identities a week," I said. "Maybe more."

"Exactly. Each identity worth four to five thousand dollars. That's..." He paused.

"Quarter million a week," I finished. "Conservatively."

"At least." Randy's grin was huge. "Danny, this is it. This is the operation that changes everything. But we can't do it without you. I can barely code a website. Jake's good with testing but not building. Colin handles money, not systems. We need someone who can actually *build* this. Someone who understands databases, automation, APIs."

"Someone who's been building criminal systems since he was sixteen," Uncle Tony added quietly.

Everyone looked at me.

This was the moment. The real moment of commitment. Not agreeing to come back to Florida. Not leaving Diana. But this. Standing in this office. Looking at what they'd built. Deciding whether to be the piece that made it all work.

I thought about David James Marcus, the identity I'd created the night I left. My insurance policy. My escape hatch. Hidden on my laptop, waiting.

The irony wasn't lost on me. I'd created a synthetic identity to protect myself from my family. Now they wanted me to create thousands more to make us all rich.

"Show me the data," I said.

Randy stepped aside, letting me sit at the main terminal. I pulled up his files. Studied the structure. The SSN database. The profile templates. The credit bureau APIs.

It was crude. Functional but inefficient. But it was expandable. And it matched the architecture I'd already been thinking about.

I could build this. Could automate the entire process. Could create a system that generated synthetic identities faster than credit bureaus could flag them.

I could make us very, very rich.

Or I could get us all sent to federal prison.

"When does Tommy want to see this working?" I asked.

"Saturday," Randy said. "After you and Dad do the skydiving thing. He wants proof of concept first. Wants to know you can actually build what we need."

"Saturday's two days away."

"Can you do it?"

I looked at the computers. At the network. At the data waiting to be processed. At Jake and Colin and Randy and Uncle Tony, all watching me. Waiting for an answer.

"I can build a basic version by Saturday. A good version will take two weeks."

Randy laughed. "I told Uncle Tony you'd say that."

Uncle Tony stood up, set down his coffee cup. "Then I'll

leave you to it. Randy, call me when the framework is ready to demonstrate. I want to see it before we show Tommy." He walked toward the door, then paused and looked back at me. "It's good to have you back, Danny. The family's stronger with you in it."

Then he was gone.

After the door closed, Jake spoke up. "Uncle Tony's been around a lot lately. More than usual."

"He's invested," Colin said, still focused on his paperwork. "Two hundred thousand in startup capital. Of course he's paying attention."

"It's more than that," Randy said. "Uncle Tony's got connections Dad doesn't have. Resources. He's the one who taught me how to filter the Death Index. Showed me which banks have weak verification. He knows things."

"What kind of things?" I asked.

Randy shrugged. "The kind of things you don't ask about. All I know is when Uncle Tony's involved, shit doesn't go wrong. Dad's been in the game forty years. Never been caught. Never even been seriously investigated. You think that's just luck?"

"No," I said quietly. "That's not luck."

"Exactly." Randy grabbed his jacket. "Look, I've got meetings today. Lining up more buyers for when we start producing at scale. Jake, keep testing. Colin, keep building the financial infrastructure. Danny..." He looked at me. "Build us something beautiful."

"No pressure," I said.

"Actually, yes pressure. This is everything. This is our shot at real money. Not Dad's petty dealing. Not small-time fraud. Real money. Life-changing money." He headed for the door. "Keys are on the desk. Alarm code is 1-9-9-0. Don't forget to set it when you leave."

After he left, Jake came over. "You good, man? You look stressed."

"I'm fine. Just processing."

"Yeah, it's a lot. When Randy first showed me what he'd built, I thought he was full of shit. Then I tested it and realized it actually works." Jake clapped me on the shoulder. "But hey, at least we're all in this together, right? All four Tyler boys. Like old times."

"Like old times," I echoed, though I knew it wasn't. It would never be like old times again.

Colin packed up his documents. "I'm heading to the bank. Need to finalize the accounts before we go operational. Danny, when you build the system, make sure it can export data in a format I can import into my accounting software. Needs to be clean. Auditable. Even fake operations need proper books."

"Will do."

They left, and I was alone in the office.

I sat at the main terminal, staring at the files Randy had created. At the proof of concept. At the evidence that this crazy scheme actually worked.

I could walk away. Could tell them I couldn't build it. Could go back to the apartment and figure out my next move.

But I wasn't going to do that.

Because Randy was right. I couldn't resist a technical challenge. And this was the ultimate technical challenge. Building a system that could fool credit bureaus. That could create people who didn't exist. That could generate wealth from nothing but ones and zeros.

It was elegant in its criminality. Beautiful in its audacity.

And I'd already figured out how to do it on a cocktail napkin at 30,000 feet.

Now I just had to build it.

I pulled up the code editor and got to work.

By the time I left the office that night, I had a basic framework. Nothing elegant, but functional. A system that could take SSNs from the database, generate synthetic profiles around them, and file reports with the credit bureaus.

It wasn't automated yet. Still required manual input at key points. But it proved the concept worked. Proved I could build what Randy and Tommy needed.

I locked up the office at nine p.m. Set the alarm. Drove back to the apartment.

Grabbed another beer. Went back out to the balcony.

The boats were still there, moving across the water in the darkness. I wondered where they were going. Wondered if the people on them were running toward something or away from something.

My phone buzzed. Text from Randy: *How'd it go?*

Good. Built the framework. Should be ready to demo Saturday.

That's my brother. Dad's going to be psyched. Uncle Tony too.

Yeah.

Three dots appeared. Then: *You okay? You've been weird since you got here.*

I thought about lying. About telling him everything was fine. About pretending I wasn't having second thoughts.

Instead, I texted: *Just adjusting. It's been a weird week.*

It has. But it's going to get better. Trust me.

I trust you.

Good. Now get some sleep. Beach tomorrow. Then Saturday you and Dad jump out of a plane and officially start this thing.

I set my phone down and finished my beer.

Tomorrow. Beach day with the family. The last day of normal before everything changed.

Saturday. Skydiving with Tommy. The symbolic jump into my new life.

And after that, the real work would begin. I'd build a criminal enterprise that would either make us rich or destroy us.

I went inside. Looked around the empty apartment. Still didn't feel like home. Might never feel like home.

I lay down on the mattress on the floor. Stared at the ceiling. Thought about Diana, alone in our old apartment. Thought about the life I'd left behind. Thought about the life I was stepping into.

My phone buzzed. Text from Tommy: *Aruba tomorrow. Two p.m. Time to talk.*

I closed my eyes and tried to sleep.

Tried not to wonder if I'd made a terrible mistake.

Tried to convince myself that this was who I really was. That this was where I belonged.

But I lay awake for hours, listening to boats moving across the water outside, wondering if I was finally becoming who I was meant to be or just becoming who my family had always expected me to be.

In the darkness of that empty apartment, I couldn't tell the difference.

5

ALL IN

I spent Friday morning fine-tuning the framework. The code was clean enough to demonstrate, rough enough to show room for improvement. Perfect for a proof of concept.

Around noon, I grabbed lunch at a Cuban place near the office. Sat in my car eating a Cuban sandwich, thinking about the meeting at Aruba. Tommy wanting to "talk" could mean anything. Another pitch. Another test. Another way to make sure I was really committed.

Or maybe he just wanted to discuss the skydiving trip.

My phone buzzed. Randy: *You heading to Aruba?*

Yeah. Two p.m.

Good. Dad's excited. This is really happening, Danny.

We'll see.

Stop being cautious. We proved it works. You're just building the machine.

He was right. The proof of concept existed. Ten identities. Forty-seven thousand dollars. Real money from fake people.

I was just making it scalable.

I finished my sandwich, drove back to the apartment to change. Couldn't show up to Aruba in the clothes I'd been coding in all morning. Put on jeans and a button-down. Made myself look like someone who had his life together.

The drive to Aruba took twenty minutes. I pulled into the parking lot at 1:45. Tommy's car wasn't there yet.

I sat in my car, engine off, watching the water. Boats moving across the Intracoastal. People on jet skis. Florida doing its Florida thing.

This was it. The moment where I stopped just thinking about the operation and started actually committing to it. Working on the framework in the office was one thing. But meeting Tommy here, discussing the details, setting the timeline, that was different.

That was choosing this life for real.

I could still drive away. Could text Tommy some excuse. Could pack up the apartment and disappear before anyone realized I was having second thoughts.

But I didn't.

At 1:55, I got out of the car and walked to the entrance.

The bar was quiet for a Friday afternoon. A few regulars watching baseball on the TV above the liquor bottles. A couple at a corner table sharing a grouper sandwich. The kind of place where locals came to drink and tourists stumbled into by accident.

I sat at the bar and waited.

A woman approached from behind the bar. Red hair, auburn rather than bright, pulled back in a way that was practical but not severe. Green eyes. Late twenties. Lean in a way that suggested discipline, not dieting. She was maybe five-eight, and she moved behind the bar with the kind of ease that said she'd been doing it for years, though something about her posture didn't quite fit. Too straight. Too aware. Bartenders slouch. This woman carried herself like someone who'd been trained not to.

She was wiping down the bar but her eyes had already done a full inventory: my watch, my shoes, the way I'd positioned myself with a sightline to both exits. The kind of pretty that doesn't try too hard because it doesn't have to. But that wasn't what caught my attention. What caught my attention was that she'd read the room faster than I had.

Most people don't notice when they're being read. I noticed because I'd been doing it to everyone else in the room.

"Hi, I'm Laura." She set a cocktail napkin in front of me. "Just you tonight?"

"My father's joining me. Running late."

"The man who raised you to always be early for meetings?"

I looked up. "Excuse me?"

She nodded toward my wrist. "You've checked your watch twice since you sat down. Either you're nervous about something or someone taught you that punctuality matters." A small smile. "Figured it was worth a guess."

"Pretty bold guess for a bartender."

"I read people." She shrugged. "Occupational hazard. You learn to size up who's going to tip well, who's going to be a problem, who's just killing time."

"And what category did you put me in?"

"Haven't decided yet." She held my gaze a beat longer than necessary. "What can I get you while you figure out if you're going to be interesting or not?"

I laughed despite myself. "Macallan 18. Neat."

"Good choice." She reached for the bottle. "Though I had you pegged for something flashier. Most guys trying to impress someone order the single malt."

"Who said I'm trying to impress anyone?"

"You ironed that shirt yourself. Recently. There's still a crease mark from the hanger." She poured. "Effort implies intention."

I took the glass. "You're either very observant or very good at making men think you're paying attention to them."

"Can't it be both?"

Something passed between us. Recognition, maybe. Two people who understood the difference between what you show and what you are. She moved down the bar to serve another customer, and I found myself watching her work. The efficiency of her movements. The way she adjusted her smile depending on who she was talking to.

Tommy arrived ten minutes later. Tan, relaxed, wearing that casual confidence like a second skin.

"There he is," he said, taking the stool next to me. "Sorry I'm late. Got held up on a call."

Laura came back over. "You must be the dad. What are you drinking?"

"Heineken," Tommy said, flashing that smile. The one that had charmed women and disarmed cops for forty years.

She grabbed his beer, set it down.

"So," Tommy said after she walked away. "You saw the office. Saw what Randy built. What do you think?"

"I think it works. The concept is sound."

"Can you scale it?"

"Yeah. I can scale it."

Tommy took a long drink of his beer. "Randy says you already figured out the SSN thing. Before you even got here."

"I worked it out on the plane. It's the logical approach if you understand the system."

"That's what I told Tony. 'Danny's gonna figure it out on

his own because he sees patterns.'" Tommy leaned back, studying me. "You know why I wanted you back? It's not just because you're good with computers. It's because you think three steps ahead. Randy's ambitious. Jake's reliable. Colin's careful. But you? You see the whole board."

"Flattery?"

"Honesty." He took another drink. "So here's what I'm thinking. We go skydiving tomorrow morning. Symbolic. Commitment. Then we go operational. You build out the full system over the next two weeks. We start producing identities at scale. By the end of the month, we're making real money."

"You already told me that."

"Quarter million a week. Maybe more if we're smart about it."

I did the math again in my head. Million a month. After Tommy and Uncle Tony got their cut and we split the rest four ways, that was $200K each. 2.4 million a year. Per person.

"That's ambitious," I said.

"We're not doing this to make pocket change. We're doing this to get rich." Tommy signaled Laura for another round. "But first, tomorrow. You and me. We jump out of that plane together. Father and son. Then we build this thing."

"Why skydiving?"

"Because you need to know you can trust me. And I need to know you're not going to back out." He smiled. "Besides, when was the last time you did something just for the thrill of it? Not for money. Not for a reason. Just because it's insane?"

He had a point. When was the last time I'd done something purely for the adrenaline? Everything in my life was calculated. Every choice was strategic. Every move was part of some larger plan.

"Tomorrow morning. What time?"

"Eight a.m. I'll pick you up." Tommy stood up, dropped cash on the bar. "I've gotta run. Got another meeting. But Danny?" He put a hand on my shoulder. "I'm glad you came back. Really glad."

He left. I sat there with my drink, processing.

When Laura came back, I had my phone out.

"Let me guess," she said. "You're going to ask for the check and tell me you have somewhere to be."

"Actually, I was going to ask if you wanted to get dinner sometime." I slid a business card across the bar. One of Randy's fronts, nothing traceable. "When you're not psycho-analyzing tourists."

She picked up the card, studied it. "Daniel Tyler. Digital consulting." Her eyebrow lifted slightly. "That's vague."

"It's supposed to be."

"Mysterious." She tucked the card into her back pocket. "I get off at eleven. There's a sushi place on the boardwalk that doesn't charge corkage if you want to bring a decent bottle of wine."

"That sounds like you asking me out."

"That sounds like me giving you a chance to be interesting." She smiled. Different from the one she'd been using on other customers. Sharper. "Don't blow it."

THE SUSHI PLACE was exactly the kind of dive a local would know. Plastic chairs, hand-written menu, the best Hamachi I'd had outside of Tokyo.

"You seem surprised." Laura watched me react to the first bite.

"I've eaten at three-star restaurants that couldn't pull this off."

"That's because they're trying too hard." She picked up her chopsticks. "Best food is usually in the ugliest rooms."

"Speaking from experience?"

"I've been places." She said it simply, no elaboration. I filed it away.

We talked about nothing important for an hour. Travel, music, the absurdity of resort towns. She was smart and funny and just guarded enough to be interesting. Every answer she gave felt considered, like she was choosing from multiple options and giving me the one she wanted me to have.

I recognized the technique. I used it myself.

"Can I tell you something?" she said, somewhere between the sake and the green tea ice cream.

"You're about to tell me you don't do this."

She stopped. "What?"

"This." I gestured between us. "Go out with customers. Give your number to strangers. You're going to tell me you're not the kind of person who does casual, so if that's what I'm looking for, I should tell you now."

Laura stared at me for a long moment. Then she laughed. Genuinely, not the performer's laugh she'd been using at the bar.

"Jesus. Does that line not work on you?"

"It's a good line. It's designed to make the guy feel special. Like he's the exception. Like you're taking a risk on him specifically."

"And you're immune?"

"I didn't say that." I took a sip of sake. "I said I recognized it. Doesn't mean it's not working."

She leaned back in her chair, studying me with new interest. "You're not what I expected."

"What did you expect?"

"The usual. Some finance guy down here on daddy's money, looking for a vacation hookup with the hot bartender. I figured I'd get a free dinner and an excuse to leave early."

"And now?"

"Now I'm wondering what digital consulting actually means and why you noticed I was reading you before I'd said a word."

"Trade secrets."

"Mmm." She reached across the table and took my sake cup, finished it. "I'm going to tell you something, and I need you to not be weird about it."

"Okay."

"I don't do this. That part wasn't a line." She set the cup down. "I've been down here six months and you're the first person I've gone to dinner with. Not because I'm picky. Because everyone else was exactly what they looked like. You're not."

"Is that a compliment?"

"It's an observation." She held my gaze. "I'm curious about you. That's rare for me. I'd like to see where it goes. But I need you to understand something. I don't know how to do casual. It's not in my programming. So if you're looking for someone to pass time with until you go back to wherever you came from, this isn't the conversation to be having."

The smart move was to keep it light. Don't commit to anything. Keep my options open.

"I'm not going anywhere," I said. "At least not for a while."

"That's not a real answer."

"No," I agreed. "But it's an honest one. I don't know what I'm looking for either. I just know I haven't been bored once in the last two hours, and that doesn't happen to me often."

She considered this. "Fair enough."

"Fair enough meaning...?"

"Meaning let's get another drink somewhere and see if you can keep it going." She stood, dropped enough cash on the table to cover her half. "I'm not going to be the girl who lets the guy pay and then owes him something. This stays even until I decide otherwise."

"You always this direct?"

"Only when it matters."

WE ENDED up at a rooftop bar overlooking the marina, trading stories that were probably fifty percent true on both sides. She'd been a bartender for three years. Traveled a lot before that. Didn't talk about family. I told her I was down here helping my father with some business. Didn't specify what kind.

At midnight, she stood up.

"I should go. Early shift tomorrow."

"Can I walk you?"

"It's three blocks and this isn't exactly a dangerous neighborhood." But she didn't say no.

We walked in comfortable silence. When we got to her building, a small apartment complex with exterior stairs, she turned to face me.

"This was good," she said. "Better than I expected."

"High praise."

"Don't let it go to your head." But she was smiling.

I wanted to kiss her. The setup was perfect. Moonlight, quiet street, the whole romantic cliché. But something about the way she was holding herself told me to wait.

"When can I see you again?"

"I'm off Tuesday."

"Tuesday then."

She nodded, started up the stairs, then stopped. Turned back.

"Danny?"

"Yeah?"

"I wasn't running game on you tonight. At the restaurant, when I said I don't do casual, I meant it. But I don't want you to think that means I know what this is either." She searched for words. "I'm not asking you to promise anything. I'm just asking you to be honest with me. Even when it's inconvenient. Can you do that?"

The irony wasn't lost on me. I was running a criminal conspiracy with my family. Honesty wasn't exactly on the menu.

But standing there, looking up at her, I said: "I'll try."

"That's all I'm asking."

She went inside. I walked back to my car replaying every moment of the evening, trying to figure out if I'd just made a terrible mistake or the best decision of my life.

MY PHONE BUZZED. Text from Randy: *Dad's pumped. Says you're ready for Tomorrow.*

I texted back: *Ready as I'll ever be.*

6

THE JUMP

Tommy picked me up at 7:45 Saturday morning in his Mercedes. He was wearing cargo pants and a T-shirt, looking more relaxed than I'd seen him in years.

"You ready?" he asked as I got in.

"As I'll ever be."

"That's the spirit." He pulled out of the parking lot, heading toward the skydiving place in Deerfield Beach. "You nervous?"

"A little."

"Good. You should be. Jumping out of an airplane is insane. But that's the point." He glanced at me. "Life's too short to only do safe things. Sometimes you gotta jump and trust the parachute works."

"Is this a metaphor?"

"Everything's a metaphor if you think about it long enough." He grinned. "But also, we're literally jumping out of an airplane. So it's both."

We drove in comfortable silence for a while. The sun was still low in the sky, turning everything orange and gold.

Florida mornings were beautiful. I'd forgotten that during my years in Maryland.

My phone buzzed. Laura.

Tuesday feels far away. You free tonight?

I stared at the message. She'd been the one holding back Friday night. Asking for honesty. Setting boundaries. Now she was the one reaching out.

Jumping out of a plane this morning. Dinner tonight?

You're jumping out of a plane?

Long story. Pick you up at six?

If you survive. Yes.

I pocketed the phone. Tommy glanced over.

"Important?"

"Just making plans for later."

"The bartender?"

"Laura. Yeah."

Tommy nodded, a small smile on his face. "Good. You need something besides work. Keeps you balanced."

Coming from him, that was almost funny. But I didn't say anything.

"Can I ask you something?" I said instead.

"Shoot."

"Why did you really want me back? I know it's about the operation. But there are other people who could build what you need. Other technical guys."

Tommy was quiet for a moment. "You want the truth?"

"Always."

"Because you're my son. And I've watched you your whole life trying to be something you're not. Trying to escape what you are. And I knew, eventually, you'd figure out that you can't outrun your own nature." He looked at me. "I wanted you back because the family is stronger with you in it. Not just because you're smart. But because you're a Tyler. And Tylers take care of each other."

"Even when we fuck each other over?"

He laughed. "Especially then. That's what family is. Fucking each other over and still showing up for dinner."

"That's dark."

"That's honest." He pulled into the skydiving facility parking lot. "Come on. Let's go jump out of an airplane before we get too philosophical."

THE FACILITY WAS SMALL. A hangar, an office, a field where people landed. The instructor's name was Mike. Mid-forties, probably done this a thousand times, completely calm about the whole thing.

"First time?" he asked.

"Yeah," I said.

"You'll be tandem with me. Tommy, you're with Rick. We'll go over the basics, get you suited up, then head up to twelve thousand feet."

"Twelve thousand?" I said.

"Standard altitude. Gives you about sixty seconds of free fall before the chute deploys." Mike smiled. "Don't worry. It's safer than driving on I-95."

"That's not comforting."

Tommy was grinning like a maniac. This was his element. Risk. Adrenaline. The edge between life and death.

We spent twenty minutes going over safety procedures. How to position your body. What happens if something goes wrong. What to do when the parachute deploys.

It all sounded simple until they started actually strapping me into the harness.

"You good?" Mike asked.

"Define good."

"You're not going to pass out or vomit, right?"

"Probably not."

"Close enough."

We walked to the plane. Small Cessna, seats removed, just enough room for the four of us and the pilot. Tommy got in first, then his instructor Rick, then me, then Mike. The door stayed open.

The engine started. We began to taxi.

"Too late to back out now," Tommy said.

"Thanks. That helps."

The plane took off. We climbed. Five thousand feet. Eight thousand. Ten thousand.

The ground got smaller and smaller. The ocean appeared in the distance. Everything looked like a toy model of the world.

"Twelve thousand feet," the pilot called back.

Mike started checking my harness. Tightening straps. Making sure everything was secure. "You ready?"

"No."

"Perfect. Let's go." He clipped himself to me. Moved us toward the open door.

Tommy and Rick went first. Tommy gave me a thumbs up, then just...stepped out. Disappeared into the sky.

"Holy shit," I said.

"Your turn," Mike said.

We shuffled to the door. I could see nothing but sky and a tiny ground twelve thousand feet below.

"On three," Mike said. "One...two..."

He didn't wait for three. We jumped.

The first sensation was pure terror. Wind hitting me at 120 miles per hour. My stomach in my throat. No sense of up or down or which way was which. Just falling, falling, falling into nothing.

Then, strangely, it got calm.

The wind was constant. The fall was steady. And I could see everything. The ocean stretching to the horizon, blue and endless. The coast, a thin line of sand between water and land. The patchwork of South Florida spread out below me like a map someone had crumpled and then tried to smooth out again.

Tommy was falling about thirty feet away, arms spread wide, grinning like a maniac. He caught my eye and gave me a thumbs up. Even at terminal velocity, even plummeting toward earth at a speed that should have been terrifying, he looked completely at ease.

I understood, in that moment, why he'd wanted to do this. It wasn't about proving anything. It wasn't about commitment or symbolism or any of the things he'd said.

It was about this feeling. This absolute freedom. This moment where nothing else mattered except the fact that you were alive and falling and trusting that the parachute would work.

Sixty seconds. That's how long we fell. It felt like both forever and no time at all.

The world rushed up at us. Details emerged from the blur. Individual buildings. Cars on roads. People who had no idea that two men were hurtling toward them from twelve thousand feet.

Then Mike pulled the chute.

The harness jerked hard against my chest and thighs as the parachute deployed. The world went from chaos to silence. One second we were falling at 120 miles per hour; the next, we were floating. Drifting. The ground still getting bigger, but slowly now. Gently.

"How you doing?" Mike asked from behind me.

"That was insane."

"Best kind of insane." He adjusted the toggles, steering us toward the landing field. "See your dad?"

I looked over. Tommy and Rick were about a hundred feet away, also floating down. Tommy was still grinning. He waved when he saw me looking.

"Yeah. I see him."

"He's done this before. Couple times. Always brings someone new. Says it's his way of testing people."

"Testing them how?"

"Seeing if they'll jump. A lot of people talk about it. Make plans. Get all the way up in the plane." Mike paused. "Then they look out that door and they can't do it. They freeze. Ask to go back down."

"What happens to them?"

"Nothing. We take them back down. No judgment. It's not for everyone." I could hear the smile in his voice. "But your dad doesn't really stay in touch with them after. Says if someone can't take the leap, they're not the kind of person he wants to work with."

I thought about that as we descended. The leap. The moment of commitment. The instant when you stop thinking and just act.

That's what Tommy was really testing. Not courage. Not trust. Just the willingness to move forward when every instinct screamed at you to stay safe.

We landed smoothly, Mike guiding us to a gentle touch-down on the grass. He unclipped the harness and I stood on solid ground, legs shaky, heart still pounding, adrenaline coursing through every cell.

Tommy landed had already unclipped from Rick. Walked over with that huge grin still plastered on his face.

"Well?" he asked.

"That was incredible."

"The feeling. Incredible. Falling through the sky. Just." He spread his arms. "Free. Nothing holding you." He looked at me intensely. "Nothing. Welcome back, son. For real this time."

We stood there in the middle of a field in Deerfield Beach, two criminals who'd just jumped out of an airplane together. Father and son. Partners, maybe, in whatever came next.

"Now what?" I asked.

"Now we go make some money." Tommy started toward the parking lot, then stopped and looked back at me. "Danny. You jumped. Not everyone does. Remember that."

"What does it mean?"

"It means when the moment comes, when you have to choose between safe and necessary, you won't freeze. You won't overthink it. You'll jump." His eyes were serious now, the grin faded. "That's the most important thing I can teach you. Everything else is just details."

I followed him to the car, thinking about his words.

Jump first. Think later. Trust the parachute.

It sounded like philosophy. But I'd seen how Tommy applied it. Jump into the drug deal. Jump into the affair. Jump into whatever felt right in the moment, and call it instinct instead of impulse.

Tommy's "code" wasn't about discipline. It was about giving himself permission.

WE DROVE BACK to the Commercial Boulevard office. Randy's car was already there. So was Jake's truck.

"They started without us?" I asked.

"I told them to get everything ready. Today is our first operational day. Figured we might as well dive in." Tommy grinned at his own pun. "Get it? Dive in?"

"I get it."

Inside, Randy and Jake had the office humming. All three workstations were running. The server was up. Monitors displayed data streams, credit reports, account verifications.

"There they are," Randy said. "How was the jump?"

"Insane," I said. "But good."

"Told you he'd love it." Randy came over, pulled me aside. "Okay, so here's the situation. We've got buyers ready to go. Today. Right now. I can move ten identities immediately if you can generate them."

"Ten? Today?"

"First day of operations, Danny. Gotta make an impression." Randy pulled up his laptop. "I've got a guy in Miami who'll take all ten. Five grand each. Fifty thousand dollars. Today."

I looked at Tommy. He nodded. "Do it. Show us what you've built."

I sat down at the main terminal. Pulled up the system I'd coded over the last two days. It wasn't pretty, but it was functional. The database was loaded with SSNs from the Death Index. The profile generator was ready. The credit bureau integration was live.

"Alright," I said. "Let's see if this works."

I started the process. The system, still in its infancy pulled a SSN from the database. Generated a profile: name, address, date of birth, employment history. I manually filed reports with all three credit bureaus. I needed to automate that part still. We'd created a complete synthetic identity in about six minutes.

"Verification's coming back clean," Jake said, watching over my shoulder.

I ran it again. Another identity. Six minutes. Then another. And another.

By noon, I'd generated ten complete identities. Ten fake people with real credit histories, real addresses, real employment records. Ten ghosts that would pass verification because every component looked legitimate.

Randy was on the phone immediately. "Yeah, I've got your ten...Everything's clean...Cash only...I'll text you the drop location...Two hours."

He hung up. Looked at me. "We just made fifty thousand dollars."

"Technically, we generated fifty thousand in credit lines and sold access to those identities for fifty thousand dollars," I corrected. "The actual fraud happens when the buyer uses them."

"Always the details guy." Randy grinned. "But yeah. Fifty K. First day. This is actually happening."

Jake had been testing each identity as I generated them. Verifying that the credit reports were filed correctly. That the accounts looked real. That nothing bounced back with flags.

"All ten passed. These are solid, Danny. Better than solid. They're invisible."

Tommy was watching from the corner, arms crossed, that proud expression on his face. "I knew you could do it. I told Tony last night, 'Danny's gonna blow our minds.' And look at this. Ten identities in a morning."

"Basic version," I said. "The full automation will take another week. But yeah, this works."

"It more than works." Randy grabbed his keys. "I'm going to meet the buyer. Make the drop. Should be back in three hours with cash."

"Be careful," Tommy said.

"Always am." Randy left to meet the buyer.

RANDY CAME BACK AROUND 5:30 with a duffel bag.

"Fifty thousand," he said, dumping it on the desk. "All there. All clean. Guy didn't even blink."

He started counting, sorting bills into piles with practiced efficiency. "Ten for Dad." His voice was flat on those words. "Seven-five for Tony's cut until he's whole on the investment." He kept counting. "Leaves thirty-two five. Eight grand each."

Jake looked up from his workstation. "Ten thousand dollars for sitting at home watching golf."

"Don't start." Randy didn't look up from the money, but his jaw was tight.

"I'm just saying."

"I know what you're saying. We're all saying it." Randy finished the count, pushed four stacks across the desk. "But that's the deal. You want to renegotiate, be my guest. I'll wait here while you call Dad and explain why his cut should be smaller."

Jake didn't reach for his phone.

I picked up my stack. Eight thousand dollars. For four hours of work. Even after Tommy's tax and Tony's return, this was more than I'd made in two months selling electronics in Maryland.

"This is insane," I said.

"This is day one" Randy finally smiled. "Wait till we scale up."

I PICKED Laura up at six. She opened the door in jeans and a black top, barefoot, hair still damp.

"You survived," she said.

"Barely."

"Tell me."

We walked Las Olas as the sun went down. I told her about the jump. The terror. The moment of calm in the middle of the fall. The way Tommy had grinned at me from thirty feet away like we were sharing the best secret in the world.

I didn't tell her what came after. The office. The identities. The thousands of dollars currently sitting in my apartment.

"So your father's idea of bonding is mutual near-death experiences."

"He has unconventional parenting methods."

"Clearly." Her hand found mine. "But you liked it. I can tell."

"I did. I don't know what that says about me."

"It says you're not as careful as you pretend to be." She looked at me sideways. "I suspected that already."

Dinner was at a place she knew, small and Italian, the kind of restaurant that doesn't need a sign because the right people already know where it is. We drank the bottle of wine I brought and ate pasta. The conversation kept almost touching something real before veering back to safe territory.

We were both still performing. But the gaps between the performances were getting shorter.

At her door, she didn't reach for her keys.

"You want to come up?"

I should have said no. I should have remembered that I was building a criminal enterprise with my family, that everything I'd told her was a lie, that getting closer to her only made the eventual reckoning worse.

Instead I thought about what Tommy had said. Jump first. Trust the parachute.

"Yeah, I do."

She led me upstairs. Unlocked her door. Turned to face me in the dim apartment, the city lights coming through the windows behind her.

"I don't do this," she said. "You know that."

"You keep saying that."

"Because I need you to understand what it means." She stepped closer. "I'm not asking you for promises. I'm not asking you to be something you're not. But if this happens, it's not casual for me. It can't be."

I thought about the fifty thousand dollars. The ten fake people I'd created that morning. The operation that was just getting started.

I thought about Diana, who'd asked me to choose a normal life, and how I'd chosen this instead.

"It's not casual for me either." And in that moment, I meant it.

She kissed me. Walked backward toward the bedroom, pulling me with her.

I followed. Because that's what I did now. I jumped.

～

I woke up before dawn with Laura's arm across my chest. For a few minutes, I just lay there, listening to her breathe, watching the early light change the shadows on the ceiling.

Twelve hours ago, I'd jumped out of an airplane. Eight hours ago, I'd made thousands creating fake people. Now I was lying in bed with a woman who'd asked me for honesty, and I'd given her everything except the truth.

I should have felt guilty. I was building something with her on a foundation of omissions and strategic silences.

But I didn't feel guilty. I felt, for the first time in months, like I was exactly where I was supposed to be.

Two leaps in one day. Tommy would be proud.

That should have worried me more than it did.

7
____

SIGNALS

The next two weeks became a rhythm. Generate, test, sell. Generate, test, sell.

I optimized the system until I could produce a clean identity in under three minutes. Jake tested them as fast as I could generate them. All passing verification, all ready to sell. Randy worked the buyers: Miami, Tampa, Atlanta, a guy in Houston who wanted bulk orders. Colin processed everything through his offshore maze until the money came out clean on the other side.

By the end of the second week, we'd cleared more than two hundred thousand dollars. After Tommy's cut and Tony's return, that still left us each with close to forty grand.

Randy wanted to push harder.

"Fifty identities a week," he said, pacing the office while the rest of us counted money. "Then seventy-five. By end of the month, we hit a hundred. Consistent. Predictable. Real volume."

"That's a lot of exposure," I said.

"That's a lot of money. There's a difference."

"Every identity is a thread someone can pull. Every transaction is a data point. You scale too fast, patterns emerge."

"Or the patterns get lost in the noise." Colin looked up from his laptop. "We're not the only ones doing this. Credit bureaus process millions of reports a month. Our thirty-five identities? Statistical rounding error. A hundred would still be invisible."

I looked at Jake. He shrugged. "The system's solid. Everything's passing verification. If we're going to get caught, it won't be because of volume."

Randy was watching me, waiting.

"Fifty a week," I said finally. "We see how that goes. Then we talk about more."

"That's all I'm asking." Randy grinned. "Fifty a week is two-fifty. After cuts, that's still fifty grand each. Per week." He grabbed his jacket. "I'm going to Miami. Got a buyer who wants to talk about recurring orders. You guys lock up."

After he left, Colin shook his head. "He's going to push for a hundred by month's end. You know that."

"I know."

"You going to let him?"

I thought about it. About the money. About the risk. About the difference between caution and cowardice.

"Probably," I said. "If the system holds."

Tommy stopped by the office once during those two weeks. Looked at the spreadsheets, nodded at the numbers, didn't ask any questions about how it worked. Just collected his cut in a brown paper bag like a landlord picking up rent.

"Nice work, boys," he said on his way out. "Keep it up."

Randy watched him go with that flat expression he got when he was biting back things he couldn't say.

"Twenty percent," Jake muttered.

"Drop it," Randy said. But he didn't disagree.

I SAW Laura three times during those two weeks. Quick dinners between operations. A Sunday afternoon walking the beach. She didn't ask too many questions about work, and I was grateful for that.

But the third time, dinner at a Thai place in Wilton Manors, she changed the rules.

We'd ordered family style, plates covering the table, a bottle of wine half empty between us. The neighborhood outside was alive with color, rainbow flags, street art, people being exactly who they were without apology. Laura had chosen this place deliberately, I realized. Testing to see if I was comfortable here.

I was.

She set down her wine glass. "Tell me something real."

"We're back to this?"

"We never left it. I just gave you a few weeks to get comfortable." She smiled, but her eyes were serious. "We've talked about surface stuff. Where we grew up. Jobs. Movies. But I want to know something that matters. Something you don't tell people."

I thought about what I could say that was true without being incriminating.

"I spent two years trying to be someone I wasn't. Had a good job. A good relationship. A future that looked exactly like it was supposed to look. And I was miserable. Every single day."

"Why?"

"Because none of it was mine. It was what I thought I was supposed to want. What everyone told me was the right choice. The safe choice." I turned my wine glass slowly on the table. "I realized I'd rather be myself and struggle than pretend and be comfortable. So I came back here. To my family. To the life that actually fits."

"Even if that life is complicated?"

"Especially if it's complicated. Simple was killing me."

She was quiet for a moment, processing that. Then she said, "My dad was military intelligence."

I waited. This felt like the beginning of something important.

"He did things he couldn't talk about. Not to my mom. Not to me. Not to anyone outside his world." She picked up her wine, held it without drinking. "I grew up knowing that my father had this whole other life. That the man who helped me with homework and coached my soccer team also did things that mattered in ways he could never explain. Things that were probably illegal, technically. Things that kept people safe."

"That must have been hard."

"It was confusing. For a long time." She finally took a drink. "But it taught me something. There are people who live in the daylight. Who only see what's on the surface, who think the world works the way they learned in civics class. And then there are people who understand that it's more complicated than that. That sometimes you have to operate in gray areas to accomplish things that matter."

My chest tightened. She was describing my life. My choices. The justifications I told myself in the dark hours when I couldn't sleep.

"Which kind of person are you?" I asked.

"I'm still figuring that out." She met my eyes. "What about you?"

"Gray areas. Definitely gray areas."

"I know." She reached across the table, took my hand. "I knew that the first time I saw you. That's why I gave you my number."

"Because I looked like I operated in gray areas?"

"Because you looked like you understood that the world isn't simple. That good people sometimes do complicated things." She squeezed my hand. "I'm tired of simple, Danny. Simple is boring. Simple doesn't understand me."

"And you think I understand you?"

"I think you might be the first person in a long time who could."

We finished dinner and walked around the neighborhood, her hand in mine. Past the rainbow flags and the street art and the bars full of people being unapologetically themselves.

"I like this place," she said. "Everyone's just...who they are."

"No performance."

"Exactly." She stopped walking, turned to face me. "Danny, I don't need to know everything about you. Not yet. Maybe not ever, depending on what it is. But I need to know that what I'm seeing is real. That you're not just showing me what I want to see."

"What you're seeing is real."

And it was. The parts she was seeing, anyway. The person who lived in gray areas. Who understood that the world was complicated. Who'd rather be authentic and struggling than fake and comfortable.

The parts I was hiding, the specifics, the details, the federal crimes, those weren't lies. They were omissions. A different kind of deception, but maybe not an unforgivable one.

At least that's what I told myself.

"Good," she said, and kissed me. "Then the rest will figure itself out."

~

I WALKED BACK to my car feeling like something had shifted in my chest. Not pain. Something else. Something I hadn't felt in a long time and had trained myself to distrust.

I sat in the driver's seat without starting the engine.

The street was quiet. Her building's exterior lights cast long shadows across the parking lot. Somewhere a dog barked twice, then stopped. I could still smell her perfume on my shirt, something subtle that I'd been breathing in all night without consciously noticing.

I replayed the evening. The Thai place with amazing food. Walking through Wilton Manors afterward, past the rainbow flags and the street art and the bars full of people being exactly who they were. Her hand finding mine somewhere between the restaurant and her apartment. The way she'd stopped under a streetlight and looked at me like she was making a decision.

But it was what she'd said about her father that kept circling back.

He did things he couldn't talk about. Not to my mom. Not to me. Not to anyone outside his world.

She understood compartmentalization. Understood that the man who helped with homework could also be someone else entirely. She'd grown up knowing that love didn't require complete transparency, that you could care deeply about someone whose full truth you'd never access.

That was rare. That was dangerous.

Because it meant she might actually be able to handle what I was. Not the sanitized version I'd given Diana the "complicated family" and "fresh start" bullshit that had crumbled the moment it touched reality. But the actual truth. The criminal. The fraud. The man who'd spent his morning generating fake identities and his evening pretending to be someone who deserved a woman like her.

I pulled out my phone. Scrolled to Randy's number. My thumb hovered over the call button.

What would I even say? *Hey, remember how you said I'd snap if I kept pretending to be someone I'm not? Well, I met someone. And the fucked up thing is, I'm not pretending with her. Or at least, I'm pretending less. And that terrifies me more than the lying ever did.*

Randy would laugh. Would tell me to enjoy it, stop overthinking, let something good happen for once. He wouldn't understand why that was exactly the problem.

I put the phone away.

The thing about Diana was that I'd always known it couldn't last. Even in the good moments, some part of me was waiting for the collapse. Preparing exit strategies. Keeping one foot out the door emotionally even while I played the role of devoted fiancé.

This felt different.

This felt like I might actually want it to work. Like I might care enough to be hurt when it inevitably fell apart. Like Laura had somehow gotten past defenses I didn't even know I had, and now I was exposed in ways that made everything more complicated.

She's a bartender. A bartender you met three weeks ago.

But she wasn't just a bartender. I'd known that from the first conversation. The way she read people. The way she'd clocked me immediately and called it out instead of playing dumb. The father in military intelligence. The international relations degree. The summer in Tokyo that she mentioned so casually, like everyone spent their college years in foreign countries.

There was more to her story. Pieces she wasn't sharing yet. Maybe pieces she'd never share.

That should have bothered me. Instead, it felt like recognition. Like finding someone who understood that the surface was never the whole truth.

I started the car. The engine turned over, and I sat there another minute, headlights illuminating the empty parking spaces in front of me.

There was a smart play here. The careful play. Keep it casual. Don't let it become something that could be used against me. Protect myself the way I'd always protected myself, by never caring too much about anything I couldn't afford to lose, but Laura didn't do casual.

I thought about her face when she'd talked about wanting something real. The vulnerability she'd shown, knowing I might use it against her or simply walk away. The courage it took to be honest when honesty was the most dangerous thing you could offer someone.

She'd asked me to be honest with her. I'd said I'd try.

Maybe trying was enough. Maybe trying was more than I'd ever given Diana, who got the performance instead of the person.

Fuck the smart play.

I was already in too deep with everything else. The operation. The family. The money flowing through accounts that would make a federal prosecutor weep with joy. What was one more risk? What was one more way this whole thing could blow up in my face?

At least this one felt like living instead of just surviving.

I pulled out of the parking lot and headed home, already

thinking about when I'd see her again. Already planning. Already falling.

The voice in my head that sounded like Tommy told me I was being stupid. That feelings were leverage other people could use. That the only safe move was no move at all.

I told that voice to shut up.

Some lessons from my father weren't worth keeping.

8

———

SOMETHING'S OFF

The next three weeks ran like clockwork.

Week two: forty identities generated and sold. $180,000 split between us. Jake refined his testing protocols. Colin streamlined the money laundering process.

Week three: fifty identities. Randy talking about pushing to seventy-five. The operation humming like a machine. Everything working too perfectly.

Week four started the same way. Monday morning, business as usual.

Then Tommy started acting strange.

"Forty identities sold this week," he announced Monday morning at the office. "That's $200,000 in sales alone. Plus another $80K from the cards we're running ourselves. Quarter million in seven days, gentlemen."

Jake raised his coffee cup in salute. Colin updated his spreadsheets. I sat at my workstation, generating more synthetic identities, watching the numbers populate on screen like I was playing God with social security numbers.

"We need to scale up," Randy continued. "Danny, can you generate more? Fifty a week instead of forty?"

"Probably. The system's pretty automated now."

"Do it. Colin, we need more buyers. Jake, you've got that connection in Atlanta, right? The guy who wanted bulk?"

"Yeah, but he's risky. Wants to pay half price for volume."

"Tell him full price or nothing. We're not desperate." Randy was pacing, energized, already spending money we hadn't made yet. "And we need to expand the card operation. I'm thinking we hit high-end retailers. Best Buy, Apple Store. Buy expensive shit, flip it immediately."

"That's more exposure," I said. "More cameras, more security, more chances to get caught."

"More money," Randy countered. "Look, we've proven the system works. Now we need to maximize profit before someone figures out how to shut us down."

"Someone like the FBI?" Colin asked quietly.

"They don't even know we exist. We're too small, too new, too clean." Randy stopped pacing, looked at each of us. "This is our moment. We either go big or we go home."

Tommy chose that moment to walk in.

He'd been mostly hands-off the first few weeks, checking in daily, reviewing the numbers, collecting his cut. But something about him this morning felt different. Off.

"Morning," he said, but his smile didn't reach his eyes. "Sounds like things are going well."

"Better than well," Randy said. "We're printing money."

"Good. That's good." Tommy pulled up a chair, sat down heavily. "I wanted to talk about operational security."

"We're secure," Randy said. "Colin's got the accounts locked down, Danny's covering our digital tracks."

"I mean physical security. People watching us. Following us. We need to be careful."

"Has someone been following you?" I asked.

"No. Maybe. I don't know." Tommy rubbed his face. "I

just think we should all be more careful. Don't talk about this on our regular phones. Don't meet at the same places all the time. Don't leave paper trails."

"Dad, we already don't do any of that," Randy said.

"Just making sure." Tommy stood up again. "Also, I need detailed records of what we're doing. Who we're selling to, how much, what methods we're using. For accounting purposes."

The room went quiet.

"Why?" Colin asked.

"What do you mean, why? So we know where the money's going. So we can track our growth."

"We have records," Colin said carefully. "But they're encrypted and minimal. Deliberately. The less detail we keep, the less evidence exists if something goes wrong."

"I'm not asking for court documents. Just basic information. Who bought what, when, for how much."

Randy and I exchanged glances.

"I'll put something together," Colin said. "But it'll be coded. Names will be abbreviations, amounts will be approximate."

"Fine. Just get it to me by end of week." Tommy headed for the door, then stopped. "Oh, and we should have a family dinner soon. All of us. Rachel wants to cook."

"When?" Randy asked.

"I'll let you know. Soon." He left without waiting for a response.

After the door closed, none of us spoke for a solid minute.

"That was weird," Jake finally said.

"Yeah," I agreed.

Randy was staring at the closed door, jaw tight. "He's never asked for detailed records before."

"Maybe he's just being cautious." Colin didn't sound convinced.

"Or maybe something spooked him," I said. "He looked nervous."

"Tommy doesn't get nervous," Randy said. "That's not how he operates."

"Everyone gets nervous sometimes," Jake said.

Randy shook his head. "Not like that. Not over nothing." He pulled out his phone, typed something, and put it away. "I want to know where he goes today. Who he talks to."

"You want to follow your own father?" Colin asked.

"I want to know why he's suddenly acting like a paranoid accountant." Randy sat down at his desk, powered up his laptop. "We're making money hand over fist. Everything's working. Why is he suddenly worried about security and asking for documentation?"

"Because we're making money hand over fist," I said. "Maybe he's just being smart."

"Maybe." Randy didn't look convinced. "Or maybe something's happening he's not telling us about."

The rest of the day felt wrong. Like when you smell smoke but can't find the fire.

I generated identities. Ran tests. Checked the system. Everything worked perfectly. But I couldn't shake the feeling that Tommy's visit had been more than just a check-in.

Around three o'clock, Randy's phone buzzed. He looked at it, frowned, walked outside to take the call. Came back five minutes later looking even more suspicious.

"That was Marco," he said. "One of Dad's old connections. Said he saw Tommy having coffee with some guy in a suit downtown. Said it looked official. Like government official."

"Could have been his lawyer," Colin suggested.

"Could have been. But Marco said the guy had that cop look. You know what I mean."

We all knew what he meant. That certain military posture, that watchful stillness, that way of sitting with your back to the wall and eyes on the door.

"Probably nothing," Jake said, but his voice lacked conviction.

"Probably," Randy agreed. "But I'm going to make some calls. See if anyone else has seen anything weird."

By end of day, we had a list:

Tommy meeting with the suit at Starbucks (Tuesday, 9 a.m.), Tommy disappearing for three hours Wednesday afternoon phone off, Tommy asking Jake weird, specific questions about our buyer network, Tommy calling Colin twice after hours asking about banking procedures, Tommy sitting in his car outside the office for twenty minutes one morning, just watching.

None of it was damning. All of it was strange.

"He's up to something," Randy said as we locked up the office. "I can feel it."

"Maybe he's planning something for the operation," I suggested. "Expansion, new angle, something he's keeping quiet until he works it out."

"Then why the secrecy? Why not just tell us?"

"Because he's Tommy. He likes being mysterious."

"This is different." Randy leaned against his Mercedes, lit a cigarette. "I've known that man my whole life. This isn't his usual power play bullshit. This is something else."

"So what do you want to do?"

"Watch him. Carefully. See what he's really up to." Randy took a long drag. "And we keep this between us for now. The four of us. If something's wrong, I don't want him knowing we're onto him."

"What if it's nothing?"

"Then we wasted some time being paranoid. But if it's something..." Randy flicked ash onto the pavement. "Then we need to know before it's too late."

THE NEXT TWO days were a masterclass in subtle surveillance.

Jake followed Tommy to lunch, watched him meet with the same suited man again. Got photos this time. The guy had that federal agent look for sure. Conservative haircut, boring suit, eyes that tracked everything.

Colin monitored Tommy's phone records. Found multiple calls to the same untraceable number. Burner phone, probably. But why did Tommy need a burner phone?

Randy dug into Tommy's recent financial records, or tried to. Found that Tommy had opened a new bank account three weeks ago. Separate from everything else. Deposits that didn't match our operation's numbers.

And me? I was watching Tommy's behavior at the office. The way he asked questions that were just a little too specific. The way he seemed interested in details he'd never cared about before. The way he left meetings early, always with some excuse.

Thursday afternoon, the four of us met at Randy's place. We spread our findings across the dining room table like detectives in a bad cop show.

"Here's what we know," Randy said. "Tommy's meeting with someone who might be federal. He's got a burner phone. He's got a secret bank account with deposits we can't trace. And he's suddenly very interested in documentation and operational details."

"That's circumstantial," Colin said. "It doesn't prove anything."

"It proves something's wrong," Jake said. "Question is, what?"

"Maybe he's planning to cut us out," I suggested. "Start his own version of the operation."

"Or maybe he's skimming," Jake offered. "Taking more than his share, hiding it."

"Or maybe..." Randy trailed off, looking at the photos of Tommy with the suited man. "Maybe he's scared."

"Of what?"

"Getting caught. Going to prison. Anthony Sr. finding out he fucked up somehow." Randy tapped the photo. "What if Dad knows something we don't? What if the feds are already watching us and he's trying to cover his own ass?"

"By doing what?" Colin asked.

"That's what we need to find out." Randy gathered up the papers. "But we can't confront him directly. Not yet. We need more information first."

My phone buzzed. Text from Tommy: "Family dinner Saturday night. Seven p.m. My place. Not optional. Bring everyone."

I showed it to the others. They all got the same text simultaneously.

"Not optional," Jake read aloud. "That's a weird way to phrase an invitation."

"Everything about this is weird," Randy said. He stared at the text for a long moment. "Saturday dinner. Fine. We'll go. We'll be polite. We'll eat Rachel's cooking. And we'll watch everything Dad does and says."

"And then what?" I asked.

"Then we figure out what the hell he's up to." Randy deleted the text. "But we need to be careful. If he's scared, if he's doing something behind our backs, we can't let him know we're suspicious. We act normal. We smile. We play the good sons."

"And if we find out he's planning something that threatens us?"

Randy's expression went cold. "Then we deal with it. As a family."

The way he said 'family' made it sound more like a threat than a bond.

THAT FRIDAY, the operation ran smooth. We generated identities, made sales, moved money. Everything clockwork perfect. But underneath the surface, we were all watching Tommy.

He came by the office twice. Both times, he stayed less than ten minutes. Both times, he made excuses to leave quickly. Both times, he checked his phone obsessively.

"He's waiting for something," Randy said after Tommy's second visit. "Or someone."

"The dinner," Colin suggested. "Maybe whatever he's planning goes down then."

"Which is why we need to be ready." Randy pulled Jake and me aside. "Tomorrow night, we go in careful. No phones. No recording devices. Nothing that could be used against us later."

"Why would we need..." I started.

"Just trust me. Something about this feels wrong. And I'd rather be paranoid and safe than relaxed and fucked."

I wanted to argue. Wanted to say we were overreacting.

But the truth was, I felt it too. That wrongness. That sense of something building toward a breaking point.

Laura called that evening. "You sound tense."

"Work stuff."

"Danny, you always say that. What's really going on?"

I was sitting in my apartment, drinking beer, trying to figure out how to explain that I thought my father might be planning to betray us without actually saying any of that.

"Family drama," I finally said. "My dad's acting strange. Can't figure out why."

"Strange how?"

"Secretive. Paranoid. Asking weird questions. We're having a mandatory family dinner tomorrow night and nobody knows why."

"Mandatory?"

"He literally texted 'not optional.'"

Laura was quiet for a moment. "Danny, be careful tomorrow."

"It's just dinner."

"If your instincts are telling you something's wrong, listen to them. I'm serious. If anything feels off, if he says or does anything that makes you uncomfortable, leave. Just get up and leave."

"You're making it sound like a mob meeting."

"Isn't it?"

I didn't have an answer for that.

"Promise me you'll be careful."

"I promise."

"And call me after. No matter how late."

"I will."

After we hung up, I sat in the dark wondering how much Laura actually knew or suspected about what my family did.

She was smart. Observant. She'd probably figured out more than I'd told her.

But she was still there. Still with me. Still warning me to be careful.

Maybe that meant something.

Or maybe it meant she was as stupid as I was for staying involved with people who made "mandatory" family dinners feel like potential last meals.

SATURDAY MORNING, I woke up to three texts from Randy:

Be there at 7 sharp.

Don't talk about the operation unless Dad brings it up first.

And Danny. Trust your gut. If anything feels wrong, we leave together.

That last text bothered me more than the others. Randy didn't get scared. Randy didn't plan exit strategies. Randy bulldozed through problems.

The fact that he was being cautious meant he was genuinely worried.

I spent the day trying to distract myself. Went to the gym. Grabbed lunch. Drove around aimlessly. But my mind kept circling back to the same questions: What was Tommy planning? Why did he need detailed records? Who was the man in the suit? Why the mandatory dinner? What the fuck?

By 6:30, I was parked outside Tommy's house, watching Randy pull up in his Mercedes. Jake arrived two minutes later. Colin three minutes after that.

We all sat in our cars for a moment, like we were preparing for battle rather than dinner.

Finally, Randy got out. We followed.

The four of us walked up to Tommy's door together. Randy rang the bell.

Rachel answered, smiled too brightly, looked relieved to see us. "Come in, come in! Dinner's almost ready."

The house smelled like roast chicken and garlic. Everything looked normal. Table set, wine breathing, soft music playing.

Tommy appeared from the kitchen, drink in hand, smile in place. "My boys. Right on time. Come, sit. Let's eat."

We filed into the dining room. Took our seats. Tommy at the head of the table. Randy to his right. Me to his left. Jake and Colin across from each other.

Rachel brought out food. Tommy poured wine. Everyone made small talk about weather, sports, nothing important.

But underneath the normal facade, I could feel it.

Tension. Thick and heavy. Like the air before a lightning strike.

We were all waiting for something to happen.

We just didn't know what.

Tommy raised his glass. "A toast. To family. To success. To the future we're building together."

We raised our glasses. Clinked. Drank.

And the performance began.

THE DOOR BURST open from the outside.

"FBI! NOBODY MOVE!"

Agents poured in. Six, eight, ten of them. All wearing vests, all carrying weapons, all shouting commands.

Rachel appeared at the top of the stairs, hands already

raised. She was calm. Too calm. Like she'd been expecting this.

"ON THE GROUND! NOW!"

"HANDS WHERE WE CAN SEE THEM!"

We did what they said. Hit the floor. Hands behind our heads. The dining room was chaos: agents everywhere, weapons drawn, Rachel being led downstairs in handcuffs.

But as they passed me, Rachel caught my eye. Just for a second. And she smiled.

Not a scared smile. Not a defeated smile.

A knowing smile.

Like this was all part of the plan.

They separated us immediately. Different rooms, different buildings, different interrogations.

～

MARCUS WEBB TOOK ME HIMSELF. "Danny Tyler," he said, sitting across from me in the small room. "You've been a hard man to catch."

"I want a lawyer."

"You'll get one. Eventually." Webb opened a folder, didn't look at it. Just let it sit there between us. "Maryland, right? That's where you were before. Nice job. Nice apartment. Nice girlfriend." He watched my face. "What made you come back?"

"Lawyer."

"Your father called. That's what we figure. Tommy needed something. Something only you could provide." Webb tilted his head slightly. "What was it, Danny? What do you do that your brothers can't?"

I kept my mouth shut. Watched his eyes. He was fishing. Trying to see what I'd give him for free.

"The thing is," Webb continued, leaning back like we were just two guys talking, "your father's operation was pretty standard stuff before you showed up. Drugs, credit cards, some identity theft, nothing sophisticated. Then you arrive and suddenly the whole thing levels up. New systems. New methods. The kind of thing that takes a certain kind of mind."

He let the silence stretch. I let it stretch longer.

"You're not going to help yourself here," Webb said. "I get it. Family loyalty. But here's what I'm curious about." He leaned forward. "Your father had connections. People looking out for him. People who don't normally get involved with small-time criminals." His eyes locked on mine. "Who was protecting you, Danny?"

"I want a lawyer."

"Yeah." Webb stood up. "You said that."

He walked to the door, then stopped. "Think about it. Think about who you want to protect and why. Because somebody's going to talk. Somebody always talks."

Then he left me alone in the room.

THE NEXT MORNING, they moved me to a different room. No handcuffs this time. Just a table, two chairs, and Adam Freeman.

"Adam, what the fuck!" I shouldn't have been surprised. Of course he was here. Of course this involved him.

"Hey, Danny." He sat down across from me, looking tired. "Hell of a mess you're in."

"Is Uncle Tony..."

"Tony doesn't know I'm making this specific offer."

Adam rubbed his face. "I'm not here as your uncle's friend. I'm here representing other interests."

"What interests?"

"The kind that can make Marcus Webb's case disappear. The kind that can get you and your brothers out of here." He looked me in the eye. "CIA, Danny."

I stared at him. "You're CIA? You've been around since I was a little kid."

"Have been for twenty years. Your uncle knows. Your father suspected." Adam leaned back. "We've been watching your father's operation for a while. Watching who he dealt with. The connections he had. Tommy did some stupid shit. So when he came to Tony Sr. with Randy's idea, saying it was his own, we knew he was full of shit. Then he started recruiting you. That's when we knew this was something bigger."

"Why?"

"Because you're the Tyler Ghost. We know how fucking smart you are. The fact you're involved means there's a system. One that we might be able to use. So we paid attention."

"Who put the FBI on us?"

Adam looked me in the eye. "That was Tommy. One of his drug ops gone bad. It happened a couple of days after you got to Florida."

"My father ratted to keep his shady ass out of jail." It wasn't a question. "On his own kids?!"

"Are you really surprised?"

"I want to be, but no." I was pissed. "So what? Now you want me to spy?"

Adam smiled, but it didn't reach his eyes. "I want you to have options, Danny. Right now you don't have any. I'm offering you some."

"That's not an answer."

"No, it's not." He leaned back. "Here's the thing. You're smart. You built something impressive. And you're sitting in a federal holding cell because your father couldn't keep his shit together. That's not fair. It's not right. But it's where we are."

"Get to the point."

"The point is that I can make this go away. All of it. Webb's case, the evidence, the charges against your brothers. Gone." He spread his hands. "Or I can walk out that door and you can take your chances with a public defender and a jury that's going to see a lot of credit card numbers with your fingerprints on them."

"And in exchange?"

"In exchange, we stay in touch. You keep doing what you're good at. And occasionally, when I need someone with your particular skills, I make a phone call." Adam shrugged. "Maybe that call never comes. Maybe it comes once a year. Maybe more. Hard to say."

"That's vague."

"That's how this works. I'm not going to hand you a contract with bullet points. I'm offering you a relationship. The kind where we help each other when we can." He stood. "You've got twenty-four hours to decide. After that, I'm out of the picture and you're on your own."

"And if I say no?"

Adam looked at me. The warmth was gone now. Just calculation.

"Then I wish you luck, Danny. I really do. But I can't save someone who doesn't want to be saved."

He walked to the door, then turned back. "One more thing. Laura is going to tell you something later. You need to listen to her, and what she tells you is one hundred percent true. Don't doubt her. Don't question it. Just listen."

"What the fuck does Laura have to do with this?"

"Just listen to her, Danny. Trust me on this."

Then he was gone.

I didn't sleep that night. Just sat in the holding cell, thinking about everything. Laura? What the fuck did Adam mean? I didn't want to go to prison.

But if I said yes to Adam, I'd be trading one kind of prison for another. Being owned by the CIA. Being an asset. Having to do whatever they asked, whenever they asked. Except I'd be free. Ish. I would be able to move around anyway. It was that or a cage for ten years.

When Adam came back the next morning, I was ready.

"I'll do it," I said.

He nodded. "Smart choice."

"What happens now?"

"Now the machinery starts moving. You and your brothers get released." Adam paused. "Your father...like I said, that's more complicated."

"What does that mean?"

"It means his choices have consequences. It means there are things in motion that can't be stopped." Adam put a hand on my shoulder. "I'm sorry, Danny. I tried. But your father made enemies. Real ones. The kind that don't forget."

"Is he going to die?"

Adam didn't answer. He just squeezed my shoulder once, then left.

⁓

THREE DAYS LATER, I was released. No charges filed. The FBI's case had collapsed. Something about evidence being classified, witnesses disappearing, the whole operation falling apart.

Randy, Jake, and Colin were released too. All of us free to go, like the arrest had never happened.

But Tommy wasn't released.

"Where's my father?" I asked the processing officer.

"Thomas Tyler is deceased. I'm sorry."

"What?"

"He was found in his holding cell yesterday morning. Apparent suicide. Preliminary investigation is ongoing."

Suicide. My father had killed himself rather than face trial. Or prison. Or whatever was coming next. Or someone had made it look like suicide. I couldn't tell which was true. Maybe I'd never know.

Marcus Webb was waiting outside the federal building when I walked out.

"Danny Tyler," he said. "You got lucky. Your father's death made you useless as a witness. The evidence we had has been classified beyond my clearance. My case just disappeared."

"How sad for you."

"I think you're relieved. I think you know exactly why that evidence got classified. I think you know who protected you." Webb stepped closer. "I'm going to keep digging. I'm going to find out what really happened. And when I do, you and your family are going down."

"Good luck with that."

"I don't need luck. I need time. And I've got plenty of that." Webb walked away, leaving me standing on the steps.

~

MARCUS WEBB STORMED BACK into the FBI building an hour later.

"Where is she?" he demanded at the processing desk.

"Who?"

"Rachel Tyler. Tommy Tyler's wife. We released her four hours ago. Standard protocol for spouses with no direct involvement. She was supposed to report back tomorrow morning for additional questioning."

"And?"

"And she's gone. Completely. No phone activity. No credit cards. No car. Security footage shows her walking out of the building and getting into a taxi. The taxi driver says he dropped her at Miami International. After that, nothing. It's like she ceased to exist."

The desk sergeant shrugged. "Sounds like she ran."

"Obviously she ran. How did she have an escape plan ready to go? Who helped her?" Webb slammed his hand on the desk. "Tommy Tyler's wife doesn't just disappear into thin air without serious help. Someone with resources. Someone with connections."

But he was talking to himself. The desk sergeant had already moved on to other paperwork.

Webb stood in the hallway of the federal building, realizing that his case, the case he'd been building for two years, had just evaporated. Tommy Tyler was dead. Rachel Tyler had disappeared. The evidence was classified. The Tyler boys were free. Someone had orchestrated all of this. Someone with power. Someone who didn't want this case going forward.

Webb was going to find out who. Even if it took the rest of his career.

RANDY FOUND me an hour later at a bar near the marina.

"You okay?" he asked.

"Dad's dead."

"I heard. Suicide, they're saying."

"You believe that?"

Randy was quiet for a long moment. "I don't know what to believe. Dad was weak. He'd been weak for years. Maybe he couldn't face what was coming. Maybe he took the easy way out."

"Or maybe someone took him out."

"Maybe. But who? The FBI? The CIA? Uncle Tony? Someone else we don't even know about?" Randy ordered a drink. "We'll probably never know the truth. That's how these things work. People die in convenient ways, and the official story is suicide or accident or natural causes. The real story gets buried."

"So we just accept it?"

"We accept that Dad's gone. We accept that his choices led to his death. We accept that we're on our own now." Randy raised his glass. "To Tommy Tyler. Whatever the hell he really was."

We drank.

THE FUNERAL WAS three days later. Small service. Rachel didn't attend; she'd disappeared completely, and nobody had been able to find her. Uncle Tony came, stood in the back, left before anyone could talk to him.

Adam Freeman came too. He approached me after the service.

"I'm sorry about your father," he said.

"Are you? Or are you relieved there's one less complication?"

"Both can be true." Adam looked at the grave. "Your father was a complicated man. He made choices. Some good, some bad. In the end, those choices caught up with him."

"Did you know? What was going to happen?"

"Danny, in this business, we all know what's going to happen eventually. We just don't know when." He put a hand on my shoulder. "Your father asked me to look after you boys if anything happened to him. I intend to honor that commitment."

"Why?"

"Because he was my friend. A huge dumbass, but also a friend. Because you're good kids who got dealt a bad hand. Because someone needs to make sure you don't end up like him." Adam squeezed my shoulder once, then let go. "Be smart, Danny. Be careful. And you already know I'll be in touch."

He walked away, leaving me standing by my father's grave, wondering what the hell had just happened.

Three days after the funeral, my phone rang. Unknown number.

"Danny Tyler?" Marcus Webb's voice.

"Agent Webb. I have nothing to say to you."

"That's fine. I'll do the talking." I could hear papers shuffling. "Rachel Tyler. Your father's wife. Any idea where she is?"

"No. Haven't seen her since before the arrest."

"That's interesting. Because she walked out of federal

custody with a fully-prepared escape plan. Fake passport, offshore accounts, safe houses across three countries. That takes preparation. That takes knowledge." Webb's voice was cold. "Your father had information about something. Something big enough that someone wanted him dead and Rachel protected."

"Tommy killed himself."

"Did he? Or did someone make it look that way? And if so, what did he know that was worth killing him over?" Papers shuffled again. "Rachel disappeared with that knowledge. Which means someone out there is very interested in finding her. And I intend to find her first."

"Why are you telling me this?"

"Because when I do find her, when I learn what Tommy knew, I'm going to come back for you and your brothers. Whatever your father was involved in, whatever got him killed, you're part of it. And I will figure it out."

He hung up.

I stood there holding the phone, thinking about Rachel's knowing smile. About the fact that she'd been prepared to disappear. About what Tommy might have known that was worth dying over.

Whatever it was, it was still out there. Waiting.

9
____

LAURA

I spent three days in a haze after the funeral.

The apartment Jake had given me was nice. Marina del Ray, high floor, water view. But it felt empty. Like a hotel room I'd never quite moved into. Boxes still stacked in corners. Nothing on the walls. No personal touches.

A place to sleep, not a place to live.

I'd been avoiding everyone. Randy called twice. I texted back: *Need time.* Jake stopped by once; I didn't answer the door. Colin sent a message: *Here if you need anything.*

I needed to figure out what the hell had just happened to my life.

Tommy was dead. That part was real, even if nothing else was.

I was now a CIA asset. That part was terrifyingly real.

Adam Freeman was CIA. Had been the whole time.

And Laura...

Adam's words kept circling: "Laura is going to tell you something later. You need to listen to her, and what she will tell you is one hundred percent true."

What did that mean?

I was sitting on my balcony Wednesday night, three days post-funeral, drinking bourbon and watching boats, when someone knocked on my door.

I ignored it.

Another knock. Harder.

"Danny, I know you're in there. I can see the light." Laura's voice.

I hadn't talked to her since before the arrest. Five days. The longest we'd gone without contact since we'd started dating.

Dating. Was that even what we'd been doing?

I opened the door.

She stood in the hallway wearing jeans and a T-shirt, hair pulled back, no makeup. She looked nervous. Laura never looked nervous.

"Can I come in?" she asked.

I stepped aside.

She walked past me into the apartment, took in the boxes, the empty walls, the general sense of temporary occupancy.

"You haven't unpacked."

"Haven't had motivation." I closed the door, leaned against it. "What are you doing here, Laura?"

"We need to talk. About who I am. About why I was at that bar the day we met."

My stomach dropped. I already knew. Had known, probably, on some level. But hearing her say it out loud was different.

"You're CIA."

"Yes."

"You were assigned to me."

"Yes."

"From the beginning. The bar. The phone number. All of it."

"Yes." Her voice was quiet but steady.

I walked to the kitchen, poured myself another bourbon. Didn't offer her one.

"So it was all fake. The dates. The conversations. Everything."

"Danny—"

"How long were you going to keep lying to me?"

"I wasn't pretending." She took a step toward me. "That's why I'm here. That's what I need to tell you."

"Tell me what? That you're a great actress? That I'm an idiot who fell for the oldest trick in the book?"

"That I broke protocol." Her voice was sharper now. "That I'm risking my career being here. That Adam didn't authorize this conversation."

"Bullshit." The word came out harder than I intended. "Adam sat across from me in that holding cell and told me, word for word, that you were going to tell me something. That I should listen. That everything you said would be one hundred percent true." I set the bourbon down. "So don't stand in my apartment and tell me he doesn't know you're here. He sent you."

That landed. I watched it hit her face. Not surprise, exactly. More like recalculation. Like she'd rehearsed this conversation and I'd just skipped ahead in the script.

"You're right," she said. "Partly. Adam authorized me to tell you that I'm CIA. That was always the plan once you agreed to cooperate. You needed to know who your handler was. That's standard." She paused. "But that's all he authorized. A professional disclosure. Officer to asset. Clean. Controlled. On his terms."

"And this isn't on his terms."

"No. This isn't." She pulled something from her pocket. A folded piece of paper. "What I'm about to show you, Adam doesn't know about. If he did, I'd be on a plane back to Langley tonight and my career would be over." She held it out but didn't let go yet. "He told you to listen to me. He told you it would be true. And it will be. But he expected me to give you the sanitized version. The version where I'm your handler and you're my asset and everything stays professional and compartmentalized."

"And instead?"

"Instead I'm giving you everything." She let go of the paper. "Read it."

I took it, unfolded it. Official CIA document. Classified header. Mission brief.

OBJECTIVE: Establish contact with Daniel Tyler. Develop relationship to facilitate intelligence gathering and recruitment.

PARAMETERS: Initial contact: casual/organic Relationship development: proceed at subject's pace Intelligence focus: family operation, financial networks, technical capabilities Recruitment coordination: with Case Officer Adam Freeman Duration: ongoing until recruitment complete or mission compromised

AUTHORIZATION: Deputy Director, Special Activities Division

HANDLER: Laura Donovan, Operations Officer

I read it twice. Then looked up at her.

"Laura Donovan?"

"My real name. My professional name, anyway. I was Laura Sullivan. Got married young, it didn't work out, kept the name for work." She paused. "Everything else I told you about my life was true. My father really was military. I really did grow up in Colorado. The summer in Tokyo. Those weren't lies."

"Just the part where you were assigned to seduce me."

"It doesn't say seduce." She pointed at the paper. "Read what it doesn't say."

I scanned it again. "It doesn't say anything about sleeping with me."

"It doesn't say anything about falling for you either."

"That's convenient."

"It's the truth." She moved closer. "I was supposed to observe and report. Build rapport, gather intelligence, facilitate your recruitment. That's it. Everything else was me going off-script."

"How do I know that? How do I know this isn't just another layer of manipulation?"

"Because I'm breaking protocol showing you this." She gestured to the paper in my hand. "That document is classified. I'm risking my career. Maybe my freedom. If this was manipulation, it would be the worst manipulation in CIA history. I just gave you everything you need to destroy me."

I sat down on the couch, still holding the mission brief.

"How long have you been CIA?"

"Eight years. Recruited out of college. Linguistics degree, fluent in three languages." She sat down across from me. "I've been an operations officer for five years. This wasn't my first assignment. But it was my first time as a romantic cover."

"How'd you get that lucky break?"

"I didn't volunteer. Adam requested someone who could blend naturally in South Florida. Someone young enough to believably approach you but experienced enough to handle the mission." She looked down at her hands. "I thought I could keep it professional. Thought I could build rapport without actually caring."

"What happened?"

"You happened." She looked up. "That first night at Aruba. You were sitting there waiting for your father, and I started reading you the way I read everyone. But you noticed. You read me back. And when I called you on the shirt crease, you didn't get defensive or embarrassed. You just said 'Can't it be both?'" She smiled slightly. "I was supposed to be profiling you. But I just liked you."

"So you slept with me."

"I dated you. There's a difference." She leaned forward. "Everything I told you about not being good at casual, about wanting something real. That was true. I shouldn't have said it. Shouldn't have gotten that personal. But I meant it."

I stared at the mission brief. "When did Adam assign you?"

"Three weeks before we met. Your father had been on CIA radar for a while. Small-time stuff. But then Adam got intel about a larger operation. Synthetic identities, technical sophistication. They wanted to know more."

"So they sent you."

"They sent me to observe. To assess whether the operation was worth CIA attention or just local criminal stuff the FBI could handle." She paused. "Then your father got arrested. And everything accelerated."

"And you reported everything to Adam."

"Not everything." She said it quietly. "I reported the operational stuff. The technical details. But the personal things? The conversations about your past, about Diana, about what you wanted from life? I kept those vague. Sanitized."

"Why?"

"Because they were ours." She met my eyes. "Because I didn't want to turn every intimate moment into intelligence."

We sat in silence for a long moment.

"So what now?" I asked. "I know you're CIA. You know I know. What happens?"

"That depends on you." She stood up, walked to the window. "I can maintain cover. Pretend I never told you. Go back to filing reports and pretending everything's professional."

"Or?"

"Or we're honest with each other. No more lies between us, even if we lie to everyone else." She turned back to me. "I'll still have to report to Adam. Still have to file mission updates. But I won't lie to you about what I'm doing. Won't pretend this is just an assignment."

"You'd risk your career for that?"

"I'm already risking it showing you that brief."

I looked at her face. At the fear and calculation and exhaustion I saw there. Two operators trying to figure out if they could trust each other.

"What are you asking me?" I said.

"I'm asking you to be my partner instead of my asset." She came back over, sat next to me. "I'm asking you to help me figure out how we survive this. Together."

"Partners in what?"

"In staying human. In protecting each other. In making sure we don't get lost in this." She leaned closer. "In building something real inside all the lies."

"That's impossible."

"Maybe. But I'd rather try than keep living the lie." She took my hand. "We're both good at playing roles, Danny.

Let's play them for everyone else. But with each other, let's just be us."

I pulled back slightly. "No more lies?"

"Not between us. I'll still have to lie to Adam, to Langley. But not to you."

Either she was telling the truth, or she was the best liar I'd ever met.

I looked at her face. At the fear and hope I saw there.

"Okay," I said.

"Okay?"

"Okay. Partners. No more lies between us." I pulled her closer. "But Laura, if this goes wrong..."

"It probably will. This kind of thing always does." She smiled. "But at least we'll go down honest."

She kissed me, and it was different from every other time. Before, there had always been something held back. Some wall neither of us could quite break through.

Now there was just us. Messy and complicated and real.

She pulled back, looked at me seriously. "I need you to understand something. I still have to report to Adam. I still have to maintain the appearance of being your handler."

"I know."

"And you'll have to play along. Pretend you don't know. Pretend you think this is all real and professional."

"I'm good at pretending."

"I know you are." She smiled. "I've been watching you do it for weeks. The way you manage your brothers. The way you handled Adam. You're better at this than they know."

"Better at what?"

"Playing the game. Reading the room. Staying three steps ahead." She traced a finger along my jaw. "They think they recruited a criminal with computer skills. They have no idea what they actually got."

"What did they get?"

"Someone smarter than them. Someone who sees systems and learns how to break them." She kissed me again. "And now you have me. An actual CIA operations officer who's on your side. Who can tell you how they think, how they operate, where their blind spots are."

"Why would you do that?"

"Because I'm tired of being used. Because I want to be on the winning side for once." She settled against me. "Because I'd rather be your partner than their tool."

We sat there in silence for a while, both processing what we'd just agreed to.

"What happens now?" I asked.

"Now we get very good at lying to everyone except each other." She stood up, grabbed her jacket. "I have to file a report in the morning. I'll tell Adam I checked on you. That you're stable. That I'm maintaining operational control."

"Is that true?"

"Parts of it." She smiled. "The parts that need to be true."

She walked to the door, then turned back.

"Danny?"

"Yeah?"

"Thank you for believing me. You didn't have to."

"Are you manipulating me?"

"No."

"Then why would I throw you out?" I stood up, went to her. "Besides, you're right. We're better together than apart."

She kissed me one more time. "Get some sleep. You've got a meeting with Adam tomorrow afternoon. He wants to discuss your role going forward."

"Will you be there?"

"Officially, yes. Your handler should be present for operational briefings." She grinned. "We'll be very professional. Very protocol."

"And afterward?"

"Afterward you come to my place. And we figure out how to stay human while doing inhuman things."

She left, and I stood in the doorway watching her walk down the hall.

Everything had changed.

Laura was CIA. My girlfriend was my handler. The woman I was falling for was the woman assigned to control me.

But she'd chosen honesty when she didn't have to.

And that meant something.

I went back inside, looked at the mission brief still sitting on my coffee table.

They thought they were running me.

But now I had Laura.

And Laura wasn't running me. She was running with me.

That changed everything.

I needed to tell Randy. Before the meeting with Adam. Before someone else shaped the story for him. He deserved to hear it from me, not from a CIA case officer in a conference room.

I'd tell him tomorrow. First thing.

I picked up my phone, almost texted him. But this wasn't a text conversation. This was face to face, brother to brother, no screens between us.

I set the phone down, looked around my empty apartment.

Time to unpack.

Time to commit.

Time to start building something real inside all the lies.

10

THE BROTHERS' BARGAIN

Randy was waiting outside my apartment at eight a.m.

I opened the door to find him leaning against the hallway wall, arms crossed, face unreadable.

"We need to talk," he said.

"Come in."

He walked past me into the apartment, took in the still-unpacked boxes, the general emptiness. "You settling in or planning your escape?"

"Haven't decided yet." I closed the door. "Coffee?"

"No." He turned to face me. "I got a call from Adam Freeman last night. Said he wants to meet with me today. Wouldn't say why, just that it was important and that you'd know what it was about."

"Okay."

"Okay? That's all you have to say?" Randy's voice was tight. "He said you'd already accepted a deal. That you were now a CIA asset. That you'd done this without talking to me."

Here it was. The conversation I'd been dreading.

"I made a choice. In that holding cell. They were going to charge all of us. I made a deal to keep us out of prison."

"Without consulting me."

"There wasn't time. Adam made an offer. I took it."

"We're supposed to be partners, Danny. Equal. Remember?" Randy's jaw was clenched. "You made a decision about both our futures without even…"

"What was I supposed to do? They had us dead to rights. We were in separate buildings. I couldn't exactly knock on your door and ask for a vote."

"I'm not talking about the holding cell, Danny. I know how that works." Randy's voice dropped. "I'm talking about after. We've been out for days. You had my number. You had every opportunity to tell me before Adam did."

"I was going to. I was figuring out the right way to explain it."

"The right way." Randy laughed, but there was no humor in it. "You were strategizing. Building your little presentation. Figuring out how to spin it so I'd react the way you wanted."

"That's not what I was doing."

"Don't bullshit me." His voice dropped. "You know what I think? I think you liked it. Making the call alone. Finally proving you're the smart one."

"Randy…"

"Four years." He cut me off. "Four years in Maryland playing house while I was here dealing with Dad's shit. His moods. His messes. Keeping Jake and Colin from killing each other. And you just…you were up there with Diana, pretending to be normal, pretending you weren't…"

"I wasn't pretending."

"Bullshit you weren't. You were hiding. And the second it fell apart, the second she found out what you really are…"

"Don't."

"What, I can't mention Diana? Can't point out that your perfect girlfriend couldn't handle..."

"I said don't."

"She dumped you, right? That's what happened? She found out about the family and she..."

"She didn't find out about anything." My voice was harder than I intended. "I left because Dad called. Because he said he needed me."

"Oh, so you came running when Dad asked. But you couldn't pick up the phone when I..." Randy stopped, shook his head. "Forget it."

"We both know Dad only called because you told him to. But what?"

"I said forget it."

"No, finish. When you what?"

Randy was quiet for a moment. Then: "When I called you. Two years ago. Dad was on one of his benders, threatening to burn everything down, and I asked you to come back. Just for a week. Help me get him stabilized."

I remembered that call. I'd been in the middle of a project at work. Diana and I had just gotten the apartment.

"You said you had it handled."

"What was I supposed to say? 'Please come back, Danny, I can't do this alone'?" Randy laughed, but there was nothing funny about it. "I'm not...I don't do that. You know I don't do that. But I needed you. And you chose her. You chose that life."

We stood there, the air thick with things we'd never said.

"I'm sorry," I said. "About not being here. About leaving you to deal with Dad alone. I'm sorry."

"Yeah, well." Randy looked away. "That's not what we're talking about."

"Isn't it?"

"No. We're talking about you making a deal with the CIA without telling me. We're talking about you deciding our futures like I'm just...like I'm one of your variables. Something to factor in."

"That's not what happened."

"Then tell me what happened. And don't give me the strategy version. Don't give me the 'I made a calculated decision under pressure' bullshit. Tell me what you were actually thinking."

I took a breath. "I was thinking that we were all going to prison. I was thinking that Dad fucked us over and you and Jake and Colin were in holding cells! I was the only one Adam was offering a deal to. And I was thinking that if I didn't take it right then, it would disappear."

"So you panicked."

"I made a choice."

"You panicked and you made a choice. Don't pretend it was only one of those." Randy sat down on the couch. "You know what the worst part is? If I'd been in that room, I probably would've done the same thing. I would've taken the deal."

"Then why are you so pissed?"

"Because you didn't trust me enough to find a way to tell me first. Because even in crisis mode, your instinct was to handle it alone." He looked up at me. "That's what Dad did. Made decisions, told everyone else later. Said it was for our protection. Said he knew best."

"I'm not Dad."

"No? Because this feels pretty fucking familiar."

I sat down across from him. "You're right. I should've found a way. I don't know how, but I should've tried."

Randy studied my face for a long moment. "You're actually sorry."

"Yeah."

"Not just saying it because it's the strategic move?"

"I'm saying it because you're my brother and I fucked up."

He was quiet. "Okay."

"Okay?"

"Okay, I believe you. And okay, I'm still pissed, but I'll get over it." He leaned back. "So. CIA. Tell me what we're actually dealing with."

"Asset status. Report to Adam. Provide intelligence and technical support when needed. In exchange: immunity, protection, and resources."

"Resources?"

"Whatever we need to operate. Within reason."

"And what's 'within reason'?"

"That's what we're going to find out at this meeting."

Randy was quiet for a moment, processing. I could see the calculation in his eyes. The anger shifting into something else.

"Adam Freeman," he said. "CIA. I should have seen that coming."

"You didn't suspect?"

"I suspected something. Guy's been around forever, never gets caught, always seems to know what's happening before it happens." Randy shook his head. "I just thought he was good at being a fixer. Didn't realize he was actually agency."

"Does it change anything?"

"Changes everything. All those years watching him operate, thinking he was one of us." Randy's jaw tightened. "He was never one of us. He was using Dad. Using all of us."

"Maybe. Or maybe he was doing both."

"That's worse." Randy stood up. "Okay. Let's say I go to this meeting. Let's say I hear Adam out. What's our play?"

"Our play?"

"Yeah. Our strategy. Because I'm not just rolling over." He looked at me directly. "What's the angle?"

This was why Randy was Randy. Five minutes ago he'd been furious. Now he was strategizing.

"The angle is we make them think they control us while we figure out how to control the situation," I said. "We give them what they want to see. We report what they expect to hear. And we hold back the things that matter."

"Never let them know your full capacity."

"Exactly."

"What about Jake and Colin?"

That was the question I'd been wrestling with.

"I don't think they should know," I said.

"What?"

"About the CIA deal. About Adam. They can't know."

"Danny, they're our brothers..."

"Which is exactly why they can't know." I stood up. "Randy, think about it. If they know we're CIA assets, they become liabilities. They're either forced to lie to protect us, which puts them at risk, or they're honest, which puts us at risk."

"So we just lie to them?"

"We protect them. By keeping them ignorant. Plausible deniability." I moved closer. "If this goes wrong, if the CIA turns on us, Jake and Colin need to be clean. They need to be able to walk away and say they had no idea."

Randy was quiet, thinking it through.

"That's cold," he finally said.

"That's practical."

"They're going to figure it out. Jake's not stupid."

"Jake's smart enough to know when not to ask questions."

Randy sat back down. "What did Dad used to say? About the family business?"

"He said a lot of things."

"He said: 'The family that plays together stays together. But the family that stays together sometimes has to keep secrets.'" Randy smiled slightly. "I always thought that was bullshit. Just Dad justifying his lies. But maybe he was right about that one thing."

"Maybe."

"Okay." Randy stood up. "I'll go to the meeting. I'll hear Adam out. I'll probably make the same deal you did." He headed for the door, then stopped. "But Danny? Next time something this big happens? You tell me first. Before you make the deal. I don't care if you're in a holding cell or on Mars. You find a way. We're in this together. That has to mean something."

"It does. And you're right. I should have found a way." I walked over to him. "I'm sorry."

Randy studied my face. "You already said that."

"I know. I'm saying it again."

He was quiet for a moment. Then he clapped me on the shoulder. "Alright. We're good. For now." He opened the door. "Adam said two o'clock. Coral Gables?"

"Yeah. I'll text you the address."

"Don't bother. I know the building." He gave me a look. "I've known Adam longer than you have, Danny. I know where he works."

~

ADAM'S OFFICE was in a nondescript building in Coral Gables. Third floor, corner suite, the kind of place that could be a law firm or an insurance agency or a front for intelligence operations.

Probably all three.

Laura met me in the lobby at 1:45.

"Ready?" she asked.

"As I'll ever be."

"Randy's already upstairs. Adam wanted to talk to him first. Separately." She pressed the elevator button. "He's pissed."

"Randy or Adam?"

"Both, probably. Randy because you made the deal without him. Adam because Randy's questioning everything."

The elevator arrived. We stepped in.

"Is that bad?" I asked.

"Depends. If Adam's smart, which he is, he'll see Randy's pushback as a strength. Independent thinker, valuable for complex operations."

"And if he's not smart?"

"Then Randy gets shut down and resentful, and this whole thing falls apart." She pressed the button for three. "But Adam didn't get where he is by being stupid."

The elevator opened. We walked down a hallway to a door marked Atlantic Consulting Group. Laura opened it without knocking.

I could hear voices. Randy's, loud and emphatic. Adam's, calmer but firm.

Laura opened the conference room door.

Randy sat at a conference table across from Adam Freeman. The tension was obvious. Randy was leaning forward. Adam's hands were folded, but his eyes were sharp.

"Danny," Adam said. "Good. We were just discussing Randy's concerns."

"Concerns." Randy laughed. "That's one word for it. I was telling Adam how fascinating it is to learn that someone I've known since I was ten has been CIA the whole time."

"Randy..." Adam started.

"No, it's great. All those years. All that advice you gave me about the business. You were running intelligence operations. Using our family."

"I was protecting your family," Adam said calmly. "There's a difference."

"Is there? Because from where I'm sitting..."

"You're sitting in a chair instead of a prison cell. That's where you're sitting." Adam's voice didn't rise, but something in it made Randy stop. "You want to be angry? Fine. Be angry. But be angry at the right things."

"The right things?"

"Your father got arrested because he was sloppy. He drew attention. He crossed lines. The FBI was going to roll up your entire operation. You, Danny, Jake, Colin. Everyone." Adam leaned forward slightly. "I made sure that didn't happen. I made sure the evidence got classified. I made sure the case collapsed. I made sure you boys walked free."

"And Dad?" Randy asked quietly.

"Your father made his own choices. In that holding cell." Adam's face was unreadable. "Whether he actually killed himself or whether someone helped him, I honestly don't know. But either way, it was his actions that led to his death. Not mine. Not yours. His."

Randy slumped back in his chair.

Laura and I sat down, she next to Adam. Me next to Randy.

"Let me be clear," Adam said, looking at Randy. "Your

brother made a deal without consulting you. From your perspective, that looks like betrayal. From my perspective, it looks like the only rational choice in an impossible situation."

"He could have waited," Randy said, but there was less heat in it now.

"For what? For you to coordinate through the prison phone system?" Adam shook his head. "Danny made his decision under extreme pressure. And he made the right call."

"For him."

"For all of you." Adam pulled out a folder. "So. Let's make a new decision. Together. I'm offering you the same deal I offered Danny. Asset status. Immunity for past crimes. Protection. Resources."

"What kind of resources?"

"Money. Equipment. Intelligence. Access. Whatever you need to operate effectively."

Randy glanced at me. I nodded slightly.

"And what do you get?" Randy asked Adam.

"Your cooperation. Your networks." Adam opened the folder. "Danny's value is technical. He builds systems. But systems don't work without people. Your father spent thirty years building relationships across South Florida. Suppliers, distributors, fixers, people who owe favors and people who collect them. That network didn't die with Tommy. It transferred to you. You're the one they trust. You're the one they take calls from." Adam looked at Randy directly. "I can find another programmer. I can't manufacture thirty years of criminal relationships."

"So we're your criminal consultants," Randy said.

"You're assets with latitude. Which means you operate with more freedom than most." Adam looked at both of us.

"Most assets have handlers who micromanage every move. I'm not offering you that arrangement."

"What are you offering?" I asked.

"Independence within parameters. You operate your business. You make your money. You live your lives. But when I call, you respond. When I need intelligence, you provide it. When I need access, you facilitate it."

"And if we say no to an operation?" Randy asked.

"Then you'd better have a good reason. This isn't a democracy." Adam pulled out two documents. "These are your asset agreements. Read them. Sign them. And we're official."

I picked up my document. Two pages. Basic terms: provide support when requested, maintain operational security, report significant intelligence.

Randy was reading his, jaw tight.

"One more thing," Adam said. "I know you're holding back. Testing boundaries. Figuring out how much control you actually have."

Randy and I went very still.

Adam smiled slightly. "I'm not an idiot. You're playing the game. That's fine. It's even healthy. If you weren't doing it, I'd be disappointed." He stood. "Just don't push so hard that you break things."

He moved toward the door.

"Questions?" he asked.

"Yeah," Randy said. "What about Jake and Colin?"

"As far as the agency is concerned, they were minor players. They've been cleared."

"They don't know about this deal," I said. "We want to keep it that way."

Adam raised an eyebrow. "Plausible deniability?"

"If this goes wrong, we want them clean."

"Smart." Adam nodded. "Fine. Jake and Colin remain unaware. Laura will handle operational details. I'll be in touch."

He left.

The three of us sat in silence.

"Well," Randy finally said. "That was something."

"He knows we're playing him," I said.

"And he doesn't care. As long as we're useful." Randy stood up, stretched. "You know what? I think I can work with that. He's not pretending this is about justice or saving the world. He's saying we're useful, he needs useful people, let's make a deal." Randy grinned. "I can respect that."

I signed my document. Slid it across.

Randy watched me, then signed his.

"Welcome to the team," Laura said, collecting the papers. "I'll brief you on protocols. Communications. Security procedures."

Randy and I followed her to another conference room.

"So you're the handler," Randy said to Laura.

"I'm a handler. Adam oversees strategy. I manage operations."

"And you manage Danny specifically?"

Laura glanced at me. "I'm his primary contact, yes."

"Interesting." Randy was grinning. "How do you like that, Danny? Having a handler?"

"It's fine."

"Just fine?"

"Randy." Laura's voice was sharp. "Whatever you think you've figured out, keep it to yourself. This is professional. Asset and handler. Understood?"

Randy held up his hands. "Understood."

But I saw the look he gave me. He suspected. And Randy

with a suspicion was almost as dangerous as Randy with the truth.

Laura spent an hour walking us through communication protocols. Code words for different scenarios. "Weather" meant all clear. "Traffic" meant surveillance detected. "Unavailable" was the panic word.

By the end, my head was swimming.

"Questions?" Laura asked.

"When's our first assignment?" Randy asked.

"Soon. Adam's working on something. You'll get briefed when he's ready."

We stood to leave.

"Danny, hang back a minute," Laura said.

Randy shot me a look but left without comment.

Once we were alone, Laura's professional demeanor shifted slightly.

"How are you doing?" she asked. "Really."

"Confused. Overwhelmed. Not sure what I signed up for."

"You signed up for survival. Everything else we'll figure out." She moved closer. "Randy's going to be a problem."

"Why?"

"Because he's reckless. Adam gave him latitude and he's already thinking about how to exploit it." She touched my arm. "Danny, Adam was serious. They'll give you room to operate, but if you cross hard lines, they'll cut you loose. Or worse."

"What's worse?"

"You don't want to know."

We stood there, close but not touching.

"I should go."

"Yeah." But she didn't step back. "Be careful with Randy.

He's smart but he's ambitious. That combination is dangerous."

"I know."

"Do you? Because ambition makes people take risks they shouldn't. Makes them think they're smarter than they are."

"Are we talking about Randy or us?"

She smiled slightly. "Maybe both."

I left her there, walked out to find Randy waiting by his car.

"So?" he asked.

"So what?"

"So are you sleeping with your handler?"

"Randy..."

"It's a yes or no question."

I looked at him for a long moment. "It's really not."

"That's not a no."

"It's not a yes either." I held his gaze. "Leave it alone."

"Thought so." He unlocked his car. "That's either really smart or really stupid."

"There's nothing to have thoughts about."

"Sure. Whatever you say." He got in, rolled down the window. "Hey Danny?"

"We're going to be okay. You know that, right? This CIA thing, it's weird and complicated, but we're going to make it work."

"How do you know?"

"Because we're Tyler boys. We don't follow rules. We find the angles." He started the engine. "Adam thinks he recruited us. He has no idea what he actually got."

"What did he get?"

Randy grinned. "Two criminals who are about to teach the CIA what 'latitude' really means."

Before he drove off, I called out, "By the way, you owe me

five hundred bucks. I actually jumped out of that plane with Dad."

We both laughed. We needed to laugh at something.

He drove off, and I stood in the parking lot thinking about what we'd just done. We'd signed our lives over to the CIA. Became assets. But Randy was right. They thought they'd recruited us. They had no idea we were already planning how to control the situation.

Never let them know your full capacity.

That was the rule.

And we were going to follow it perfectly.

11

EASY MONEY

Three weeks after signing with Adam, we were back in business.

Not the same business. The synthetic identity operation was too hot, too exposed. Marcus Webb might be off the case, but the methodology was burned. We needed something new.

Randy found it in real estate fraud.

"It's perfect." He spread documents across the table in our new office. Smaller than the last one, tucked into a business park in Pompano Beach. "We're not creating fake people anymore. We're creating fake transactions."

"Explain."

"Straw buyers. We find people with decent credit who need money. They 'buy' properties we control temporarily. Vacant homes, pre-foreclosures, estate sales sitting in probate. Places that are real, that an appraiser can walk through and photograph, but where the ownership is muddy enough that we can forge our way onto the title. We process the mortgage applications through shell companies, our appraiser signs off on an inflated value, the banks approve the loans, wire the money. By the time they realize the title was fraudulent and the buyer's gone, we've already moved the cash through three layers of offshore accounts."

"That's mortgage fraud."

"That's real estate investment." Randy grinned. "And it's lower risk than identity theft. Banks lose money, not individuals. No victim to file complaints. Just institutions writing off bad loans."

"How much are we talking?"

"Each transaction? $200k to $500k. We can run ten transactions a month. That's two to five million." He leaned back. "Split four ways, even after expenses, we're looking at $300k to $600k each. Per month."

I did the math. That was $3.6 million to $7.2 million a year. Each.

"And the CIA is okay with this?"

"Why wouldn't they be? We're not hurting national security. We're just redistributing bank assets." Randy's smile widened. "Besides, Adam said we have latitude. This is us using it."

Laura had been copied on my report about the new operation. Her response was brief: "Proceed. But keep detailed records for audit purposes."

Which meant: do it, but make sure we can prove we're not completely out of control.

THE OPERATION RAMPED UP FAST. Randy had buyers lined up. I built the database systems to track everything. Colin managed the shell companies and money flows. Jake vetted each transaction, making sure the paperwork would pass initial scrutiny.

It was smooth. Almost too smooth.

Two weeks into the new operation, something happened that tested everything I thought I believed.

Her name was Maria Santos. Forty-three years old, single mother, two kids in middle school. She worked as an office manager for a medical supply company and had credit good enough to qualify as one of our straw buyers. Randy had recruited her six months ago, back when we were still running the synthetic identity operation. She'd needed money for her son's medical bills. We'd needed someone clean.

The deal was simple. She'd "buy" a vacant property in Pompano Beach that we'd temporarily put ourselves on the title for. We'd process the mortgage with our appraiser, collect the funds, and give her ten thousand dollars for her trouble. The bank would eventually figure out the fraud, but by then the money would be untraceable. Maria would claim she'd been deceived, a victim of a scam she didn't understand. Banks rarely prosecuted the straw buyers. It wasn't worth the legal fees.

That was the theory.

"They're charging her," Randy said, tossing a document onto my desk. "Federal wire fraud. The U.S. Attorney's office picked up her case as part of some task force initiative. They're making examples."

I read the indictment. Maria Santos, named as a co-conspirator in a mortgage fraud scheme. Facing up to twenty years if convicted.

"She was supposed to be protected," I said. "You told me these buyers never get charged."

"They usually don't. This is bad luck. Wrong place, wrong time, wrong prosecutor." Randy shrugged. "It happens."

"It happens? Randy, she has two kids. She did this because her son needed surgery."

"She did this because we paid her ten grand to sign some papers. She knew it wasn't legitimate. She's not innocent."

He wasn't wrong. Maria had known. We'd never lied to her about what the deal was. She'd made a choice, eyes open, because the money mattered more than the risk.

But she'd made that choice because I'd told her the risk was minimal. Because I'd looked her in the eye and said, "The banks never go after people like you. You're too small. They write it off and move on."

I'd been wrong. And now she was facing twenty years because I'd been wrong.

"We need to help her," I said.

Randy stared at me. "Help her how?"

"A lawyer. A real one."

"A federal defense attorney costs fifty grand minimum. Probably more like a hundred if this goes to trial."

"Then we pay a hundred grand."

"For a straw buyer?" Randy's voice rose. "Danny, we've got thirty people like her on our books. What happens when the next one gets charged? And the one after that?"

"We'll deal with that when it happens."

"No. We deal with it now, by not setting a precedent we can't afford." He jabbed a finger at the indictment. "She knew what she was signing. She took ten grand to commit fraud. That's on her."

"I told her it was safe."

"You told her what we tell everyone."

"And I was wrong." I stood up. "Randy, I sat in her kitchen. Her kids were doing homework at the table."

"That's not our problem."

"It is now."

"Danny—"

"I'm not asking."

Randy went quiet. That was new. I didn't pull rank. I didn't make demands. That was his thing.

"You're serious," he said.

"Hundred percent."

"This is a terrible precedent."

"I don't care."

"People are going to expect…"

"Good. Let them."

He stared at me, calculating. I could see him running the numbers, weighing the cost against something he couldn't quite name.

"Adam's not going to like this," he finally said. "Using operational funds for something like this."

"Adam doesn't need to know. This comes out of our cut. Yours and mine."

"Fifty grand each."

"Yup."

Randy shook his head slowly. But the resistance was fading. "You know this changes things. If we start protecting our people, really protecting them, word gets out. Everyone's going to expect the same treatment."

"Then we'll be more careful about who we recruit."

"Or we'll bleed cash every time someone gets unlucky."

"Then we build legal costs into our planning." I held his gaze. "Randy, I'm doing this. With or without you. The only question is whether you're in."

He held my stare for a long moment. Then he nodded.

"Fine. I'll find her a lawyer. A good one." He picked up the indictment, looked at it again. "But Danny? This better be worth it."

I TOLD myself I was going to her house to explain the situation. To let her know we were getting her a lawyer, a real one, someone who could make this go away. That was the professional thing to do. Keep your people informed. Manage expectations.

But that wasn't why I went.

I went because I needed to see what I'd done.

Maria lived in a duplex in Margate, one of those stucco places painted the color of a faded sunset. The lawn was patchy but mowed. A bicycle lay on its side near the front steps. Kid's bike, purple with streamers on the handlebars.

I sat in my car for five minutes before I got out. Rehearsing what I'd say. How I'd frame it. The lawyer we're hiring is one of the best. Federal cases like this, he knows how to work the system. You're going to be okay.

All true. All bullshit.

She answered the door in scrubs. Must have just gotten home from work. Her eyes went wide when she saw me, then careful. Guarded.

"Danny." Not a question. Not a greeting. Just my name, sitting there between us.

"Can I come in?"

She stepped aside without a word.

The living room was small and clean. Photos on the walls. School pictures of her kids, gap-toothed smiles and awkward poses. A crucifix above the television. The smell of something cooking. Rice and beans, maybe.

"Kids are at my mother's," she said, reading my glance toward the hallway. "I didn't want them here when...I didn't want them to see me like this."

"Maria, I came to tell you we're getting you a lawyer. A

good one. Federal defense specialist. He's handled cases like this before."

"Cases like this." She almost smiled. "You mean cases where someone was stupid enough to sign papers they knew were fake."

"You weren't stupid. You were desperate. There's a difference."

"Is there?" She sat down on the couch, and for the first time I saw how tired she looked. Not just tired. Hollowed out. "Twenty years, Danny. The lawyer I talked to, the public defender, he said I could get twenty years. My kids would be grown by the time I got out. They'd be strangers."

"That's not going to happen."

"You don't know that."

"I know the lawyer we're hiring. I know what he can do." I sat down across from her, leaning forward. "Maria, I'm not going to let you go to prison for this."

She looked at me for a long moment. I waited for the anger. The accusations. *You told me this was safe. You said the banks never prosecute. You lied to me.*

Instead, she said: "Why?"

"Why what?"

"Why are you helping me? I'm nobody to you. I signed some papers, you paid me, that was supposed to be the end of it." She shook her head slowly. "A lawyer like you're talking about costs money. Real money. Why would you spend that on me?"

Because I sat in this room six months ago and told you the risk was minimal. Because I watched your son limp in from the other room, the one who needed surgery, and I thought about how ten thousand dollars was nothing to us and everything to you. Because I used your desperation and told myself it was a victimless crime.

"Because it's the right thing to do."

She laughed. Short and sharp, no humor in it. "The right thing. That's funny, coming from you."

"Yeah. I know."

"You know what I keep thinking about? That morning when I signed the papers. Miguel was at the table doing his math homework. He looked up and asked what I was signing, and I told him it was work stuff. Boring grown-up things." Her voice caught. "I lied to my son so I could commit a crime. And now I might go to prison, and he's going to find out his mother is a criminal, and he's going to remember that morning. He's going to remember that I lied."

"Maria..."

"I'm not blaming you." She said it quietly, firmly. "I need you to understand that. I knew what I was doing. You explained it to me, and I said yes, and I took the money. That's on me. Not you."

That should have made me feel better. It didn't.

"The lawyer's name is Richard Stein," I said. "He's going to call you tomorrow. Whatever he needs, documents, meetings, anything, you give it to him. Don't talk to anyone else about the case. Not the public defender, not the FBI, nobody. Just Stein."

She nodded.

I stood up. There was nothing else to say. No way to fix what I'd broken with words.

At the door, she stopped me.

"Danny." I turned. "Thank you. For trying."

I wanted to tell her not to thank me. I wanted to tell her that I was the reason she was in this mess, that my assurances had been worth exactly nothing, that the ten thousand dollars I'd paid her might end up costing her everything.

"I'll make this right."

I didn't know if that was a promise or a prayer.

The drive home took forty minutes. I don't remember any of it.

THREE MONTHS LATER, I was at the office when the call came.

Richard Stein's voice was calm, professional, satisfied. "Misdemeanor plea. Six months' probation, no jail time. Judge accepted it twenty minutes ago."

I closed my eyes. Let out a breath I hadn't realized I'd been holding for ninety days.

"She's okay?"

"She's okay. Walked out of the courthouse a free woman. Well, a woman on probation, but that's paperwork. She keeps her nose clean for six months, this whole thing disappears."

"Thank you, Richard."

"Thank your checkbook. That's what made this happen." He paused. "For what it's worth, she's a good woman. Wrong place, wrong time. I'm glad we could help her."

After I hung up, I sat at my desk staring at nothing. Relief, yes. But something else too. Something that felt like getting away with it.

Randy appeared in my doorway. "Stein called?"

"Misdemeanor. Probation. No jail."

"Good." He nodded once. "That's good, Danny."

"Yeah."

He waited, like he expected me to say something else. When I didn't, he left.

I should have felt better. I'd kept my promise. Maria wasn't going to prison. Her kids weren't going to grow up visiting their mother through plexiglass. The system had bent, just this once, in favor of someone who deserved a break.

But I couldn't stop thinking about all the other Maria Santoses out there. The ones we'd recruited who hadn't gotten unlucky yet. The ones who might get unlucky tomorrow, or next month, or next year. Were we going to hire Richard Stein for all of them?

Could we afford to?

Could we afford not to?

I buried myself in work for the rest of the day. Database updates. Transaction reviews. The mechanical stuff that didn't require me to think about anything but numbers and systems.

Around six, Jake stuck his head in. "You staying late?"

"Just finishing up."

"Don't work too hard." He disappeared down the hall.

I was packing up to leave when I heard the front door open. Footsteps in the reception area. Then Colin's voice, surprised: "Can I help you?"

"I'm looking for Danny Tyler."

My stomach dropped. I knew that voice.

I walked out of my office to find Maria Santos standing in our lobby. She was holding a foil-covered dish in both hands, like an offering. Her hair was pulled back, and she was wearing a nicer blouse than the scrubs I'd seen her in before. Sunday clothes on a Tuesday.

Colin looked at me, eyebrows raised. I gave him a small nod, and he retreated to his office without a word.

"Maria. What are you doing here?"

"I wanted to thank you. In person." She held out the dish. "It's arroz con pollo. My mother's recipe. It's not much, but..."

"You didn't have to do that."

"I know. I wanted to."

I took the dish. It was warm through the foil. "How did you find this place?"

"Mr. Stein. I asked him where to send a thank you card, and he gave me the address." She smiled, just barely. "I decided a card wasn't enough."

"Maria, you really didn't have to come all the way out here."

"Danny." She said my name the way she had that night at her house. Direct. Unadorned. "I spent three months thinking I was going to prison. Three months watching my kids and wondering how many more dinners we'd have together. Three months waking up at three a.m. running through worst-case scenarios." She paused. "And then it was over. Just like that. The judge said some words, Mr. Stein shook my hand, and I walked out into the sunshine a free woman."

"That's...I'm glad."

"You paid for that. You and your brother. Don't think I don't know what a lawyer like that costs. Don't think I don't understand what you did for me."

"We owed you. We put you in that situation."

"No." She shook her head. "I put myself in that situation. I made a choice. You gave me a way out when you didn't have to." She stepped closer. "My son, Miguel, the one who needed the surgery? He's doing better. Running around like nothing ever happened. And last week, he asked me if everything was okay, because he could tell I'd been worried about something. And I got to tell him yes. Everything's okay. Because of you."

I set the dish on the reception desk. I didn't know what to say. I'd prepared myself for her anger, her blame, her resentment. I hadn't prepared for this.

"Thank you," she said. "I'll never be able to repay you, but thank you."

She hugged me. Quick, firm, then gone. The kind of hug you give someone when words aren't enough.

"I should go," she said. "I just needed you to know. What you did mattered. It mattered to me, and it mattered to my kids, and I won't forget it."

She walked out the door before I could respond. I stood there holding arroz con pollo, watching her car pull out of the parking lot.

Colin emerged from his office. "Who was that?"

"Someone we helped."

"She seemed grateful."

"Yeah."

He waited for more. I didn't give him any. After a moment, he shrugged and went back to his desk.

I took the dish to the break room. Put it in the refrigerator. Stood there with the door open, cold air washing over me.

We'd spent a hundred and twenty thousand dollars on Maria Santos. A hundred and twenty grand to fix a problem we'd created. To save a woman we'd put in danger. To keep two kids from losing their mother.

Worth every penny.

But here's the thing about doing the right thing when you're in the wrong business: it doesn't make you good. It just makes you slightly less bad. You don't get to feel righteous about cleaning up your own mess.

Maria Santos walked out of that courthouse because we had money and connections and a willingness to spend both. But she walked into that courthouse in the first place because of us. Because I'd sat in her kitchen and told her the risk was minimal. Because I'd needed her signature more than I'd needed to tell her the truth.

I'd kept my promise. I'd made it right.

But I'd never be able to make it like it never happened.

I closed the refrigerator and went home.

"MONTH-END FIGURES," Colin announced at our weekly meeting. "$2,347,000 gross. Expenses totaled $507,000. That's operating costs, legal reserves, and the twenty percent allocation. Net distribution: $460,000 per principal." He paused, looked up from his laptop. "Each. Per month. In case that wasn't clear."

Jake whistled. "That's a 400% increase over the same period under the previous structure."

"I'm aware." Colin closed his laptop. "I ran the numbers three times because I thought I'd made an error."

"Because we're smarter than Dad," Randy said. "We're not greedy. We're not sloppy. We take calculated risks."

"And we have protection," I added.

Everyone looked at me.

"What kind of protection?" Jake asked.

Shit. I'd said too much.

"Lawyers," Randy jumped in smoothly. "Danny means we have better legal protection. Real attorneys on retainer. Not Dad's cut-rate guys who'd sell us out for a plea deal."

Jake studied us both but didn't push. "Good. Because this is working. Let's not fuck it up."

"Agreed," Colin said. "I've set up the offshore accounts to cycle every 90 days. By the time any bank starts investigating, we're three jurisdictions removed. Technically untraceable."

"Beautiful," Randy said. "Let's scale up. I want to hit fifteen transactions next month."

"Randy, that's aggressive," I said.

"That's ambitious. There's a difference." He looked around the table. "We have an opportunity here. We're making money hand over fist and nobody's even looking at us. Why would we not capitalize on that?"

"Because getting too big is what got Dad caught," Jake said.

"Dad got caught because he was stupid and careless. We're neither." Randy stood up. "Look, I'm not saying we go crazy. I'm saying we recognize that we have a window. Eventually, someone will figure out this scheme. Eventually, the banks will tighten their verification processes. But right now? Right now we print money."

He wasn't wrong. But something about the way he said it made me nervous.

After the meeting, I pulled Randy aside.

"You're pushing too hard," I said.

"I'm pushing appropriately."

"Fifteen transactions is a 50% increase. That's going to draw attention."

"From who? The banks? They lose billions every year to fraud. We're rounding errors." He clapped me on the shoulder. "Relax, Danny. I know what I'm doing."

That was what worried me.

∼

The offer came a week later.

Randy had scheduled a meeting with a new buyer. Someone referred by one of our regular clients. "Big money," Randy said. "Wants to discuss a partnership."

We met at a restaurant in Aventura. Upscale Italian place, the kind where mobsters and politicians shared the same dining room and pretended not to see each other.

The buyer's name was Dimitri. Late forties, expensive suit, Eastern European accent. He had two guys with him. Security, probably. They sat at the bar while Dimitri joined us at our table.

"Randy Tyler," Dimitri said, shaking hands. "I've heard good things."

"All true, I'm sure." Randy gestured to me. "This is my brother, Danny. He handles the technical side."

"Technical is good. I like technical." Dimitri ordered vodka, neat. "Your operation is impressive. Efficient. Professional. This is why I wanted to meet."

"What can we do for you?" Randy asked.

"I have a business opportunity. Different from what you do now, but complementary." Dimitri sipped his vodka. "I move merchandise. High-value merchandise. It requires clean money, proper documentation, logistics. You understand?"

"What kind of merchandise?" I asked.

Dimitri smiled. "The kind that walks on two legs."

The temperature in the room dropped.

Randy's expression didn't change, but I saw his jaw tighten. "You're talking about people."

"I'm talking about a business with incredible margins. Minimal risk if you have the right systems." Dimitri leaned forward. "You have the systems. The shell companies, the transaction processing, the money laundering infrastructure. We partner, you process my transactions, everyone makes money. Very good money."

"How much money?" Randy asked, voice flat.

"Five million a month. Your cut would be forty percent. Two million, just for processing paperwork."

Two million a month. Twenty-four million a year.

For helping traffic human beings.

Randy finished his drink slowly. Set down the glass. Looked at Dimitri directly.

"Not interested."

Dimitri raised an eyebrow. "You didn't even hear the full proposal."

"Don't need to." Randy stood up. "We're thieves, not slavers. Get the fuck out."

"Randy, think about this..."

"I said get out. Now. Before I have you thrown out."

Dimitri's security guys stood up from the bar. Randy didn't flinch.

"This is a mistake," Dimitri said, standing. "You're turning down..."

"I'm turning down nothing because there's nothing to turn down. We don't do that. We'll never do that." Randy's voice was cold. "And if I hear you're operating in our territory, if I catch even a whiff of your 'merchandise' in South Florida, I'll make sure every cop and fed from here to Miami knows exactly what you're doing."

Dimitri's smile vanished. "You threaten me?"

"I'm telling you how it is. This is my city. My operation. My rules." Randy stepped closer. "Now leave. While you still can."

Dimitri stared at Randy for a long moment. Then he nodded to his guys and walked out.

After they left, Randy sat back down. Ordered another drink. His hand was shaking slightly.

"That was risky," I said quietly.

"That was necessary."

"He could be connected. He could come back at us."

"Let him try." Randy took a long drink. "Danny, there are lines. Things we don't do. Things I won't do. Stealing from banks? Fine. Credit fraud? Whatever. But that?" He shook his head. "Never. Not for any amount of money."

"I know. I agree completely."

"Dad would have taken that deal. You know he would have. Dad would have rationalized it, said business is business, said money is money. That's why Dad's dead and we're not."

He was right. Tommy would have absolutely taken that deal.

"I'm calling Laura," I said. "She needs to know about this."

"Agreed. And let's find out who this asshole really is."

THAT NIGHT, I filed my report to Laura. Detailed everything: the meeting, the offer, Randy's refusal. I emphasized Randy's exact words: "We're thieves, not slavers."

Laura called fifteen minutes later.

"Dimitri Kovalenko," she said without preamble. "Ukrainian national. He's been on our watch list for two years. Human trafficking, mostly Eastern European women, some from Southeast Asia. Operates through Miami and Fort Lauderdale."

"Can you shut him down?"

"We've been trying. He's slippery. Always uses intermediaries, never touches the merchandise himself. But this…" I could hear the satisfaction in her voice. "This is the first time we have him on record making a direct offer. Your report gives us something concrete."

"What happens now?"

"I'm passing this to the trafficking task force. They'll coordinate with FBI and local law enforcement. Dimitri's going to have a very bad month." She paused. "Danny, you and Randy did the right thing. You know that, right?"

"I know. We both know. That's not something we'd ever touch."

"Good. Because that's a hard line for us too. The agency has a lot of gray areas, but trafficking isn't one of them. You refuse that kind of operation, you have our full backing. Always."

"What about Randy threatening him? Is that going to be a problem?"

"No. It establishes you as hostile to his network. Makes it clear you're not going to be assets he can flip or compromise." Laura's voice was firm. "Randy handled it exactly right. Made your position clear, drew a hard boundary, showed you're not afraid of him. That's good tradecraft."

"Laura, we didn't refuse because it was strategic. We refused because it's fucking evil."

"I know that. And that's exactly why it works." Her voice softened. "Danny, you can do the right thing and have it benefit you strategically. Those things aren't mutually exclusive. Randy has principles. That makes you both more valuable as assets, not less. The agency wants criminals who can be trusted, who have boundaries, who won't go completely off the rails."

"So it's a win-win."

"Exactly. You maintain your integrity, we get reliable

assets, and Dimitri gets taken down. Everyone wins except the bad guys." She paused. "I'll keep you updated on the Kovalenko operation. In the meantime, keep doing what you're doing. The real estate fraud is clean, it's profitable, and it doesn't cross any hard lines."

After we hung up, I sat in my apartment feeling better than I had in weeks.

Randy and I had done the right thing. Not because it was strategic. Not because it looked good to the CIA. But because it was right.

The fact that it also benefited us was just a bonus.

Maybe we could do this. Maybe we could be criminals with the CIA's protection while still maintaining some kind of moral compass.

Maybe we could find a way to stay human in this inhuman system.

Or maybe I was just rationalizing. Telling myself pretty stories to make the compromises easier to swallow.

Either way, we'd drawn a line. And that meant something.

THE NEXT DAY, Jake cornered me at the office.

"Something's shifted with you and Randy. The communication patterns are different. What changed?" he asked.

"Nothing. Why?"

"Because you two have been acting weird since the arrest. Having private conversations. Making decisions without consulting me and Colin. Something's different."

"We're just being more careful. After what happened with Dad…"

"Bullshit." Jake moved closer. "I'm not stupid, Danny. I

know when I'm being managed. When I'm being kept out of the loop. So what is it? What aren't you telling me?"

I could tell him the truth. Tell him about Adam, about the CIA, about the deal Randy and I had made. He was my brother. He deserved to know.

But if I told him, he'd be exposed. He'd know too much. If anything went wrong, if the CIA turned on us, Jake would be implicated.

Keeping him ignorant kept him safe.

"We're just being paranoid," I said. "After everything that happened, Randy and I are probably being too careful. But there's nothing to tell. We're running the same operation, just with better security."

Jake studied my face. "You're lying to me."

"I'm not..."

"Danny, I've known you since you were born. I know when you're lying. I can see it." He stepped back. "But you know what? I'm going to let it go. Because I trust you. Both of you. I trust that whatever you're doing, whatever you're not telling me, it's for a good reason. But don't forget we're brothers. All four of us. Not just you and Randy."

He walked away, leaving me standing there feeling like shit.

That night, Colin sent a text: "Jake's upset. What happened?"

I called him. "He thinks Randy and I are keeping secrets."

"Are you?"

"Yes."

Colin was quiet for a moment. "Are these secrets that are going to get us arrested?"

"No. The opposite. These secrets keep us out of prison."

"Then I don't need to know what they are." Colin's voice

was pragmatic, clinical. "Jake's emotional about family stuff. I'm not. If you and Randy have some arrangement that protects us, I don't need details. I trust you to do what's necessary."

"You're okay not knowing?"

"I'm okay with plausible deniability. If shit hits the fan, I want to be able to honestly say I had no idea what you were doing." He paused. "That's the play, right? You're protecting us by keeping us ignorant?"

"Yeah."

"Then keep doing it. I'll handle Jake."

After he hung up, I poured myself a bourbon and stood at the window.

This was the cost Laura had warned me about. The cost of being an asset. The cost of protection.

Randy and I got to operate with CIA backing. We got immunity, resources, latitude. But in exchange, we had to lie to our brothers. We had to isolate them. We had to make them feel excluded and managed.

We were protecting them.

But it felt like we were betraying them.

My phone buzzed. Text from Randy: *Adam wants a meeting tomorrow. Something about a job.*

What kind of job?

The kind where we actually earn our protection.

Great.

I finished my bourbon and went inside. Looked at the photos on my phone. Pictures from years ago. All four brothers together. Jake and Colin and Randy and me. The Tyler boys. A family.

But families kept secrets. Families lied to protect each other. Families made choices that hurt in order to prevent worse harm.

That's what I told myself, anyway.

That's what I needed to believe.

Because if I was wrong, if keeping them in the dark wasn't protection but betrayal, then everything we were doing, all the deals we'd made, all the lies we'd told, were for nothing.

I buried the thought and went to bed.

Tomorrow we'd find out what the CIA actually wanted from us.

Tomorrow the real work began.

12

VIENNA

Adam's call came the next morning.

"Conference room. One hour. Both of you."

He hung up before I could respond.

I texted Randy: "Adam's calling us in."

His response was immediate: "About fucking time. Been waiting for them to actually use us."

Laura met us in the lobby of Adam's building, looking more official than usual. Suit instead of casual clothes. Hair pulled back. All business.

"International?" Randy asked, reading her body language.

"Vienna," she said.

"Perfect. I've always wanted to see Austria." Randy grinned. "What are we stealing?"

"Information. And you're not tourists." She pressed the elevator button. "Adam will brief you."

The conference room was different this time. Larger. A projector screen on one wall. Files spread across the table. This wasn't a recruitment meeting. This was operational.

Adam was already there, along with two people I didn't

know. A man in his fifties, salt-and-pepper hair, wearing a suit that screamed federal agent. A woman in her thirties, sharp eyes, arms crossed.

"Danny, Randy," Adam said. "This is Special Agent Michael Chen, FBI Cyber Crimes. And Sarah Mitchell from Treasury's Financial Crimes division. They're coordinating the domestic side of this operation."

We shook hands. Chen had a firm grip. Mitchell studied us like we were evidence.

"Must be important if you've got FBI and Treasury in the room," Randy said, sitting down without waiting for an invitation. "What are we looking at?"

Adam clicked a remote. The screen lit up with a photograph. A man, late thirties, expensive suit, cold eyes.

"Viktor Antonov. Russian national, operates out of Vienna. He runs one of the most sophisticated identity theft networks in Europe."

"How sophisticated?" Randy asked. "Scale, revenue, geographic reach?"

Adam raised an eyebrow. "Impressed. Those are the right questions."

"I'm in the business. I know what matters." Randy leaned forward. "So how big is his operation compared to what we were running?"

"International scope. Revenue estimated at $200 million annually. He's operating at a level that makes your Florida business look like a lemonade stand."

Randy whistled. "And you want us to what, compete with him?"

"We want you to infiltrate him." Adam clicked to the next slide. A network diagram, dozens of connections spreading across multiple countries. "Antonov's network provides identities to various criminal organizations. Drug cartels, arms dealers, and most importantly, terrorist cells."

That got my attention. Randy's expression sharpened.

"His customers have been linked to three attempted attacks in the last two years," Sarah Mitchell said. "London, Paris, and Berlin. The identities he provided allowed operatives to move freely, rent vehicles, purchase materials. One of those attacks nearly succeeded."

"London truck bomb," Randy said. "I remember that. Detonator failure."

"You follow terrorist attacks?" Agent Chen asked.

"I follow anything that might affect markets or draw law enforcement attention." Randy shrugged. "Professional interest. So Antonov's selling to terrorists. That makes him a priority target. What's the plan?"

Adam clicked to another slide. A building in Vienna, elegant architecture, looked like an office complex.

"Antonov operates from here. Legitimate import-export business on the surface. The identity operation runs through the basement. Completely isolated network. No outside connections. No way to hack in remotely."

"So you need boots on the ground," Randy said. "Someone who can get inside, map the system, get out clean."

"Exactly." Adam looked at me. "That's Danny."

"What am I working with?" I asked. "What's the system architecture? Standalone servers or networked? What operating systems? What kind of encryption?"

Adam nodded at Laura. She pulled up a file.

"Best guess from signals intelligence: isolated local network, no internet connection, custom encryption. We don't know the OS. We don't know the database structure.

That's part of what makes this hard. Every remote approach we've tried has hit a wall."

"So I'm going in blind."

"You're going in with the best technical skills we have access to and four hours to figure it out." Adam looked at me directly. "Can you do it?"

"Depends on what I find. Four hours is tight if the encryption is layered. If it's a single-key system, I can map the whole thing in two."

"And if it's something you've never seen before?"

"Then I adapt. That's what I do."

"And I'm the pretty face who gets us in the door," Randy said. "I like it. What's our approach?"

"You go as yourselves. Danny and Randy Tyler. Actual criminals from Florida looking to expand operations into Europe."

Randy's grin widened. "No legends? No fake identities? Just walk in as ourselves?"

"Your real background is your credential," Adam said. "Antonov vets everyone. Runs deep background checks. Has people inside law enforcement across three continents. We send in agents with fake identities, he spots them in a week. But you two? You're real. Your criminal operation in Florida is real. Everything will verify because it's all true."

"Except the part where we're working for you," Randy said.

"Except that. Which is why this is dangerous." Adam's expression was serious. "If Antonov figures out you're CIA assets, he won't just kill you. He'll use your real identities to come after everyone you know. Your brothers. Your associates. Everyone."

"Then we don't let him figure it out." Randy's voice was

confident. "What's our value proposition? Why would Antonov want to work with us?"

"You don't go in asking to learn. A man like Antonov doesn't take meetings with students." Adam clicked to the next slide. A map of Antonov's network, dense across Europe and Asia, almost nonexistent in the Americas. "See that gap? He's been trying to establish a US pipeline for two years. Moving money through American banks, laundering through US real estate, building domestic shell companies that pass regulatory scrutiny. He can't do it from Vienna. Every proxy he's sent has either gotten flagged by FinCEN or burned by the FBI within months." Adam looked at us. "You two walk in with a functioning US operation. Shell companies across three jurisdictions. Banking relationships. A laundering infrastructure already processing millions a month. You're not his students. You're the missing piece he's been looking for."

"So we're offering a merger, not an apprenticeship." Randy nodded. "That's a stronger position. He needs us as much as we need him." He leaned forward. "What's his personality? Is he ego-driven? Does he negotiate or dictate?"

"All of the above," Laura said. "He's arrogant but not stupid. He likes being recognized as the best in his field. He respects criminals who are successful and ambitious. But he's also paranoid. He'll test you."

"Good. I can work with ego and paranoia." Randy looked at Adam. "Timeline?"

"You leave Friday. First week is establishing contact. Making the approach, passing his vetting. If he bites, and that's an if, he's hosting a reception the following week. That's our window. You get invited to that reception, Danny finds a way into the basement, and he has approximately four hours to access the systems, map the network, and get out." Adam paused. "If Antonov doesn't take the meeting, or if he takes it and doesn't trust you, we pull you out and find another way in. This isn't a suicide mission. But it is our best shot."

"What happens after we map it?" Randy asked.

"Coordinated takedown. FBI, Interpol, European authorities. We hit every node simultaneously. Dismantle the whole thing in one night." Agent Chen stepped forward. "But we need the complete network first. Miss one node, they rebuild. We only get one shot at this."

"And when you take it down," Randy said, "what happens to the infrastructure? The systems, the servers, the architecture?"

Adam's expression didn't change. "It's seized. Dismantled. Standard procedure."

Randy smiled slightly. "Right. Standard procedure. Got it."

I could see Adam register that Randy didn't believe him, but he let it pass.

"Any other questions?" Adam asked.

"Yeah," Randy said. "If this goes sideways, if Antonov makes us, what's the extraction protocol?"

Laura spoke up. "Panic word is 'unavailable.' Work it into any phone conversation. We'll have a team there within thirty minutes."

"Thirty minutes is a long time when someone's trying to kill you," Randy said. "But I assume that's the best you can do given the constraints."

"It is," Laura said.

"Then we'll make sure we don't need it." Randy stood up. "When do we prep?"

"Starting tomorrow," Laura said. "Two days of briefings, surveillance detection, counter-interrogation basics."

"Perfect. Danny and I will study up on Antonov tonight. Get a feel for who we're dealing with." Randy headed for the door, then stopped. "One more thing, Adam. When we pull this off, when we hand you a $200 million criminal network on a silver platter, we're going to want to discuss compensation. And by compensation, I mean more than just 'good job, boys.'"

"We'll discuss it after the operation," Adam said.

"Looking forward to it." Randy grinned. "Come on, Danny. We've got homework."

THAT NIGHT, Randy came to my apartment with his laptop.

"Okay, let's game this out." He spread the briefing materials Adam had given us across my table. "Antonov. Russian national. Vienna based. $200 million operation. Sells to terrorists."

"You seem excited."

"I am excited. This is the real shit, Danny. This is what being CIA assets is supposed to mean. Not just running our little operation in Florida. Actually going up against major players." He pulled up a file. "Antonov's been operating for eight years. No arrests, no major exposure. That means he's smart, cautious, and connected. We need to respect that."

"I thought you were cocky, not careful."

"I'm cocky about things I'm good at. I'm careful about things that can kill me. Antonov can definitely kill us." Randy leaned back. "So let's rehearse Adam's pitch. Make sure it sounds like us, not like something a case officer wrote on a whiteboard. How do we sell it?"

"Because we're ambitious?"

"Not enough. Ambitious criminals are everywhere. We

need something specific. Something that makes us inter-esting to him." Randy thought for a moment. "What if we tell him we've maxed out the US market? That we need European connections to scale, and he needs American infrastructure to expand? A partnership. Equals, not employer and employee. That positions us as valuable, not desperate."

"Flattery and ambition."

"Exactly. We're not threatening his territory. We're offering to fill a gap he already knows exists. And we let him think the partnership was his idea. People commit harder to things they believe they chose."

"What if he decides we're not worth it?"

"Then we had a nice trip to Vienna and we come home. No harm, no foul." Randy grinned. "But he's going to think we're worth it. Because we're actually good at what we do. We're not pretending to be criminals. We are criminals. That's the beauty of this whole thing."

"You're really enjoying this, aren't you?"

"Hell yeah. This is what I've been waiting for. A real challenge. A real operation." He looked at me seriously. "Danny, we've been playing small-time for too long. Even before Dad died, we were just doing what he taught us. Following his playbook. But this? This is us operating at the next level. Learning from the best, understanding how the big players work. This is how we become something more than just Florida criminals."

"Randy, we're doing this to map his network for the CIA. Not to actually become international criminals."

"Sure. But there's no reason we can't learn something while we're at it." Randy's smile was calculating. "You saw that network diagram. Antonov built something sophisti-cated. Something elegant. Why wouldn't we study it? Figure out what makes it work? Even if we're helping the CIA take it down, we can learn from how it was built."

That was Randy. Always seeing the opportunity inside the mission.

"Just don't get us killed."

"Please. I'm way too smart to get killed by some Russian in Vienna." He closed his laptop. "Now let's talk about what you're going to do in that basement. Four hours to map an entire network. That's tight, but doable if you know what you're looking for."

We spent the next hour going over the business side. Randy walked me through every detail of our portfolio, quizzing me on property addresses, acquisition dates, mortgage terms. The kind of questions Antonov's people would ask to test whether we were real.

"If they ask about the Shell Island deal, keep it vague on the timeline," Randy said. "Say we're waiting on permits. That buys ambiguity without sounding evasive."

When he'd run out of scenarios, Randy grabbed his jacket. "The tech stuff is your world. I'd just slow you down."

After he left, I spent another two hours on my own, working through the network mapping. What to look for. How to prioritize the data the CIA would need most. How to do it all in four hours without leaving a trace..

When I was done,I sat in my apartment thinking about what was coming.

Randy was right. This was the next level. This was what being assets really meant, but I couldn't shake the feeling that He was playing his own game. That he wasn't just learning from Antonov to help the CIA.

He was learning to build something of his own.

THE NEXT TWO days were intense.

Laura drilled us on operational security. How to spot surveillance. How to lose a tail. How to communicate in code. Emergency extraction procedures.

But mostly, she prepared us for Antonov's vetting process.

"He's going to ask questions," she said in our first prep session. "Detailed questions about how you run your business. What properties you've acquired. How you process the mortgages. Where you bank. He's going to verify everything."

"Good thing it's all real," Randy said. "Makes lying so much easier when you're telling the truth."

"Walk me through your last five transactions," Laura said.

We spent hours going over details. Properties we'd acquired. Shell companies we'd used. Banks we'd worked with. Randy knew every transaction cold, could recite details without hesitation.

"What about the FBI investigation?" Laura asked. "Your father's arrest. The case that collapsed. Antonov will ask about that."

"We tell him the truth," Randy said. "Dad got arrested on drug charges. Died in custody. FBI's case fell apart because the evidence wasn't as strong as they thought. We walked away clean."

"He's going to dig deeper. Ask why the case collapsed. Whether you made deals."

"Then we tell him the FBI was sloppy. They built their case on a confidential informant who turned out to be unreliable. When that fell apart, everything else did too." Randy's voice was smooth, confident. "It's not unusual for cases to collapse. Happens all the time. Antonov will understand that."

Laura looked at me. "What if he asks about your father's death specifically? Whether it was really suicide?"

"I tell him I don't know," I said. "That Tommy was depressed, facing serious time, and made a choice. If Antonov wants to believe it was something else, that's his business. But I'm not going to speculate."

"Good," Laura said. "Don't volunteer information. Answer questions directly and move on."

On the second day, she taught us counter-surveillance. How to spot a tail. How to identify surveillance cameras. How to move through a city without leaving a trace.

Randy picked it up fast. Too fast.

"You've done this before," Laura said.

"I've avoided cops before. Same principle." Randy grinned. "You learn quick when getting caught means prison."

"This is different. These aren't cops. These are intelligence professionals."

"Even better. Higher stakes means I pay more attention."

Laura looked at me. "Your brother is either going to be brilliant at this or get you both killed."

"Fifty-fifty chance," I said.

"Those aren't great odds."

"They're better than you think," Randy said. "I know how good I am. I also know my limits. I'm not going to do anything stupid in Vienna. I'm going to be careful, professional, and smart. Because I want to come home. And I want to come home having learned everything I can from Antonov before we burn him."

Laura studied him for a long moment. "You're not doing this just for the mission, are you?"

"I'm doing it for lots of reasons. The mission is one. Learning from the best is another. Proving to Adam that we're valuable assets is a third." Randy's smile was sharp. "But yeah, I'm also doing it because I want to see how the best in the world operates. Sue me for being curious."

"Just don't let curiosity get you killed."

"I won't. I'm too smart for that."

The night before we left, Laura came to my apartment.

"You ready?" she asked.

"As ready as I'll ever be."

She sat down on my couch. "I'm worried about Randy."

"Why?"

"Because he's treating this like a learning opportunity instead of a dangerous operation. He's excited, not cautious."

"Randy's always like that. It's how he operates. But he's not stupid. When shit gets real, he'll be careful."

"I hope you're right." She took my hand. "Danny, if anything feels wrong over there, if Antonov seems suspicious, if the situation goes sideways, you get out. You use the panic word and you get out. Don't try to salvage the mission. Don't try to be heroes. Just get out alive."

"We will."

"Promise me."

"I promise."

She kissed me, and it felt different. Desperate. Like she thought it might be the last time.

"Come back to me," she said.

"Always."

But as I said it, I wondered if that was a promise I could keep.

∾

Vienna, Austria

Dimitri Kovalenko stood in the doorway of Antonov's study and waited to be acknowledged. The room smelled of leather and old wood. Antonov was reading something on his laptop, his face lit by the pale glow of the screen.

"The Tyler brothers," Dimitri said. "They landed in Vienna this morning. Hotel Imperial. First class."

Antonov didn't look up. "These are the ones from Florida."

"The same. I approached them three weeks ago about processing logistics for one of our transport lines. They turned it down."

Now Antonov looked up. "Why?"

"They said they don't touch trafficking. Walked away from six figures in annual revenue without negotiating."

Antonov closed the laptop. His eyes were the color of dishwater, flat and assessing. "Either they're law enforcement, or they have principles. Both are unusual in this business."

"I ran them thoroughly. Father was Tommy Tyler, ran mortgage fraud and drug operations out of South Florida. Arrested by the FBI, died in custody. Both sons walked clean. Their operation is real. Small compared to ours, but sophisticated for Americans."

"And now they're in Vienna."

"Spending money. Not hiding. Using their real names."

Antonov was quiet for a long moment. "Men who use their real names are either very stupid or very confident. And men who turn down easy money on principle..." He stood and walked to the window that overlooked the Ringstrasse. "They're worth a conversation. Take Pavel with you tomorrow. The restaurant near the cathedral. Keep it casual."

"And if they're not what they appear to be?"

Antonov's reflection smiled in the glass. "Then we find out what they really are."

Vienna was beautiful.

We flew first class, stayed in a two-bedroom suite at the Hotel Imperial, moved through the city like wealthy Americans with money to spend. Everything was real. The credit cards were in our actual names. The reservations were under Danny and Randy Tyler. We weren't hiding.

Randy loved it.

"This is how we should always travel," he said, looking out at the city from our hotel suite. "First class, expensive hotels, no pretending to be someone we're not. Just being successful criminals enjoying the fruits of our labor."

"We're here on a CIA mission," I reminded him.

"Details." He grinned. "Laura picked up chatter overnight. Antonov's people are planning to approach us tomorrow, feel us out, report back. If we pass the test, we get invited to the reception."

"What if we don't pass?"

"We will. Because we're exactly who we say we are. That's our superpower, Danny. We're authentic."

Laura stayed at a different hotel, maintained professional distance in public. But she coordinated everything. Briefings in our suite. Updates on Antonov's schedule. Intel on his security.

"I intercepted a communication last night," she said on our second day. "Antonov's people have been watching you since you checked in. They're planning to approach you at lunch tomorrow." She pulled up profiles on her laptop.

"These are the two men who'll make contact. Pavel Kozlov and Dimitri Kovalenko. Both ex-Russian intelligence. Both dangerous."

"Wait," Randy said. "Dimitri Kovalenko? The guy who tried to recruit us for trafficking?"

Laura nodded. "Same person. He works for Antonov. And based on the chatter I picked up, your refusal is exactly what got their attention. Turning down easy money on principle was unusual enough to get reported up the chain."

Randy and I exchanged a glance.

"That could be a problem," I said. "If Dimitri's hostile about how we left things."

"Or it's an opportunity," Randy said. "We already established we have standards. We turned down trafficking. That might actually make us more credible to Antonov. Shows we're not desperate. Shows we have boundaries."

"It could go either way," Laura said. "Dimitri might recommend you or bury you."

"Then we address it head-on. If Dimitri brings it up, we own it. Tell Antonov we have lines we don't cross. See how he reacts." Randy's voice was confident. "Criminals respect other criminals who have standards. It shows self-control. Discipline. Those are valuable traits."

"It also shows you're willing to make enemies," Laura said.

"We're criminals. We have enemies. That's normal." Randy stood up. "Look, if Dimitri's hostile tomorrow, we deal with it. But I'm not going to stress about something we can't control."

After Laura left, I turned to Randy. "You really think the Dimitri situation works in our favor?"

"I think it shows we're real. Real criminals with real principles and real enemies. That makes us credible." Randy was grinning. "Besides, if Dimitri's working for Antonov, it means Antonov tolerates trafficking. And if we turned down Dimitri but want to work with Antonov, it means we're being selective. That we see value in what Antonov does that we didn't see in what Dimitri offered. That's smart positioning."

"You've thought about this."

"I think about everything." Randy headed to his room. "Get some sleep. Tomorrow's going to be interesting."

The next day, we had lunch at a restaurant near St. Stephen's Cathedral. Expensive place, the kind where the wine list was longer than the criminal code and nobody asked how you earned your money. Halfway through our meal, two men approached. I recognized them from Laura's briefing. Pavel Kozlov and Dimitri Kovalenko.

Dimitri's eyes widened slightly when he saw us. Then narrowed.

"Mr. Tyler," Pavel said to Randy. Not Dimitri. Pavel was running this. "My employer would like to speak with you."

"Which employer?" Randy asked casually, like he hadn't noticed Dimitri at all.

"Viktor Antonov. You're in Vienna asking questions about his operations. He's curious why."

"We're looking for a European partner. We have US infrastructure that might interest Mr. Antonov. We've heard he's been looking to expand westward."

Pavel studied Randy for a moment. Then glanced at Dimitri. "Have you met my associate before?"

"We have." Randy finally acknowledged Dimitri. "In Miami. He made us a business proposal. We declined."

"Why?" Pavel asked.

"Because we have standards. We're thieves, not slavers." Randy's voice was calm, matter-of-fact. "Dimitri wanted us to process transactions for human trafficking. We don't do that. We won't ever do that. I made that very clear."

Dimitri's face was red. "You threatened me."

"I told you to stay out of my territory or I'd make sure law enforcement knew what you were doing. That's not a threat. That's a boundary." Randy looked at Pavel. "Does Mr. Antonov have a problem with us refusing to work with Dimitri? Because if he does, we can end this conversation now. No hard feelings."

Pavel was silent for a long moment. Then he smiled slightly.

"Mr. Antonov appreciates criminals who have principles. He also doesn't particularly like human trafficking. Too much attention, too much risk, not enough profit." He pulled out a card. "He'll see you tomorrow. Two o'clock. His office."

He handed Randy the card and walked away. Dimitri followed, shooting us a look that promised trouble.

After they left, I let out a breath. "That went better than it could have."

"That went exactly how I said it would." Randy tucked Pavel's card into his pocket. "Dimitri was pissed, but Pavel was impressed. You could see it. The standards play worked."

"Dimitri's look when he walked away didn't scream 'impressed.'"

"Dimitri's not the one making decisions. Pavel reports to Antonov, and Pavel liked what he saw." Randy was buzzing. "We just established ourselves as principled operators who aren't desperate for a deal. That's exactly the position we wanted."

Back at the hotel, Laura was waiting.

"How did it go?" she asked.

"Pavel gave us a card. We meet Antonov tomorrow at two." Randy dropped into a chair. "Dimitri was hostile, just like you predicted. But Randy's refusal of the trafficking offer did exactly what we hoped. Pavel seemed to respect it."

Laura nodded slowly. "Antonov values discipline. If Pavel reports that you stood your ground against one of his own people over a matter of principle, that tells Antonov you're not easily pushed around. That's a quality he looks for in partners."

"See?" Randy grinned at me. "Exactly what I said."

"It also means Dimitri's going to be a problem," Laura said. "You embarrassed him in front of his colleague. Men like that don't forget."

"Let him hold a grudge. By the time it matters, we'll be too valuable for Antonov to care what Dimitri thinks."

The next day, we took a car to Antonov's building.

Antonov's office was on the top floor. Elegant, expensive, with a view of the city that probably cost more than most people's houses.

He was younger than his photo suggested. Maybe thirty-five. Well-dressed, cultured, nothing about him screaming "dangerous criminal."

"Mr. Tyler," he said, standing to shake Randy's hand. His English was perfect, barely accented. "And Mr. Tyler. Brothers in business. I appreciate that. Family is important."

"It is," Randy said.

"Please, sit." Antonov gestured to expensive leather chairs. "Pavel tells me you had an interesting interaction with Dimitri."

"We did," Randy said. "He made us an offer we couldn't accept. Nothing personal. Just business."

"Dimitri operates in areas I find...distasteful. But he's

useful for certain clients." Antonov sat down across from us. "You refused him because you have standards?"

"We refused him because human trafficking is evil. We're criminals, Mr. Antonov. We steal money. We defraud banks. But we're not monsters." Randy's voice was confident. "There are lines. Things we won't do regardless of profit. Trafficking is one of them."

Antonov studied Randy for a long moment. Then smiled.

"I like you. You have principles. That's rare in our business." He leaned back. "I've been hearing about your operation in Florida. Real estate fraud. Very clever. Straw buyers, phantom properties, the banks don't realize they've been defrauded until months later. You've moved nearly fifty million in the last year."

"We do alright."

"You do better than alright. But you want to do better still. That's why you're here."

"We want to propose something," Randy said. "You've built something impressive over here. Multi-country operations, identity systems at scale, money moving without leaving traces. But from what we can see, you don't have a reliable US pipeline. We do. Shell companies across three jurisdictions, banking relationships that are already processing millions a month, a laundering infrastructure that's never been flagged. We're not here to ask for lessons. We're here to offer you the piece you're missing."

"And what would I get in return?"

"You've got the product. We've got the distribution channel. You help us handle the European side, we run your operations through the US financial system. Clean, fast, and already built."

Antonov considered this. "You're proposing a real partnership."

"We are. Equal terms. We're not looking for a job. We're looking for a partner who makes our operation bigger and whose operation we make bigger in return."

"That requires trust. And trust takes time." He stood up, walked to the window. "I'm hosting a reception Friday night. Potential investors, business partners, people I work with. You'll attend. I'll introduce you to some associates. We'll see if there's compatibility."

"We appreciate the opportunity," Randy said.

"Don't thank me yet. This is an audition, not an acceptance." Antonov turned back to face us. "I'll be verifying everything about you this week. Your operation, your finances, your background, your father's death, why the FBI case collapsed. If anything doesn't match up, if I find any indication that you're not who you say you are..." He let the threat hang.

"Everything will check out," Randy said. "Because we're exactly who we say we are."

"We'll see." Antonov smiled. "Enjoy Vienna, gentlemen. I'll see you Friday."

Outside, Randy was practically bouncing.

"That went perfectly," he said.

"He's going to investigate everything."

"Good. Let him. Everything's real. Our operation, our background, our father's arrest and death. It all checks out because it's all true." Randy grinned. "This is the beauty of not using legends. We don't have to remember lies. We just tell the truth."

Back at the hotel, Laura was waiting.

"Antonov bought it," Randy said.

"For now. He'll be running background checks all week."

Laura pulled up her laptop. "I'm monitoring what databases he accesses. So far he's looking at your property records, your banking information, your father's arrest record."

"Let him look," Randy said. "He's not going to find anything suspicious. Because there's nothing to find except that we're exactly who we say we are."

The rest of the week was tense. Waiting. Knowing that Antonov's people were digging into our background. Hoping that nothing raised flags.

Randy spent the time learning everything he could about Antonov. Reading articles, watching videos, studying his business practices.

Laura brought us an updated briefing on Thursday. A partial map of Antonov's operation that CIA analysts had pieced together from signals intelligence and asset reports.

Randy studied it for an hour. "The guy's a fucking artist," he said. "Look at how he structured this. The compartmentalization. The way no single person sees the whole picture. The layers between him and any transaction that could be traced. This is beautiful."

"You're admiring the criminal network we're supposed to take down."

"I can admire good work and still want to stop terrorists." Randy looked at me. "Danny, when you get into that basement, when you're mapping his network, pay attention. Really pay attention. This is graduate-level criminal infrastructure. We should learn from it."

"Randy..."

"I'm not saying we should build something like it. I'm saying we should understand how it works. Knowledge is power. And the more we understand about how these systems function, the more valuable we are to Adam. The more latitude we get."

"He had a point. But Randy's curiosity had a way of turning into ambition before anyone noticed the shift."

On Friday afternoon, Randy got a call.

Mr. Tyler. A car will be at your hotel at eight p.m. Formal attire.

"We'll be ready."

After he hung up, Randy looked at me. "This is it. Tonight we either pull this off or we die trying."

"Let's aim for pulling it off."

"Obviously. I have too much to live for." He grinned. "Plus, I want to see how this network actually functions. Four hours in that basement, Danny. Make them count."

That night, Laura came to my room after Randy had gone to get ready.

She didn't say anything at first. Just checked my suit for anything that could identify me, straightened my collar, adjusted my cuffs. Professional. Methodical. The way she got when she was trying not to feel something.

"If Dimitri makes a move, it'll be when you're separated from Randy," she said. "Stay visible. Stay in the main rooms. Don't let anyone lead you somewhere isolated until you're ready to go to the basement."

"I know the plan, Laura."

"I know you know." She stopped fussing with my collar. Her hands stayed there. "I just need to say it out loud. So I know I said it." She stepped back, operational again. "At midnight, I'll take the security cameras offline from the outside. You'll have a four-hour window before the morning shift resets the system. Get in, map everything, and get out before the clock runs."

I covered her hands with mine. "I'll be careful."

"You'd better be. I don't have time to train a replacement."

She smiled, but it didn't reach her eyes.

THE BLACK MERCEDES picked us up at exactly eight p.m.

Randy looked sharp in his suit. Confident. Excited, even. Like we were going to a party instead of a potential death trap.

"You ready?" I asked.

"Been ready for this my whole life."

We drove through Vienna to Antonov's building. The reception was on the second floor. Maybe a hundred people, all wealthy, all connected. Criminals, corrupt businessmen, people who moved money and power through channels that would never appear in any official record.

Antonov worked the room like a politician. Charming, gracious, showing no sign of being one of Europe's most dangerous criminals.

"Mr. Tyler," he said when we found him. "I'm glad you could make it. Your background checked out. Everything you told me was true."

"We don't lie about business," Randy said.

"Good. I respect honesty." Antonov gestured to the room. "These are people I work with. People I trust. Perhaps, in time, you'll join that group. But first, let's see how tonight goes."

I watched Randy work the room for an hour.

It was like watching a master class. He'd found Antonov's head of European distribution, a German named Kellerman who controlled logistics across six countries, and somehow gotten the man laughing within five minutes. I couldn't hear what they were saying, but I could read the body language. Kellerman leaning in. Opening up. Responding to whatever Randy was selling.

This was Randy's gift. The thing that made him dangerous and valuable in equal measure. He could read a room the way I could read a network diagram. See the connections. Identify the nodes that mattered. And then insert himself exactly where he needed to be.

I drifted closer, pretending to examine a painting on the wall.

"The problem with most Americans," Randy was saying, "is they think bigger is better. More volume, more transactions, more exposure. They don't understand that elegance is more profitable than scale."

Kellerman nodded. "This is true. The Americans I've worked with, they want everything fast. No patience."

"Exactly. But my brother and I, we learned from our father. Old school. Quality over quantity. You build relationships first, infrastructure second, profit third." Randy sipped his champagne. "Profit always comes if the first two are solid."

"Your father taught you this?"

"He taught us a lot of things. Some good, some bad. The good stuff we kept. The bad stuff killed him." Randy's voice carried just the right amount of weight. Honest without being maudlin. "That's why we're here. Learning from people who've figured out what he never did. How to operate at scale without becoming a target."

Kellerman was nodding along, completely hooked. Randy had found the angle: respect for European sophistication, humility about American limitations, the tragic backstory that made him sympathetic. All true, technically. All calculated perfectly.

Then Randy pushed it one step further.

"Between us," he said, lowering his voice just enough that Kellerman had to lean closer, "I think Antonov's network is the most elegant operation I've ever seen. The compartmentalization alone is worth studying for years."

I tensed. That was too specific. Too much like intelligence gathering.

But Kellerman just smiled, pleased by the compliment. "Viktor has spent fifteen years building this. Every piece designed to function independently. Even if one part fails, the others continue."

"Resilient systems. That's the key, isn't it?" Randy gestured with his glass. "Most operations are fragile. One arrest, one informant, and everything collapses. But something built like this? You'd have to take down every node simultaneously to stop it."

"Exactly so." Kellerman was beaming now, proud of an architecture he probably hadn't built but felt ownership over. "This is why Viktor is Viktor. He thinks like an engineer, not a criminal."

Randy laughed. "Maybe that's the secret. Stop thinking like criminals and start thinking like engineers."

I moved away before I could hear more. Randy was getting exactly the kind of information Adam would want. Confirmation of the network structure. Insight into how Antonov's people thought about their own vulnerabilities. Valuable intelligence, gathered through nothing more than charm and well-placed flattery.

But he was also dancing on a line. One wrong word, one question that felt too pointed, and Kellerman would remember this conversation differently. Would wonder why the American had been so curious about how to take down the network.

That was the thing about Randy. He was brilliant at this.

Better than me, maybe better than anyone I'd ever seen. But he always pushed right up to the edge. Always trusted his ability to pull back before he went too far.

One day that confidence was going to cost him.

I checked my watch. Eleven forty-five. Fifteen minutes until the cameras went down.

Across the room, Randy had moved on to a new target. A woman this time, someone's wife or mistress, laughing at something he'd said. Gathering information or just enjoying himself, I couldn't tell. With Randy, it was usually both.

Time to do my part.

At 11:45, I excused myself. "Restroom?"

"Third floor. End of the hall," someone told me.

I took the elevator up, found the bathroom, waited. At exactly midnight, my phone buzzed. Text from Laura: "Cameras down. You have four hours."

I found the maintenance corridor exactly where she'd said. Followed it down two flights of stairs. The basement door was locked, but not with anything sophisticated. Thirty seconds with the bypass tool Laura had given me, and I was in.

The room was larger than I expected. Server racks lining two walls, floor to ceiling, LED status lights blinking in patterns that told stories if you knew how to read them. Three workstations arranged in a U-shape facing the door. Multiple monitors, all dark now, waiting for morning shift. The hum of cooling fans filled the space, white noise that would mask small sounds but not careless ones.

I stood still for thirty seconds, letting my eyes adjust, cataloging everything. Emergency exit in the far corner. Loss Prevention 101: always know your way out. Security camera in the ceiling corner, red light dark. Laura's work. But I'd learned not to trust disabled cameras completely.

Some systems had redundant recording. Some had motion-triggered backups.

I moved along the wall, staying out of the camera's theoretical sight line anyway. Old habits.

The main terminal was password-protected, but that was expected. I pulled out the first USB drive, the one with the bypass tools I'd built specifically for this kind of system. European security software. Different architecture than American systems, but the same fundamental weaknesses. Everyone trusted their encryption too much and their physical security too little.

Ninety seconds to crack the login. Faster than I'd hoped.

The desktop that loaded was clean. Organized. Whoever ran this system was a professional. Folders labeled in German with alphanumeric codes. No helpful labels like "ILLEGAL OPERATIONS" or "CUSTOMER DATABASE." Just strings of letters and numbers that meant nothing without context.

But I had context. Days of briefings. Laura's intelligence on Antonov's organizational structure. The patterns I'd observed during my conversations with his people upstairs.

I started with the network architecture. Plugged in the second USB, the mapper, and let it run while I explored manually. The software would capture the technical infrastructure. I needed to understand the logic. How Antonov thought. How he'd built this.

The first folder I opened contained identity templates. Thousands of them. Pre-built profiles for different nationalities, different age ranges, different purposes. A menu of fake people, ready to be customized and deployed.

I recognized the structure immediately. It was elegant. More elegant than what I'd built in Florida. Antonov had created modular components: identity cores that could be mixed and matched with different employment histories, different credit backgrounds, different family structures. Like building blocks. Snap together the pieces you need, generate a complete person in minutes.

I took notes. Not on paper, nothing that could be found, but mental notes. The architecture. The logic. The efficiency.

Randy was right. This was graduate-level work.

The mapper beeped softly. Twenty percent complete. I checked the time. Forty-seven minutes since I'd entered. Three hours and thirteen minutes remaining.

I moved to the financial systems. This was what Adam really wanted. The money trails. The client connections. The evidence that would let them roll up the entire network in one coordinated strike.

The financial database was better protected. Three layers of encryption. Biometric backup that I couldn't bypass. But the mapper was designed for this. It would capture the encrypted data, let Langley's cryptographers crack it later. My job was just to make sure it got everything.

While the software worked, I explored the client files.

Names I didn't recognize. Organizations I'd never heard of. But patterns I understood. Payment structures. Communication protocols. The rhythm of criminal enterprise, the same everywhere in the world even when the specifics differed.

And then I found the terrorist connections.

A subfolder, buried three levels deep, with a different encryption signature. Newer. More sophisticated. Someone had added this recently, and they'd been more careful about it than the rest.

I couldn't crack the encryption in the time I had. But I could see the metadata. The creation dates. The access logs.

Antonov had been selling to these clients for less than a year. The same timeframe Adam had mentioned. London. Paris. Berlin. The attacks that had nearly succeeded.

I stared at the folder icon, thinking about the people who'd almost died because of what was in there. The people who would die if Antonov kept operating.

For a moment, I understood why Adam's original plan had been to simply kill him. Clean. Final. No more identities flowing to people who wanted to blow up trains and marketplaces.

But that wasn't who we were trying to be.

The mapper beeped again. Fifty percent. I'd been in the basement for an hour and forty minutes. The reception upstairs would be winding down soon. Guests leaving. Security tightening back up.

I moved faster now. Financial records. Communication logs. Client databases. Everything the mapper could reach, I directed it toward. Everything it couldn't reach, I documented the location of so Langley would know where to look once they had physical access.

Two hours in, I heard footsteps above me.

I froze. The basement was supposedly isolated. Separate entrance, separate security, no direct connection to the floors above. But supposedly wasn't the same as certainly.

The footsteps passed. Faded. Just someone walking to the bathroom, probably. Or leaving early.

I realized I'd been holding my breath. Let it out slowly. Reminded myself that panic was the enemy of precision.

Two hours and thirty minutes. The mapper was at seventy-eight percent.

I used the remaining time to do what Randy had asked. To really look at what Antonov had built. Not just capture it, but understand it.

The identity generation system was brilliant. The financial architecture was sophisticated. But what impressed me most was the compartmentalization. Antonov had built a network where no single person knew enough to bring down the whole thing. Even his most trusted lieutenants only saw pieces. Only he saw the complete picture.

Until now.

I pulled out my phone. This wasn't part of the mission. Adam hadn't asked for this. But Randy was right. We should learn from the best, even when we were helping to destroy them.

I photographed the network diagrams. The system architecture. The logic flows that showed how Antonov had structured everything. Not the data itself; that was for the CIA. But the design. The thinking. The patterns that made this operation work.

If we ever needed to build something similar, something for ourselves, outside of Adam's control, these photos would be invaluable.

The mapper beeped. Ninety-five percent.

I checked my watch. Three hours and twenty minutes. Forty minutes remaining, but I didn't want to push it. The reception was definitely ending now. People would be leaving. Security would be returning to normal protocols.

Ninety-eight percent.

Ninety-nine.

Complete.

I pulled the USB drives. Pocketed them. Did a final scan of the room to make sure I'd left no traces. The chair I'd sat in, positioned exactly as I'd found it. The keyboard, no fingerprints. I'd worn gloves the entire time. The monitors, still dark, still waiting for morning.

I moved to the door. Listened. Silence from the corridor.

One more look back at the server racks, their lights still blinking their patient patterns. In seventy-two hours, this room would be swarming with law enforcement from four countries. These servers would be seized. This operation would be over.

And I'd have a copy of the architecture in my pocket, ready for whatever came next.

I slipped out the door and started the long walk back to the reception.

The service corridor was empty. I moved quickly but not too quickly, a man who belonged here, a guest who'd gotten turned around looking for a bathroom. The USB drives in my pocket felt like they weighed ten pounds each.

I took the maintenance stairs up two flights, pushed through a door marked with German I couldn't read, and found myself in a carpeted hallway. Muffled sounds of the reception filtered from somewhere ahead. Almost there.

"Mr. Tyler."

I stopped. Turned slowly.

Dimitri Kovalenko stood at the far end of the hallway, a glass of vodka in his hand. He wasn't moving toward me. Just watching. The way a cat watches a bird it hasn't decided to chase yet.

"Dimitri." I kept my voice casual. "Good party."

"You've been gone a long time." He walked closer, each step deliberate. "I noticed you leave. That was more than three hours ago."

"Stomach trouble." I gestured vaguely behind me. "The schnitzel, maybe. I found a bathroom on the third floor. Quieter up there."

"The third floor." His eyes moved over me, cataloging details. Looking for something out of place. "That's a long way to go for a bathroom."

"The one down here had a line." I smiled. "You know how it is at these things."

Dimitri didn't smile back. He stopped about six feet away, close enough for conversation, far enough to watch my whole body. Professional distance. The distance of a man who'd been trained to read people.

"Your brother is very charming," he said. "Everyone loves him. Mr. Antonov especially."

"Randy has that effect on people."

"Very smooth. Very convincing." Dimitri sipped his vodka, eyes never leaving mine. "In Miami, you told me you were thieves with principles. That you don't cross certain lines. Very noble. Very American."

"It's true."

"Perhaps." He tilted his head slightly. "But I've learned that men who talk about principles are often the most dangerous. They believe their own stories. They think they're the heroes." A thin smile crossed his face. "In my experience, the heroes are the ones you have to watch most carefully."

"I'll take that as a compliment."

"Take it however you want." He stepped aside, clearing my path to the reception. "Enjoy the rest of the evening, Mr. Tyler. I'm sure we'll see each other again."

I walked past him, feeling his eyes on my back the entire way. At the door to the main room, I paused and looked back.

Dimitri hadn't moved. He stood in the hallway, vodka in hand, watching me with an expression I couldn't quite read. Suspicion, certainly. But something else too. Patience. The look of a man who was willing to wait for answers.

I pushed through the door and found Randy holding court with three of Antonov's associates, telling some story that had them laughing. He caught my eye across the room. I nodded slightly. Mission accomplished.

But as I made my way toward him, I spotted Dimitri entering through a side door. He found a position near the bar where he could see the whole room. See us.

He watched us for the rest of the night. Every handshake, every conversation, every smile. Taking mental notes. Building a file.

Randy noticed too. "Our friend from Miami," he murmured during a quiet moment. "He's been staring at us for an hour."

"He caught me coming back from the basement level. Asked questions."

"What did you tell him?"

"Bad schnitzel."

Randy laughed, but his eyes stayed serious. "He didn't believe you."

"No."

"Problem?"

I watched Dimitri watching us. In seventy-two hours, this whole operation would be rolled up. Antonov would be in handcuffs. His network would be dismantled. None of this would matter.

But Dimitri wasn't Antonov. Dimitri was a survivor. The kind of man who slipped through nets that caught everyone else.

"Maybe," I said. "Not tonight. But eventually? Maybe."

Randy raised his glass in Dimitri's direction. A toast. A taunt.

Dimitri didn't react. Just kept watching.

Some enemies you make by accident. Others you make by choice.

Dimitri Kovalenko was going to be both.

LAURA WAS WAITING in our suite.

"You got it?" she asked.

I handed her the USB drives. "Complete network map. Every node, every connection, every account."

"Any problems?"

"Dimitri is suspicious, but security never saw me."

"We will need to keep a closer eye on Mr. Dimitri Kovalenko." She plugged the drive into her laptop, started uploading. "This goes to Adam tonight. Takedown happens in seventy-two hours."

"What happens to the infrastructure?" Randy asked.

Laura looked up. "What?"

"The systems. The servers. The architecture. What happens to all of it after you take Antonov down?"

"It's seized. Dismantled."

Randy laughed. "Come on, Laura. You can lie to Adam if you want, but don't lie to us. You're not going to dismantle that network. It's too valuable."

Laura's fingers stopped moving on the keyboard. "What are you talking about?"

"The CIA is going to repurpose it. Use it for your own operations. Why build your own criminal network when you can just take over someone else's?" Randy sat down, completely relaxed. "It's smart. Efficient. No paper trail, no congressional oversight, completely deniable. I'd do the same thing."

Laura looked at me. I shrugged. Randy had figured it out. No point denying it.

"What you're suggesting would be highly illegal," Laura said carefully.

"Unless it's for national security. Then it's just operational necessity." Randy's smile was sharp. "Look, I'm not judging. I actually think it's brilliant. Antonov built something valuable. You'd be stupid to destroy it. Better to control it. Use it for legitimate purposes."

"This conversation never happened," Laura said.

"Of course not." Randy stood up. "I'm going to bed. Long flight home tomorrow."

He left Laura and me alone in the suite.

"Your brother is too smart for his own good," Laura said.

"He's right though, isn't he? The CIA is going to repurpose that network."

She was quiet for a long moment. Then: "Yes. We are."

"Why?"

"Because the system isn't evil. It's just a tool. What made it evil was how Antonov used it. But the tool itself..." She trailed off. "It's useful. For intelligence operations. For tracking other criminal networks. For controlled operations where we need to move money or establish identities without leaving CIA fingerprints."

"So you take over criminal infrastructure and run it yourselves."

"We repurpose it. Carefully. With oversight. For legitimate national security purposes."

"And who decides what's legitimate?"

"People above my pay grade." She closed her laptop. "Danny, I'm telling you this because you deserve to know. But this is classified. The kind of thing that ends careers if it becomes public."

"I understand."

"Do you? Because your brother just figured it out in about thirty seconds. And if he figured it out, other people might too."

"Randy won't tell anyone. He sees the value in keeping

secrets." I moved closer. "My question: what else does the CIA repurpose? How many criminal networks are you running?"

She looked at me for a long moment. Then: "More than you'd imagine. Less than conspiracy theorists claim. When we find something useful, something we can turn to our advantage...yes. We use it."

"Jesus."

"It's not about being evil. It's about being practical." She touched my face. "Does this change how you see me?"

"I don't know yet."

"Fair enough." She kissed me softly. "Get some sleep. We fly to Prague tomorrow."

"Prague?"

"Two-day layover before we head back. Adam's orders. Lets the operation cool down before the takedown. Gives distance between you and Vienna before the takedown. If anything went wrong in that basement, we don't want you still in the city when they find it."

She smiled slightly. "Also gives us some time away from Vienna. Somewhere we can actually relax."

"Can we relax after this?"

"We can try."

∾

WE COULDN'T SLEEP. The Antonov operation had gone clean, but the adrenaline was still working through both of us. "Laura had found a bottle of wine somewhere, and we'd ended up on the couch in the suite, curtains open, watching the Vienna lights through the window."

She was quiet for a long time.

"I was twenty-three," she said finally, her wine glass

catching the moonlight. "Junior analyst at State, assigned to the embassy in Tokyo. Boring work. Cable traffic, diplomatic scheduling, the kind of thing they give you when you're too new to trust with anything real."

I waited. Watched the way the shadows played across her face. I'd learned not to push her. Laura told stories when she was ready, and pushing only made her retreat behind that professional mask she wore so well.

"There was a reception. Some trade delegation, I don't even remember which one. I was there to take notes and look decorative." A ghost of a smile crossed her lips. "I ended up talking to this Japanese businessman. Older guy, very polished. He asked me questions about American policy that I definitely wasn't authorized to answer."

"But you answered them," I said.

"I gave him nothing. Smiled, deflected, fed him the same talking points he could have read in any newspaper." She took a sip of wine. "But I did it in a way that made him think I was being indiscreet. Made him feel like he was pulling secrets out of me, when really I was just watching him work."

"Watching him work?"

"He was intelligence. Chinese, not Japanese, despite what his business card said. I'd read his file two weeks earlier when it crossed my desk by accident." Her eyes met mine, and I saw something there I recognized. Pride. The satisfaction of having outplayed someone who thought they were outplaying you. "I spent forty-five minutes letting him think he was recruiting me, while I figured out exactly what he was actually after."

"Someone noticed," I said. It wasn't a question.

"They did." She set down her glass. "Three days later, a woman from the seventh floor asked me to lunch. Very casual. Just two professionals getting to know each other. Except she knew everything about that conversation. Every word, every pause, every moment where I'd steered him without him realizing."

"And she offered you a job."

"She offered me a question. She asked what I'd felt, sitting across from a man who was trying to manipulate me." Laura's voice went quiet, and I leaned closer to hear. "I told her the truth. I felt alive. I felt like I was finally doing something that mattered. Like all the games I'd been playing my whole life, reading people, figuring out what they really wanted, being whoever they needed me to be, finally had a purpose."

I understood that. The relief of finding a place where the skills that made you strange everywhere else suddenly made you valuable. I'd felt it too, the first time I built something Tommy actually needed.

"She said I had a gift," Laura continued. "That most people can't do what I did. Can't stay calm when they're being worked. Can't think three moves ahead while pretending to think zero moves ahead." A pause. "She said the Agency could teach me to use that gift. To do real good with it."

"Did she tell you about the cost?"

Laura looked at me for a long moment. The moonlight carved shadows across her face, and for an instant she looked older than her years. Tired in a way that had nothing to do with sleep.

"She told me everything has a cost. That the work would change me. That I'd have to become someone who could lie to anyone, about anything, without hesitation." Laura picked up her wine glass again. "She asked if I could live with that."

"And you said yes."

"Maybe too quickly." Her smile was thin, sad. "I was twenty-three. I thought I knew what I was agreeing to. I thought becoming someone else wouldn't mean losing myself."

"Did it?"

She was quiet for a long time. Then: "There was an asset in Karachi. Hamid. A university professor who'd been feeding us intelligence on weapons procurement networks for two years. Brave, principled, the kind of person who risks everything because he believes it matters." She turned the wine glass in her hands. "I ran him for eighteen months. Did everything by the book. Every protocol, every precaution, every safeguard the Agency had ever designed." She stopped. "They found him in his office. Made it look like a robbery. I was three blocks away when it happened."

I didn't say anything. There was nothing to say.

"I did everything right, Danny. And he still died." She set the glass down. "That's what the cost looks like. Not losing yourself. Losing someone who trusted you."

We sat with that for a while. The Vienna lights below us, the wine going warm, neither of us needing to fill the silence.

PRAGUE WAS DIFFERENT.

No missions. No briefings. No looking over our shoulders. Just two days of being tourists. Walking along the Charles Bridge. Drinking in old pubs. Pretending to be normal.

Randy stayed in Vienna one more day, maintaining

appearances. Meeting with more of Antonov's associates. Playing his role. That left Laura and me alone in Prague.

On our second night, we sat by the river, watching the castle light up as the sun set.

"Can I ask you something?" Laura said.

"Always."

"Why didn't you run? When you had the chance. After the arrest. After Adam made his offer. You could have disappeared. Used your skills to create a new identity and vanished. Why didn't you?"

I thought about it. "Same reason you became my handler even though you didn't want to."

"What reason is that?"

"Because we're both good at things we're not sure we should be good at. And we can't stop being good at them just because we want to." I looked at her. "I could have run. Created a new identity. Disappeared. But then what? Spend the rest of my life looking over my shoulder? Wondering when they'd find me? That's not freedom. That's just a different kind of prison."

"So you chose this prison instead."

"I chose latitude. The illusion of freedom. It's not perfect, but it's better than the alternatives." I took her hand. "What about you? Why did you really become a CIA officer?"

"Same reason, I think. I was good at languages. Good at reading people. Good at lying convincingly. Those aren't normal skills. Those are spy skills. And once I realized I had them, I couldn't unknow it. Couldn't pretend to be some normal person with a normal job. So I leaned into it."

"Do you regret it?"

"Most days, no. Some days, yes. Days like today." She squeezed my hand. "When I realize that every relationship I have is transactional. Every friend is a potential asset. Every conversation is calibrated. It's exhausting. Being yourself is exhausting when you're trained to be whoever the situation requires."

"Is that what you're doing with me? Being whoever the situation requires?"

"No. That's what makes this terrifying." She turned to face me. "With you, I'm just me. No performance. No calculation. Just Laura. And I don't know how to do that anymore. How to be just myself. I forgot how."

"Then we'll figure it out together. How to be ourselves inside all the lies."

"That's impossible."

"Probably. But we can try."

We sat there watching the sun set over Prague, two people who'd forgotten how to be normal trying to remember together.

"Danny?" Laura said quietly.

"Yeah?"

"Adam's going to ask you to run Antonov's network. Repurpose it for the CIA. You just proved you understand the architecture better than anyone."

"How do you know?"

"Because that's what I'd do. Why build from scratch when you've already mapped every node?" She looked at me. "When he asks, what are you going to say?"

"I don't know yet."

"You should think about it. Because that's the kind of request you can't refuse without consequences. But accepting it means becoming something more than an asset. It means becoming infrastructure. The kind of person the CIA depends on."

"Is that good or bad?"

"Depends on whether you want to be indispensable or expendable." She smiled slightly. "Indispensable means they can't get rid of you. But it also means they'll never let you go."

"So I'm trapped either way."

"Everyone in this game is on a leash. The only thing you get to choose is how long it is."

I thought about that as we walked back to our hotel.

The next morning, we flew back to Miami. Randy met us at the airport, grinning.

"Antonov's people kept checking on me right up until I left. Verification after verification." He looked at both of us, and for the first time, the grin faded. "Seventy-two hours. Then either we pull off the biggest takedown the CIA's run in a decade, or Antonov figures out what we did in that basement." He paused. "No pressure."

THE SEVENTY-TWO HOURS between Prague and the takedown were the longest of my life.

We flew back to Miami on day two, maintaining the cover of businessmen returning from a European trip. Randy talked about expansion plans the whole flight, loud enough for nearby passengers to hear. Building the legend even when no one was watching. That was good tradecraft, Laura had taught us. You never knew who might remember a conversation later.

But underneath the performance, we were both wound tight.

Laura called on the second night. Encrypted line, but I could hear the tension in her voice.

"Antonov's people are running final verification," she

said. "Deep background. They're checking everything again."

"They already checked us once."

"This is different. More thorough. They're pulling records we didn't expect them to access."

I sat down on my couch, suddenly aware of my heartbeat. "What kind of records?"

"Travel history. Your father's arrest files. Communication metadata from the last six months." A pause. "Someone flagged your trip to Prague. They're wondering why you didn't fly directly back to Miami."

"We told them we had business in Prague. Meeting with potential partners."

"I know. But they're verifying it. Looking for the partners you supposedly met with."

Randy was in my kitchen, pouring himself a drink. He could tell from my face that something was wrong.

"What do we do?" I asked.

"Nothing. We've built cover for Prague. A consulting firm that will confirm you had meetings with them. It'll hold up to scrutiny." Laura's voice steadied. "But Danny, this is close. Closer than I'd like. If they dig much deeper, if they find something we didn't anticipate..."

"They'll find two American criminals who came to Vienna to learn from the best. That's all there is to find."

"I hope you're right."

After I hung up, Randy handed me a bourbon. "Problem?"

"Maybe. They're running additional checks. Verifying our cover story."

"Let them verify. They're not going to find anything in twenty-four hours that they didn't find in the last week." Randy dropped into the chair across from me. "The clock is on our side now, Danny. They can dig all they want. By the time they hit anything real, it won't matter." "Except the part where we work for the CIA."

"Which they won't find because it doesn't exist on paper." He took a long drink. "Relax, Danny. We did the job. We got the data. In twenty-four hours, Antonov's whole network comes down and none of this matters."

He was right. Logically, I knew he was right.

But I couldn't shake the image of Dimitri in that hallway. The patience in his eyes. The way he'd watched us for the rest of the night, cataloging every detail.

"Dimitri knows something's wrong," I said.

"Dimitri suspects something's wrong. There's a difference. And in twenty-four hours, Dimitri's going to have bigger problems than us."

"What if he doesn't get picked up in the raids?"

Randy shrugged. "Then he goes back to trafficking and forgets about us. We're not his problem. Antonov was his meal ticket, and Antonov's about to disappear."

I wanted to believe him. Randy had a gift for making complicated situations feel simple. For cutting through the noise to find the clean line.

But I'd been in that hallway with Dimitri. I'd seen his face.

That wasn't a man who forgot.

The next morning, Laura called again. Two words: "We're clear."

Antonov's verification had confirmed everything. The Prague cover held. The background checks found exactly what they were supposed to find. Two ambitious American criminals with a dead father and a growing operation, looking to expand into Europe.

We were clean.

That night, the news broke.

"International Identity Theft Ring Dismantled. Dozens Arrested Across Three Continents."

They showed footage of the raids. Vienna, Berlin, London, Moscow. Synchronized takedowns. Antonov being led out in handcuffs. Servers being confiscated. The whole network collapsing at once.

Randy watched with satisfaction.

"We did that," he said. "Used our real names, our real backgrounds, our real operation. And we just took down a $200 million criminal network."

"You're proud of yourself," I said.

"Hell yeah I'm proud. This is exactly what I wanted. A real challenge. A real operation. Proof that we can operate at the highest level." He turned to me. "And now Adam's going to ask you to run the one we just took. Antonov's network, his infrastructure, all of it. You know that, right?"

"Laura mentioned it."

"What are you going to say?"

"I don't know yet."

"Well figure it out fast. Because that ask is coming."

He was right. My phone buzzed. Text from Adam: "Excellent work. Let's discuss next steps. Tomorrow, two p.m."

Here it came. The request I'd been expecting. The one I couldn't refuse.

The one that would change everything.

13

THE LONG GAME

Four days after Vienna, we celebrated.

Adam had called it a "debrief," but it felt more like a victory lap. Antonov's network was fully integrated into CIA infrastructure. His servers, now scrubbed and relocated, were processing identities for three separate intelligence operations. The money laundering channels had been redirected to fund assets in Eastern Europe. Everything I'd mapped, everything Laura had helped coordinate, was now generating value for the United States government.

And we'd been rewarded. A bonus deposited into accounts we didn't know we had. A handshake from someone whose name I was told I'd never hear again. Laura got a commendation that would sit in a classified file no one would ever read.

"You should feel good about this," Adam said, pouring bourbon in his office. Real bourbon, not the stuff he kept for regular meetings. "Vienna was clean. Professional. Exactly what we needed."

I took the glass he offered. "Thank you."

"I mean it." He settled into his chair, studying me. "You

exceeded expectations. Both of you. There's a future here, Danny. A real one."

Laura stood by the window, her glass untouched. I could see it in her posture, the slight tension in her shoulders. She was thinking what I was thinking.

A future. But whose version of it?

LATER THAT NIGHT, we sat on my balcony watching the boats move across the Intracoastal. Laura had kicked off her shoes and pulled her feet up onto the chair, her shoulder pressed against mine. The celebration was over. Now came the part we couldn't say in Adam's office.

"He's got us mapped out. The next five years. Probably the next ten. Every operation, every deployment, every mission." She paused. "You and Randy are assets. Valuable ones. And I'm the handler who fell for her asset. That makes all three of us the worst kind of useful."

"Because valuable assets get used."

"Until they're not valuable anymore." She turned to look at me. "And then they get retired. One way or another."

I'd been thinking about this since Vienna. Not the mission itself, which had gone exactly as planned, but what came after. The way Adam looked at us. The way he talked about "the future" like it was something he'd already written.

We were tools. Sophisticated ones, sure. Well-compensated. But tools nonetheless.

"What if we changed the equation?" I asked.

Laura raised an eyebrow. "Meaning?"

"Right now, we're employees. We do what they tell us, go

where they send us, execute their plans. The CIA sets the terms. We follow them."

"That's how it works."

"But it doesn't have to be that way." I leaned forward. "Think about what they actually need. Not us specifically. What the CIA needs from criminal networks."

Laura was quiet for a moment, processing. She'd been agency long enough to know where this was going.

"Access," she said slowly. "They need access. To infrastructure. To contacts. To operations they can't officially run."

"Exactly. They don't want to run criminal networks. Too much liability. Too much oversight risk. What they want is a partner. Someone who can provide what they need without them having to own it."

"A vendor," Laura said. "Not an employee."

"A vendor with leverage."

She shook her head, but I could see her working through it. "That's dangerous thinking. We start maneuvering against them, Adam figures it out, and we're done. Worse than done."

"Adam sees what he expects to see. A grateful recruit. A useful asset. Someone who's happy with their bonus and their attaboys." I finished my drink. "He doesn't see someone building an exit strategy."

"Is that what this is? An exit strategy?"

"No." I met her eyes. "It's a leverage strategy. We don't run away. We become too valuable to control. Too connected to cut loose. We make it so they need us more than we need them."

"So your plan is to out-spy the spies." She laughed quietly. "You know how insane that sounds, right?"

"Coming from the woman who seduced her own asset

and then decided to commit treason with him? Yeah, I'll take my chances."

She elbowed me in the ribs, but she was smiling. "I didn't seduce you. You were embarrassingly easy."

"Ouch."

"I'm serious. Two dates and you were already looking at me like I'd hung the moon."

"You had good intel. You knew exactly what I wanted to hear."

"Please. I barely had to try." She leaned her head against my shoulder. "That's how I knew you were trouble. The easy ones always are."

Laura was quiet for a long time. The boats moved across the water below us, their lights reflecting on the dark surface.

"How?" she asked finally.

~

WE STARTED THAT NIGHT.

The first rule was simple: every contact we made through the CIA, we would cultivate independently. Adam would introduce us to an asset, and we'd follow up on our own time. Build the relationship outside of official channels. Make them loyal to us, not to a handler they'd never meet.

Eduardo in Caracas was our first test case. Adam had connected us during the Antonov operation, a minor logistics provider who could move equipment across borders without questions. Standard operational support.

I reached out directly. No official channels. Just a secure message through the network I'd built during our Florida operation.

"I have a proposal," I told him. "Independent of our mutual friend."

Eduardo was skeptical at first. People in his line of work survived by being skeptical. But I offered him something Adam couldn't: terms that favored him. Better percentages. More autonomy. Less oversight.

Within a month, Eduardo was reporting to me first, Adam second. The information flow hadn't changed. The CIA still got what they needed. But now it came through us.

"That's one," Laura said when I told her. "We need more than one."

"I know. But it's proof of concept. The model works."

The second rule was harder: never let them see you building. Every move we made had to look like initiative, not strategy. Adam wanted motivated assets? We'd be the most motivated assets he'd ever seen. We'd anticipate problems before he knew they existed. Solve issues before they became issues.

And in the process, we'd make ourselves indispensable.

"He'll notice eventually," Laura warned. "You don't get to his level by being naive."

"He'll notice we're good at our jobs. That's not suspicious. That's exactly what he wants."

"And when we're too good? When we know too much, have too many connections, control too many pieces?"

I smiled. "Then we have a conversation about terms. And for the first time, we'll be the ones setting them."

WE SAT at the kitchen table until two in the morning and built ourselves a conscience.

Not operational rules. Not the kind Adam would

approve. These were ours. The lines we wouldn't cross, no matter how much leverage we built or how much power we accumulated.

Laura started. "No trafficking. Of any kind. People, organs, children. We don't touch it, we don't facilitate it, we don't look the other way."

"Agreed. That's one."

"No terrorism. We don't provide resources, intelligence, or cover to anyone targeting civilians."

"Two."

We went back and forth for hours. Some were obvious. Some required debate. By the time we finished, we had fifteen.

We finished the list around two a.m.

Fifteen hard lines. Fifteen things that would never be negotiable, regardless of what Adam wanted or what opportunity presented itself. Written on a piece of paper that could end both our careers if the wrong person found it.

"If we're going to build something," Laura said, looking at the list, "it has to be better than what came before. Otherwise what's the point?"

"The point is survival."

"Survival isn't enough. I've seen what happens to people who survive without principles. They become the thing they were fighting against." She tapped the paper. "These keep us honest."

Laura folded the list carefully and slipped it into her pocket. Then she sat back on my couch and looked at me with an expression I couldn't quite read.

"Do you understand what we just did?" she asked.

"We wrote down some principles. Guidelines for how we want to operate."

"No." She shook her head. "We just committed conspiracy. Together. On paper." She laughed, but there was no humor in it. "A CIA operations officer and her asset, documenting their plan to build leverage against the agency. If Adam found this, we wouldn't just lose our jobs. We'd disappear."

I hadn't thought about it in those terms. But she was right. The list wasn't just ethics. It was evidence.

"Then why did you write it down?"

"Because I needed it to be real." She pulled her legs up onto the couch, wrapped her arms around her knees. For a moment she looked younger than I'd ever seen her. Vulnerable in a way that didn't match the competent handler I'd come to know. "In my head, I can rationalize anything. I can tell myself I'm still doing my job, still serving the mission, still loyal to the agency. But this?" She touched her pocket where the paper sat. "This is a line. Once I cross it, I can't pretend anymore."

"And you wanted to cross it."

"I wanted to stop pretending." She met my eyes. "Danny, I've been an intelligence officer for eight years. I've run assets on four continents. I've done things I can't talk about, things that still wake me up at night. And through all of it, I told myself I was one of the good guys. That the mission justified the methods. That I was serving something larger than myself."

"And now?"

"Now I'm not sure the good guys exist. I think there's just people with power and people without it. And I'd rather build my own power than keep serving someone else's." She reached out and took my hand. "But I can't do that alone. And I can't do it if I'm still pretending this is just an operation."

I understood what she was saying. What she was offering.

"So this is real," I said. "Whatever this is. It's not handler and asset anymore."

"It stopped being that a while ago. I just wasn't ready to admit it." She squeezed my hand. "Partners. Co-conspirators. Two people betting everything on each other. That's what this is now."

"That's terrifying."

"Yes." She smiled, and for the first time it reached her eyes. "But it's also the first honest thing I've done in years."

I pulled her close, and we sat there in the darkness, bound by a piece of paper that could destroy us both.

Partners.

The word felt like a promise and a threat at the same time.

I looked at her. Really looked at her. This woman who'd been assigned to seduce me, who'd broken protocol by falling in love with her mark, who was now planning to outmaneuver the agency that trained her.

"You really think we can do this?" I asked. "Build something ethical in a world that rewards ruthlessness?"

"I think we can try. And trying is more than anyone else is doing."

RANDY CALLED THE NEXT MORNING.

"Where've you been?" His voice had that edge it got when he felt left out. "Haven't heard from you in a week."

"Busy. Post-Vienna stuff." I kept my tone casual. "Adam had some follow-up."

"Follow-up. Right." A pause. "You know, it's interesting. Ever since you got back from Europe, you've been different."

"Different how?"

"I don't know. More...focused. Like you're playing a game I can't see."

I felt a chill run through me. Randy wasn't stupid. We'd grown up together, worked together, built an operation together. He knew me better than almost anyone.

"Just learning the ropes," I said. "The CIA stuff is more complicated than I expected."

"Yeah." He didn't sound convinced. "Look, we should get together. Catch up. TJ's been sending some new business our way. High-end clients. Not something I want to get into on the phone." TJ was from the neighborhood, a kid Anthony and I'd helped out years ago, ran off some guys who were beating on him. He'd gone on to Wall Street, but never forgot the favor.

"Sure. This week."

After I hung up, I stood at the window for a long time.

Randy was family. More than family. He'd had my back since we were kids stealing from the same stores, running the same streets. When I'd left Florida four years ago, he'd been the one who understood. When I came back, he'd welcomed me without judgment.

And now I was keeping secrets from him.

Not small secrets. Not the kind of things brothers hold back from each other. I was building something that would change everything, and he didn't even know it existed.

But I couldn't tell him. Couldn't risk it. If Randy knew what Laura and I were planning, he'd want in. And if he was in, Adam would find out. Randy was many things, but subtle wasn't one of them.

So I'd lie. I'd compartmentalize. I'd be the brother he thought he knew while building something he'd never see coming.

It's what you do when you love someone enough to protect them.

You lie.

And you hope they never find out.

THREE DAYS LATER, Laura showed up at my apartment with coffee and a question.

She let herself in with the key I'd given her two weeks ago, set the cups on the counter, and kissed me before I could say good morning. She tasted like the latte she'd been drinking on the drive over.

"You're up early," I said.

"Couldn't sleep." She handed me my coffee, black, no sugar, and settled onto the couch with her legs tucked under her. "How long has Adam been in your life?"

I sat down next to her, close enough that our knees touched. "Since I was a kid. He's one of Tony's guys. Been at every family barbecue, every birthday. Why?"

"And you never knew he was agency."

"Not until the holding cell. I thought he was just another one of Tony's business associates." I watched her face. "What are you getting at?"

"I'm getting at the timing." She wrapped both hands around her cup. "Your father gets arrested. Within hours, Adam's there with an offer. Not the FBI. Not the DEA. The CIA. He had the whole deal ready. Immunity, terms, every-thing. That's not something you put together overnight."

I'd wondered about it, actually. In the chaos after Tommy's death, there hadn't been time to question how quickly Adam had appeared with a fully-formed proposal. But now, with distance, the timeline did seem...convenient.

"You think he was waiting for it."

"I think Adam doesn't do anything without a plan. And I think his plan for you started long before that night in the holding room." She sipped her coffee. "I've been doing some quiet digging. Nothing that would raise flags. But Adam's operation is bigger than I thought. Older, too. Some of his relationships go back decades."

"Like his relationship with Tony."

"Exactly." She shifted, leaning into me slightly as she talked, the way she did when she was working through something complicated. "Every time I trace a connection back far enough, I hit a wall. The same wall. Like there's something, or someone, at the center of all this that I can't quite see."

I thought about my father. About the arrest that seemed staged. About Adam appearing like he'd been waiting for exactly that moment.

And I thought about Uncle Tony. The way he'd counseled patience when my father demanded action. The way he always seemed to know more than he was saying. The chess lessons that were never really about chess.

But that was paranoid thinking. Uncle Tony was family. He'd looked out for me my whole life.

Hadn't he?

"What are you suggesting?" I asked carefully.

"I'm not suggesting anything. Not yet." Laura set down her coffee. "I'm saying we should keep our eyes open. Ask questions. Pay attention to things we might have missed before."

"Like what?"

"Like how smoothly everything has gone for us. Vienna. The Antonov operation. Even the way Adam recruited you in the first place." She met my eyes. "Doesn't it feel a little too easy? A little too...orchestrated?"

I wanted to argue. To tell her she was being paranoid. But the truth was, she was right. Things had gone smoothly. Too smoothly for two people who were supposedly gaming a system designed by professionals.

"What do we do about it?"

"Same thing we were already planning. Build our network. Gain leverage. Make ourselves indispensable." She stood, moving toward the door. "But we do it with our eyes open. And we don't assume we're the only ones playing the long game."

She paused at the door.

"Your Uncle Tony taught you chess, right? All those lessons about thinking ten moves ahead?"

"He did."

"Good advice." She opened the door. "Just remember, in a real game, you're not the only one thinking ahead. Sometimes the best players let you think you're winning."

The door closed behind her.

I sat alone in my apartment, turning her words over in my mind.

Uncle Tony. Adam. The timing of everything.

It was probably nothing. Probably just Laura's training making her see shadows where there weren't any.

But I couldn't shake the feeling that somewhere, somehow, someone was watching our moves with a smile. Like a chess master watching two students finally learn the game he'd been teaching them all along.

I pushed the thought away. We had work to do. A network to build. Leverage to accumulate.

Whatever game was really being played, I intended to win it.

At least, that's what I told myself.

14

THE PARTNERSHIP

MONTH ONE

The first rule of building leverage is making sure no one knows you're building it.

Adam assigned us to our first routine operation a few weeks after the debrief. Communications support for an asset in Morocco. Standard stuff. Monitor the channels, flag anything unusual, report back through proper channels.

We did exactly what he asked. And then we did more.

I rebuilt the communication infrastructure from scratch. The existing system was functional but clunky, legacy tech that had been patched together over years. I replaced it with something elegant. Faster. More secure. Harder to trace.

"You didn't have to do that," Adam said when he saw the results. "The old system worked."

"The old system had vulnerabilities. Three different entry points that a sophisticated actor could exploit." I pulled up the technical specs on my laptop. "This one has none. Plus it's faster and uses less bandwidth."

Adam studied the diagrams for a long moment. "You built this in two weeks?"

"I had some free time."

What I didn't tell him was that the new system routed everything through servers I controlled. Not to spy on the CIA. I wasn't that stupid. But to understand the traffic patterns. To see the shape of the network I was becoming part of.

Knowledge is leverage. And I was quietly accumulating both.

Laura worked a different angle. She'd been agency long enough to know where the real power lived. Not in the corner offices or the briefing rooms, but in the administrative layers. The analysts who processed reports. The support staff who saw everything and were seen by no one.

"I've made a friend," she told me one night. "Jennifer. Works in operations coordination. She knows every active operation Adam is running."

"Is that safe?"

"I'm not pumping her for information. I'm just building a relationship. Being friendly." She smiled. "And Jennifer has been passed over for promotion three times because Adam doesn't think analysts deserve career advancement. She has opinions about that."

This was the second rule of accumulating power: never take more than you need. Small moves. Nothing that would trigger alarms.

We were playing a game measured in months, not days.

Eduardo called at the end of the first month with a problem. FARC was squeezing his shipments through Colombia. I connected him with a fixer from the Antonov files, negotiated terms that worked for everyone, and his cargo moved without incident.

Adam never knew it happened. But Eduardo did. And now he owed me.

That's how you build a network. One favor at a time.

MONTH TWO

I met Randy for lunch at a place in Pompano Beach. He'd been texting more frequently, checking in with questions that felt like probes.

"You're different," he said, studying me over his beer. "Ever since Vienna. "

"I'm learning a lot."

"Learning what, exactly?" He leaned forward. "You're not just running operations for Adam. You're building something. I can feel it."

This was the danger of working with family. They knew you too well.

"I'm making myself useful," I said carefully. "That's the job."

"Danny, I've known you my whole life. You don't do anything just to be useful. You're always playing an angle."

"And if I am?"

"Then I want in." His voice dropped. "Whatever you're building, I want to be part of it. We're brothers."

I felt the pull of it. The temptation to bring him in. Randy was loyal. Capable. He could be an asset.

But he was also Randy. Impulsive. Emotional. If Adam suspected anything, he'd read it on Randy's face in thirty seconds.

"The best thing you can do right now is exactly what you're doing," I said. "Run Florida. Build the operation. Make money."

"While you do what?"

"While I figure out how to make sure we both stay free." I met his eyes. "I'm playing a long game, Randy. One that requires being invisible. And you, brother, are many things. But invisible isn't one of them."

He stared at me for a long moment. I could see the hurt there, the frustration.

"Fine. I'll do my job." He stood up, dropping cash on the table. "But when this game of yours comes to a head, when you need someone you can trust with your life, you call me. That's what brothers are for."

He left without looking back.

I sat there wondering if I'd just protected him or pushed him away.

ADAM CALLED me into his office the next week.

"Budapest operation. Asset went dark three days ago. I need someone to figure out what happened."

"Send a team."

"I can't. This is off-book." He leaned back. "But you're not official. Assets don't require paperwork."

Two days later, Laura and I were on a plane.

Kovacs's apartment told us what we needed to know. Heart attack, according to the local police. But the body position was wrong, the tea on the counter suggested poison, and someone had been in that apartment who knew his routine.

"The wife's circle," Laura said. "That's the vulnerability. Wives talk."

We spent the first day watching the widow. Two visitors. The first was Dr. Farkas, a cardiologist from the hospital where Kovacs died. He'd signed the death certificate. That seemed too convenient, so we burned twelve hours investigating him.

Dead end. Farkas was clean. Just a doctor being kind to a grieving widow.

"We wasted a day," Laura said.

"We eliminated a possibility. What about the second visitor?"

"Tomas Varga. Brother-in-law. Works for a security company called Sentinel." She pulled up the file. "Looks legitimate. Corporate clients, government contracts. Nothing that screams intelligence."

"Everyone's legitimate on paper."

It took another day to find the thread. Sentinel had a consulting contract with Gazprom's Budapest office. Russian state energy. Thin, but interesting.

I followed Tomas the next morning. Gym, office, nothing unusual. I was about to give up when he left for lunch and walked six blocks to a park.

He sat on a bench. Waited. Twenty minutes later, a woman joined him. They exchanged an envelope and a phone. Then they left in opposite directions.

I followed the woman to the Belarusian embassy.

Close enough to Moscow.

That night, I dug into Tomas's digital footprint. Found an old Instagram photo: Tomas in a Moscow restaurant, arm around a man my Ukrainian intelligence contact identified as Alexei Morozov. FSB. Three years ago.

Travel records confirmed it. Tomas had been in Moscow two weeks before Kovacs died. And again three days after.

"Reporting in," Laura said. "First to get the order. Then to confirm completion."

"But how did he do it? The poison was in the tea. He needed access to the kitchen."

I went back to Marta's social media. Found a photo posted the morning of the death. A box of chocolates on the counter, next to the tea kettle. Caption: "Tomas spoils me!"

"He brought her chocolates," I said. "Gave him an excuse to be in the kitchen while she opened the box."

We spent the next two days destroying him. Three channels: a journalist in Berlin who'd expose Sentinel's Russian connections, an anonymous tip to their biggest client, and a document drop to their hungriest competitor.

Within a week, Sentinel was under investigation. Tomas fled to Moscow, his career in ruins.

He wasn't dead. He wasn't in prison. But he'd never hurt anyone again.

"It's messier than killing him," Laura said.

"Messier but better. He gets to live with what he did."

We flew back to Miami. Adam never knew the full extent of what we'd done. He only knew we'd solved the problem.

That was enough.

MONTH Three

Adam was impressed.

"You solved the Kovacs problem without making a mess. Without needing your hand held." He studied me from across his desk. "I'm starting to think you might actually be as good as you think you are."

"I just did what you asked."

"No. You did more than I asked. You anticipated problems I hadn't considered." He paused. "That's not a criticism. That's an observation."

He meant it as a compliment. What he didn't realize was that he was also describing the threat I posed.

"I have something bigger for you," Adam continued. "Caracas. A network that's been running for years, but it's becoming unstable. Internal conflicts. Power struggles. If it collapses, we lose intelligence capabilities we've been building for a decade."

I thought about Eduardo. The relationship I'd been building independently.

"When do I leave?"

"Next week." Adam stood. "Don't disappoint me."

THE CARACAS SITUATION was worse than Adam knew.

Eduardo had been warning me for weeks. A rival cartel called Los Diablos was making moves, pressuring operators to switch allegiances. They'd already turned three key people.

"They came to me last night," Eduardo said over an encrypted call. "Offered me double. Said if I didn't take the deal, they'd make an example."

"Give me five days."

I called Laura. "We fix this ourselves. Before Adam has a chance to screw it up."

"How?"

"Information warfare. We find something on Los Diablos leadership. Something they don't want public."

Finding the leverage was easy. Their leader, Castillo, had a brother in a Colombian prison. A brother he'd been quietly paying to keep protected. If that money stopped, the brother would lose everything.

We didn't threaten. Just made sure Castillo knew we knew.

Two days later, Los Diablos withdrew their offers. The network was off limits.

I called Eduardo. "It's done. They're backing off. You're safe."

The relief in his voice was palpable. "Danny, I don't know how to thank you."

I hung up feeling good. Clean. We'd solved the problem without violence, without Adam, without anyone getting hurt.

That feeling lasted three days.

EDUARDO'S VOICE was different when he called. Flat. Hollow.

"They burned my cousin's warehouse. Last night. His whole inventory."

My stomach dropped. "What? Castillo agreed to back off."

"Castillo did. But one of his lieutenants, Rojas, didn't like being told to stand down. He wanted to make a point." Eduardo's voice cracked. "My cousin wasn't even part of this, Danny. He just stores auto parts. Twenty years of work, gone."

"Is he okay?"

"He wasn't in the building. But he lost everything. His business. His livelihood." A long pause. "He doesn't know why it happened. I can't tell him."

I didn't have an answer.

"You said nobody would get hurt," Eduardo said. "You said you had it handled."

"I thought I did."

"You were wrong."

The line went dead.

Laura found me in my hotel room an hour later. I told her everything.

"You couldn't have predicted that," she said. "Castillo gave the order."

"But I didn't account for the ego of some mid-level asshole who felt disrespected." I walked to the window. "I was so proud of myself, Laura. So fucking clever. Blackmail the boss, skip the violence, nobody gets hurt. And now some guy who fixes cars for a living has nothing because I thought I was smarter than I am."

"What do you want to do?"

"I want to fix it. Pay for the warehouse. Set the cousin up somewhere else."

"And Rojas?"

I thought about it. The anger was there, hot and ready. It would be easy to destroy him the way we'd destroyed Tomas.

But that was the same thinking that had gotten me here.

"Nothing. If we go after him, his people go after Eduardo. Next time it won't be a warehouse."

"So he just gets away with it?"

"That's the cost of my mistake." The words tasted like ash. "I have to live with it."

WHEN ADAM ARRIVED in Caracas the following week, he found there wasn't a crisis.

"What happened?" he asked. "My intelligence said this operation was falling apart."

I thought about the warehouse. About Eduardo's cousin.

"The rival group backed off. Internal politics." I met his eyes. "Sometimes problems solve themselves."

"Good work. However it happened."

I should have felt proud. Another test passed.

Instead, I felt sick.

THAT NIGHT, Laura and I went for a walk along the marina. We'd started doing that when we needed to talk without walls around us.

"Eduardo reports to us first now," I said. "So does the fixer in Bogota. Jennifer is feeding you information about Adam's other operations. We're becoming essential."

"Essential how?"

"Indispensable means they need us. Essential means they can't function without us." I took a drink. "We're not there yet. But we're closer than we were."

Laura was quiet for a moment. "Sometimes I wonder if we're fooling ourselves. Playing a game we think we're winning while someone else moves the pieces."

"Maybe. But what's the alternative? Accept our role as assets? Do what we're told and hope for the best?"

"No."

"Then we keep building." I met her eyes. "And we stay alert. Trust each other, even if we can't trust anyone else."

She reached over and took my hand. "Partners."

"Partners."

We sat there in the darkness. After a while, I spoke again.

"I keep thinking about the cousin. The one whose warehouse burned."

"I know."

"I don't even know his name. I destroyed his life and I don't know his name."

Laura squeezed my hand. "Do you want to know it?"

I thought about it. Really thought about it.

"No. Because if I know his name, I'll look him up. I'll see his family. His kids, if he has them." I stared at the water. "I'm not strong enough for that. Not yet."

"That's not cowardice. That's human." She leaned her head against my shoulder. "We can't carry every consequence. We'd break."

I wanted to argue. But I was tired. And she was warm against my shoulder. And the boats kept moving across the water like they did every night, indifferent to the small disasters of small people.

Three months into a game that might take years to win.

And I was already learning what it cost.

15

CONFRONTATION

I was on the phone with Eduardo when Randy walked in.

I hadn't heard him come through the office door. Hadn't heard his footsteps on the carpet. One second I was alone, talking through the logistics of the new shipping route through Panama, and the next second my brother was standing six feet away with an expression I couldn't read.

"The customs contact is solid," Eduardo was saying in my ear. "But he needs assurance that the protection extends to his family. The last group he worked with couldn't deliver on that."

"Tell him it's handled," I said, watching Randy. "We protect our people. That's non-negotiable."

"He'll want to hear that from you directly."

"Set up a call. Tomorrow, his time. And Eduardo, the Los Diablos situation is contained?"

"Completely. They've moved on to other targets. We're clear."

"Good. Talk tomorrow."

I ended the call. Randy hadn't moved.

"Eduardo," he said. "Customs contacts. Los Diablos. Protection for families." His voice was flat. "That doesn't sound like CIA intelligence gathering, Danny."

"Randy, I can explain."

"I'm sure you can. You're very good at explanations." He walked to the window, looked out at the parking lot. "I came by to talk about the TJ situation. He's got three new clients for us, Wall Street guys who need clean identities. Big money. I thought you'd want to know."

"That's great. We can talk about it."

"But that's not what we're going to talk about, is it?" He turned to face me. "Because what I just heard wasn't you running an operation for Adam. That was you running something Adam doesn't know about."

"You're not just working for them," Randy said slowly. "You're working around them."

"You're right," I said finally. "It's not sanctioned. Eduardo reports to me, not Adam. I've been building relationships outside official channels. Solving problems Adam doesn't know exist."

"Why?"

"Because Adam sees us as assets. Tools. Things to be used until we're not useful anymore, and then discarded." I leaned forward. "Laura and I decided we weren't going to accept that. We're not rebelling. We're repositioning."

"Repositioning to what?"

"To a place where we have leverage. Where they need us more than we need them. Where we're not employees, we're partners. Real partners, with real power to set terms."

Randy was quiet for a long moment. I could see him processing, weighing what I'd told him against everything he thought he knew.

"How long?" he asked.

"Three months. Since right after Vienna."

"And you didn't tell me."

"I couldn't tell you. If Adam suspected anything, if he looked at you and saw that you knew, everything would fall apart. You're not..."

"I'm not subtle. I know." His jaw tightened. "That's what you were going to say, right? Randy can't keep a secret. Randy's too emotional. Randy would give it away."

"That's not..."

"It's exactly what you were going to say. And you know what? You're probably right." He stood up, paced to the window and back. "I would have given it away. I would have looked at Adam wrong, said something stupid, tipped him off. Because I'm not built for this cloak-and-dagger bullshit. I'm built for running operations. Making money. Handling problems directly."

"Randy..."

"I'm not done." He stopped in front of me. "You kept me out because you thought I'd screw it up. Fine. But that doesn't mean it doesn't hurt. We're brothers, Danny. We're supposed to be in this together. And instead, you and your CIA girlfriend have been building something without me. Planning a future that doesn't include me."

"That's not true."

"Isn't it? What's my role in this leverage play of yours? What's my place in the empire you're building?"

I hesitated. Because the truth was, I hadn't thought that far ahead. Laura and I had been so focused on strengthening our position against the CIA that we hadn't planned what came after.

"That's what I thought," Randy said.

He walked toward the door.

"Randy, wait."

He stopped but didn't turn around.

"I should have told you. I was wrong. But I was trying to protect..."

"Don't." Now he turned. His eyes were cold in a way I'd never seen from him. "Don't say you were protecting me. That's what Dad used to say. Every time he lied. Every time he kept us in the dark. 'I'm protecting you boys.' It was bullshit then and it's bullshit now."

"This is different."

"Is it? Because from where I'm standing, it looks exactly the same. You made a decision about my life without asking me. You decided what I could handle. You decided what was best." He shook his head. "That's not protection, Danny. That's control. And I've had enough of being controlled to last a lifetime."

He left without another word.

I SAT in the conference room for an hour, replaying the conversation, wondering if I'd just lost my brother.

Laura found me there.

"Randy called me," she said, sitting down across from me. "He's not happy."

"I noticed."

"He asked me if this was my idea. Building leverage. Keeping him out."

"What did you tell him?"

"The truth. That it was both of us. That we made the decision together." She paused. "He hung up on me."

"He compared me to Tommy."

Laura winced. "That's...harsh."

"He's not wrong." I stared at the table. "I made decisions

about his life without consulting him. I decided what he could handle. That's exactly what Dad used to do."

"You're not Tommy."

"No? Because Randy seems to think I'm following the playbook pretty closely."

Laura was quiet for a moment. "He'll come around. He's hurt, not broken. Give him time."

"And if he doesn't?"

"Then we figure out how to move forward. But I don't think it'll come to that. Randy loves you. That doesn't disappear because you kept a secret."

I wanted to believe her. But the look on Randy's face when he left, the coldness in his eyes, it reminded me of Diana. Of all the other people I'd hurt by keeping them at arm's length.

Maybe that was who I was. Someone who protected people by pushing them away.

Maybe that was all I knew how to do.

TOMMY'S OLD HOUSE, **Fort Lauderdale**

Randy called two days later.

"Come to Dad's place," he said. "We need to talk. All of us."

His voice was flat. Professional. The voice he used with business associates, not family.

I hadn't been to Tommy's house since before his death. Rachel had taken some things when she left, but most of it remained, preserved like a museum to a man none of us fully understood.

Randy was in the living room when I arrived. Jake and Colin were already there, sitting on the couch, looking uncomfortable.

"Laura's not invited," Randy said when he saw me looking around. "This is family."

"Laura is..."

"Laura is your partner. Your girlfriend. Your handler. Whatever." Randy's voice was controlled. Too controlled. "But she's not a Tyler. And right now, we need to talk as Tylers."

I sat down in Tommy's old chair. It felt strange, like I was taking a place I hadn't earned.

"I told them," Randy said, gesturing to Jake and Colin. "The basics. That you've been running operations Adam doesn't know about. That you're building some kind of leverage play against the CIA."

Jake's expression was unreadable. Colin looked worried.

"We have questions," Colin said. "Concerns."

"I'm sure you do."

"The main one being: what the fuck are you thinking?" Jake leaned forward. "The CIA, Danny. You're playing games with the CIA. These are people who make problems disappear. And you're what, trying to outmaneuver them?"

"I'm trying to create a situation where we're not disposable. Where they can't just cut us loose when we stop being useful."

"By going behind their backs."

"By making ourselves essential. There's a difference."

Colin shook his head. "This is insane. You know that, right? You're building a shadow operation inside a shadow operation. If they find out..."

"They won't."

"You don't know that."

"I know that we've been doing this for three months and they haven't noticed. I know that every operation we run makes us more valuable. I know that we're solving problems they can't solve without us." I looked at each of them in turn. "I know that the alternative is spending the rest of our lives as assets. Tools. Things to be used and discarded."

The room was quiet.

Randy hadn't said a word since I sat down. He stood by the window, arms crossed, watching but not participating.

"What do you need from us?" Jake asked finally.

"Keep doing what you're doing. Run your parts of the operation. Make money. Be visible. Be the Tyler operation everyone sees."

"While you work in the shadows."

"While I build something that can protect all of us. If Adam ever decides we're more trouble than we're worth, if he tries to cut us loose or worse, we need options. Leverage. Something to negotiate with."

Jake nodded slowly. "I don't need the operational details. Cleaner that way. But if you need something handled. Logistics, physical security, deniable actions. I'm available."

Colin spoke next. "Agreed. Exclude me from operational planning. Plausible deniability is quantifiable protection. But if you need financial routing, documentation, or accounting cover, those are my areas."

I looked at Randy. He was still staring out the window, his back to the room.

"Randy?"

"I heard."

"And?"

He turned around. His face was blank. Closed off. "I'll keep running Florida. That's what I was doing before this conversation, and it's what I'll keep doing after."

"That's it?"

"That's it." He walked toward the door. "Jake, Colin, I'll

see you at the office tomorrow. Danny, you know where to find me if you need something."

He left. Not angry, not emotional. Just gone.

Jake and Colin exchanged glances.

"He'll come around," Jake said, but he didn't sound convinced.

"Will he?"

"He's Randy. He runs hot, but he cools down. Give him a week."

I wasn't so sure. The Randy who just left wasn't hot. He was cold. Distant. Professional.

That was worse.

Danny's Apartment, Later That Night

Laura was waiting when I got home.

"How did it go?"

I dropped onto the couch beside her. "Jake and Colin are in, in their own way. Plausible deniability, but they'll help if we need them."

"And Randy?"

"Randy's out. Or in. I can't tell." I rubbed my face. "He said he'll keep running Florida. That's it. No emotion. No argument. Just...business."

"That doesn't sound like Randy."

"It's not. That's what worries me." I leaned back, stared at the ceiling. "He accused me of making decisions about his life without asking. Calling it protection when it's really control."

Laura was quiet for a moment. "Is he wrong?"

"No. That's the worst part. He's not wrong."

"So what do you do?"

"I don't know. Apologize? I tried that. He doesn't want to

hear it." I looked at her. "Maybe some things can't be fixed. Maybe I burned this bridge and now I have to live with it."

"Danny..."

"I kept him out, Laura. For three months. I looked my brother in the eye and lied to him, over and over, because I decided he'd blow it. That he wasn't subtle enough to keep it from Adam. That's not something you just get over."

Laura took my hand but didn't argue. She knew I was right.

"There's something else," she said after a moment. "I heard from Jennifer today. Adam's been asking questions."

I sat up. "What kind of questions?"

"Nothing specific. Just checking on our activities. Wanting to know where we've been, who we've talked to. Normal oversight stuff, on the surface."

"But?"

"But he's never asked before. We've been operating for three months, and he's never once followed up on our movements outside of official operations." She met my eyes. "Something's changed."

I thought about the Caracas operation. About Eduardo. About all the moves we'd made without Adam's knowledge.

Had we slipped somewhere? Made a mistake that caught his attention?

"What do we do?" I asked.

"Nothing different. We keep doing exactly what we've been doing. If we change our behavior now, that's suspicious. We act normal, hit our marks, exceed expectations." She took my hand. "We just do it more carefully."

"And if he's onto us?"

"Then we deal with it when it becomes a problem. Right now, it's just questions. Curiosity. That's not the same as suspicion."

I nodded, but the unease remained. Adam asking questions. Webb, the FBI agent who'd sworn to take us down, still building his investigation somewhere. Randy cold and distant. The walls we'd built around our operation were starting to show cracks.

"We're running out of time," I said.

"We were always running out of time. That's how this works." Laura squeezed my hand. "The question is whether we can build enough leverage before the clock runs out."

"Can we?"

"I don't know." She looked toward the window, toward the lights of the city beyond. "But I know we have to try. Because the alternative is spending the rest of our lives as someone else's tools. And I didn't come this far to end up like that."

Neither did I.

We sat together in the darkness, partners in a game we might not win.

But now there was something else in the room. The weight of Randy's absence. The knowledge that my brother was out there somewhere, thinking of me as a liar. Thinking of me as Tommy.

Some victories come with costs you don't expect.

This one had cost me my brother.

I just didn't know yet if I could get him back.

16

THE HARD CHOICE

Six months into our leverage play, and I'd learned that sometimes there are no good options.

Only less-bad ones.

Randy hadn't been to one of Adam's briefings since I'd told him about the leverage play. Adam had handled the split quietly, assigned Randy his own handler, a guy named Derek Hale who ran operations out of the Miami station. Randy was still an asset, still running jobs, but on a separate track now. His operations, his briefings, his chain of command. Adam told me it was "operational efficiency." I knew it was something else. You don't keep brothers working together when one of them starts building leverage against you.

The meeting was at Adam's office in Coral Gables, the one that officially belonged to a consulting firm that didn't do any consulting. Someone in the building had strung Christmas lights along the balcony railing outside. Laura sat next to me. Adam across the table, laptop open, files spread in front of him.

"Congressman Michael Carver," Adam said, pulling up a

photo on his screen. Mid-fifties, Florida tan, politician's smile that had graced billboards across Miami's 27th district. "On the surface, he's a rising star. Anti-corruption platform. Tough on crime. Leads the South Florida Counter-Terrorism Task Force."

"On the surface," Laura said.

"Yes, on the surface." Adam clicked to the next slide. Bank records. Offshore accounts. Money flows traced through shell companies in the Caymans, Panama, the Isle of Man. "Underneath, he's been taking cartel money for three years. The Sinaloa organization, primarily. Not huge amounts. Fifty to a hundred thousand at a time. Enough to be useful to them, not enough to draw immediate attention."

"What does he give them in return?" I asked, studying the financial trails.

"Information. About DEA operations. FBI investigations. Border security measures. He's careful. Never directly compromises operations. Just...delays them. Redirects resources. Creates small windows of opportunity." Adam pulled up another document. "Last month, a major shipment made it through the Port of Miami because Carver's office requested a reallocation of customs inspectors to Fort Lauderdale. Coincidentally timed, of course."

"So take him down," I said. "Expose the corruption. End his career. Seems straightforward."

"We would," Adam said. "Except for this."

He clicked to another slide. Intelligence briefing. Classified markings that shouldn't have been in this room. Photos of men I didn't recognize. Surveillance footage. Arabic writing on documents spread across a table.

"Terrorist cell," Adam continued. "Operating out of Miami for the past four months. Seven members. Five

Iranian nationals, two with confirmed ties to Hezbollah. They entered the country on student visas, scattered across three different universities, then quietly dropped out and disappeared into the community."

Laura leaned forward. "Planning what?"

"We don't know yet. But the chatter suggests something significant. High-casualty. Public venue. Timeline is unclear, but we believe it's imminent."

"And Carver's task force is tracking them," Laura said, seeing where this was going.

"His task force is the only agency actively tracking them. FBI's focused on domestic extremist threats. CIA's watching international movements but doesn't have domestic jurisdiction. DHS is stretched thin across a dozen different priorities. But this cell? They slipped through every crack. Carver's people stumbled onto them by accident three weeks ago during routine surveillance on a different target. Now they're the only ones with eyes on the operation."

I understood the problem now. "So if we take Carver down..."

"His task force gets frozen. Congressional inquiry, leadership vacuum, every ongoing investigation goes under review. The cell doesn't need to notice a thing, the bureaucracy does the work for them. By the time a new chair is appointed and read in, we've lost weeks." Adam closed the laptop. "Maybe that matters. Maybe it doesn't. But it's a risk."

The air conditioning hummed, traffic sounded from the street below.

"So what's the call?" I asked, though I already knew what answer I'd get.

"We take him down anyway," Adam said. His voice was flat, clinical. "Carver's compromised. He's a liability to multiple operations. The longer he stays in place, the more damage he does. The terrorist cell is someone else's problem. FBI will figure it out. They always do."

"And if they don't figure it out in time?"

"Then people die. That's unfortunate. But it's not our responsibility." Adam's eyes met mine. "Our responsibility is to the network. To protecting our operations. Carver threatens that. The cell doesn't."

Laura spoke up. "What if there's another way?"

"There isn't."

"But what if there was? What if we could neutralize Carver and stop the attack?"

Adam studied her for a long moment. I couldn't read his expression. Interest? Skepticism? Both?

"I'm listening," he said finally.

"Give us forty-eight hours. Let us look at the situation. If we can find a way to accomplish both objectives, we do it our way. If not, we follow your plan."

"Forty-eight hours is a long time when you're dealing with an imminent threat."

"It's also a long time for Carver to do more damage," I added. "Unless we use that time productively."

Adam was quiet. I could see him calculating, weighing the risks against whatever he was seeing in us. Whatever test this represented.

"Forty-eight hours," he said finally. "Not a minute more. And if your plan doesn't work, we do it my way. No arguments."

"Agreed."

He stood, gathering his files. "I hope you know what you're doing. Because if this goes wrong, if the attack happens and it comes out that we had information that could have prevented it..."

"It won't come to that," Laura said.

"For all our sakes, I hope you're right."

He left without another word. The door clicked shut behind him.

Laura turned to me. "Okay. Clock's running. What's our play?"

Danny's Apartment, Two Hours Later

We spread everything across my kitchen table. Carver's financial records. The task force's organizational structure. What little we had on the terrorist cell. Maps of Miami. Timelines. Connections.

"The problem isn't either situation individually," Laura said, pacing. "Carver's corruption is straightforward. We have the evidence. We know who to feed it to. Taking him down is a matter of timing and execution."

"And the cell?"

"Also straightforward, if we had more information. Seven men. A target. A timeline. Standard counterterrorism work." She stopped pacing. "The problem is the intersection. We can't do one without affecting the other."

"Unless we control the sequence," I said slowly, an idea forming. "What if we don't have to choose which problem to solve first? What if we solve them simultaneously?"

"Explain."

I pulled up Carver's task force structure on my laptop. "Carver's the head, but he's not doing the actual work. His people are. Analysts. Field agents. Surveillance teams. They're the ones who found the cell. They're the ones tracking it."

"So?"

"So what if we accelerate their investigation? Give them the information they need to identify the target and timeline. Let them do their jobs, stop the attack. And then, immediately after, while everyone's celebrating the victory, we drop the corruption evidence."

Laura considered it. "Carver takes credit for stopping the attack. Becomes a hero. And then, within hours, he's arrested for corruption. Maximum contrast. Maximum impact."

"The task force doesn't collapse because the threat's already neutralized. The cell gets stopped because we helped make it happen. And Carver goes down harder because he fell from a greater height."

"It's elegant," she admitted. "But it requires us to have information the task force doesn't. Information about the cell's target and timeline."

"Then we find it."

"In forty-eight hours."

"In forty-eight hours."

She looked at me. "You know this is crazy, right? We're not counterterrorism specialists. We're criminals who happened to become intelligence assets. We're not equipped for this."

"We're equipped to find information people don't want found. We're equipped to connect dots people don't want to be connected. We're equipped to solve problems that don't have clean solutions." I met her eyes. "That's exactly what this requires."

"And if we're wrong? If we miss something, make a mistake, and people die because of our plan instead of Adam's?"

The question hung in the air. The real question. The one that made this different from every other operation we'd run.

"Then we live with that," I said. "But at least we tried. At least we didn't just accept that innocent people have to die because it's convenient for us."

Laura was quiet for a long moment. Then she nodded. "Okay. Let's do this."

Hour 6

The first step was understanding the cell.

Adam had given us the basics. Seven members. Iranian nationals. Hezbollah connections. Four months in-country. But basics weren't enough. We needed details. Patterns. The small mistakes that every operation makes, no matter how careful.

I started with their digital footprint. The first layer was always the easiest.

I pulled immigration records through a backdoor Laura had given me access to months ago. Student visas for five of them, tourist visas for two. Standard cover for this kind of operation. The student visas gave them eighteen months of legitimate presence, time to establish patterns, build routines, become invisible.

But invisible people still leave traces.

I started mapping their digital exhaust. Credit card transactions. ATM withdrawals. Cell tower pings. Not the content of their communications, that was encrypted six ways from Sunday, but the metadata. Where they went. When they went there. How long they stayed.

The first pattern emerged around two a.m.

"Three of them, originally enrolled at different universities across Miami, were pinging the same cell tower in Hialeah at least twice a week." Never during class hours. Always between ten p.m. and three a.m.

I pulled up satellite imagery of the area. Industrial.

Warehouses, light manufacturing, a few auto shops. Nothing that would draw college students in the middle of the night.

"Found something," I told Laura. She came to look over my shoulder.

"Hialeah. That's their base?"

"Has to be. But I need more than cell tower data to confirm."

The rental car company was my next target. Laura had requested their records through proper channels, but proper channels took days. We had hours.

Their network security was exactly what I expected from a mid-tier rental company in Opa-locka. Firewall that hadn't been updated in eighteen months. Password policy that allowed "password123." I was in their system within forty minutes.

The van was registered to a name that matched one of the tourist visa holders. GPS tracking showed twelve trips in three weeks. I downloaded the complete history and started plotting coordinates.

Warehouse in Hialeah. Confirmed.

Home Depot in Kendall. Materials.

Marine supply store in Fort Lauderdale. Interesting.

And then, four times in three weeks, the Port of Miami.

I zoomed in on the GPS data for each port visit. Same route every time. Past the cargo terminals. Past the administrative buildings. The van stopped at the same location each time, idling for twenty to forty minutes before leaving.

Cruise Terminal F.

I pulled up the terminal schedule. Three ships operated out of Terminal F. The largest was Royal Caribbean's newest flagship, carrying six thousand passengers plus crew. Embarkation days were chaos. Thousands of people crowded into security lines, waiting areas, boarding queues.

A bomb in that crowd wouldn't just kill hundreds. It would be broadcast around the world within minutes. The footage would play on every news channel for weeks.

"Laura," I said. My voice sounded strange. Distant.

She looked at the screen. At the cruise schedule. At the GPS coordinates that kept returning to the same spot.

"When's the next embarkation?" she asked.

"Tomorrow. Noon."

Neither of us said anything for a long moment. The weight of it settling over us. Seven men with timer switches and trips to marine supply stores. A van that could carry a significant payload. A target that would maximize casualties and media coverage.

"We need to move faster," Laura said.

I was already typing. Cross-referencing the marine supply purchase against inventory databases. Looking for bulk orders. Fertilizer. Chemicals. Anything that could be weaponized.

The clock on my laptop read 3:47 a.m.

Eight hours until embarkation began.

Hour 14

Laura worked the human angle while I refined the data.

She had a contact in the FBI's Miami field office. Not someone she could ask directly, but someone she could steer. A supervisor named Martinez who owed her a favor from a previous operation.

"I need you to run some names through your system," she told him over the phone. "Quietly. No flags. Just tell me if anything pops."

I could only hear her side of the conversation, but I could tell Martinez was hesitant.

"I know," Laura said. "But I also know you trust me. And I'm telling you this matters. Lives might depend on it."

A long pause while Martinez talked.

"Send me what you can. And thank you. You won't regret this."

She hung up, turned to me. "He'll run the names. But he's nervous. Asked a lot of questions I couldn't answer."

"Will he stay quiet?"

"For now. But if this goes wrong, he's going to want explanations."

"Then we better make sure it doesn't go wrong."

Two hours later, Martinez called back. I watched Laura's face as she listened, watched her expression shift from anticipation to confirmation to something harder.

"What kind of van?" she asked.

She grabbed a pen, wrote something down.

"When was this? Last week? And you're sure about the capacity?"

More writing.

"Thank you. I mean it. When this is over, I'll explain everything I can."

She hung up. Looked at me.

"Two of our names hit on a low-priority watchlist. Suspected Hezbollah sympathizers, no active investigation. But one of them rented a van last week. Commercial vehicle. Large capacity."

"Same van I tracked?"

"Has to be. Martinez said it's the kind you'd use for moving equipment. Or cargo." She paused. "Or a large amount of explosives."

I pulled up the cruise schedule. Three departures in the

next week, but only one that made sense as a high-casualty target. The Royal Caribbean flagship, leaving tomorrow at noon. Six thousand passengers plus crew. Laura checked her watch. Less than eighteen hours.

Hour 18

The next step was the hardest.

We had the information. The warehouse location. The van. The target. The timeline. Now we needed to get it to Carver's task force without revealing how we got it.

"It has to be convincing," Laura said as she built the anonymous source profile. "Detailed enough to be actionable, vague enough to be believable. If we give them too much, they'll wonder how a random citizen knows all this. If we give them too little, they won't move fast enough."

"What's the right balance?"

"The warehouse location. The van description. The fact that they've been watching the cruise terminal." She paused. "But not the timeline. Let them figure that out themselves. It'll be more convincing if they reach the conclusion on their own."

She created a burner email. Routed it through three different countries. Crafted a message that read like a concerned citizen who'd noticed suspicious activity, not an intelligence professional who'd hacked rental car companies and traced cell phone metadata.

"Last chance to back out," she said, finger hovering over the send button.

"Send it."

She did.

"Now we wait," I said.

"Now we wait. And hope they move fast enough."

· · ·

HOUR 22

No response.

Laura checked her phone for the fifth time in ten minutes. Nothing from her contact in the task force. Nothing from any of the channels we'd been monitoring.

"It's been four hours," I said. "They should have moved by now."

"They should have." Laura's voice was tight. "Something's wrong."

She made a call. Stepped into the other room. I could hear fragments of the conversation, her voice shifting from professional to urgent to something that sounded like pleading.

When she came back, her face told me everything.

"They're treating it as a crank," she said. "Low priority. The duty officer flagged it as 'unverified anonymous tip' and put it in the queue."

"The queue? There's a terrorist attack happening in fourteen hours."

"I know." She sat down heavily on the couch. "The tip was too clean. Too detailed. The duty officer thinks it reads like someone trying to manipulate them into a response. Maybe a competitor trying to get them to raid a rival operation. Maybe someone testing their protocols."

"So they're just going to ignore it?"

"Not ignore. Evaluate. Which means it sits on someone's desk until morning shift, when a supervisor reviews overnight reports and decides what's worth following up."

"By morning the ship starts boarding."

"I know."

We sat in silence. The clock on my laptop showed 2:47 a.m. Nine hours until embarkation began. Nine hours until thousands of people crowded into a terminal that seven men with explosives had been watching for weeks.

"We could call it in again," I said. "Different channel. Add details that make it harder to dismiss."

"More details means more exposure. If we know too much, they start asking how we know." Laura shook her head. "We're already pushing the line. Any more specific and they'll start looking for the source instead of the threat."

"Then what? We just wait and hope someone decides to take it seriously?"

Laura was quiet for a long moment. I could see her calculating, weighing options I probably couldn't even imagine.

"Martinez," she said finally. "My contact in the FBI field office. He owes me. If I call him directly, tell him to push this up the chain as a personal favor, he might be able to get the right people looking at it."

"And if he asks questions?"

"I tell him I got a tip from a source I can't name. That I trust the source. That people will die if they don't move." She met my eyes. "It burns some credibility. Maybe a lot of credibility. But it gets the tip in front of someone who can act on it."

"Do it."

She made the call. I watched her pace the room, voice low and intense, calling in whatever favors she had left.

Twenty minutes later, her phone buzzed. She read the message. Let out a breath.

"Martinez got it to the night supervisor. They're mobilizing a team to verify the warehouse location." She looked at me. "It's moving."

"How much did that cost you?"

"More than I wanted to spend." She sat down beside me. "But less than letting those people die."

Hour 30

The tip had been sent. The task force was mobilizing. All we could do was wait.

Laura hadn't slept in more than twenty-four hours. I could see it in the way she moved, careful and deliberate, compensating for exhaustion with discipline. She'd taken up position by the window, watching the street below like she expected threats to materialize from the shadows.

"You should rest," I said.

"Can't." She didn't turn around. "If something goes wrong, if the task force misses something, if the cell accelerates their timeline..."

"Then being exhausted won't help you fix it."

"No. But being awake means I'll know the moment it happens." She finally turned to face me. "I've lost assets before, Danny. Lost operations. Lost people I was supposed to protect. The not knowing is worse than any of it. The hours when you're waiting to find out if your decisions got someone killed."

I crossed the room to stand beside her. Outside, Miami was going about its business. Cars moving through intersections. People walking dogs. A normal night in a city that had no idea what was about to happen.

"This is different," I said. "We did everything right. The information is solid. The task force is competent."

"I know." She leaned against me, let some of her weight rest on my shoulder. "But there's always something you didn't account for. Some variable you missed. Some person who makes a decision you didn't predict." Her voice dropped. "That's what happened in Karachi. I did every-thing right. Every protocol, every precaution. And Hamid still died."

I put my arm around her. Felt the coiled energy that had nowhere to go.

"If this goes wrong," she said quietly, "if people die because we tried to be clever instead of following Adam's plan..."

"Then we live with it. Together."

She looked up at me. "You mean that."

"I mean that." I turned her to face me fully. "Laura, six months ago I was a criminal running identity fraud in Flor-ida. Now I'm trying to stop a terrorist attack and take down a corrupt congressman in the same forty-eight-hour window. I'm in way over my head. The only reason I'm not drowning is because you're here."

"I'm in over my head too."

"I know. That's why we work." I kissed her forehead. "Two people in over their heads, holding each other up. That's what this is."

She was quiet for a moment. Then she laughed, soft and exhausted.

"That might be the most romantic thing anyone's ever said to me."

"Criminals aren't known for their poetry."

"No." She pulled me closer. "But sometimes they surprise you."

We stood there by the window, watching the city, waiting for dawn to bring either vindication or disaster.

Together.

Whatever came next, we'd face it together.

· · ·

HOUR 38, Four a.m.

I watched the raid from a coffee shop across the street from the federal building where Carver had set up his command post.

Laura had advised against it. Too much exposure, she'd said. Too many cameras, too many people who might remember a face that showed up in the wrong place at the wrong time. But I needed to see. Needed to understand the man we were about to destroy.

Carver arrived at 3:15 a.m., fifteen minutes before the synchronized raids began. He moved with the energy of a man who'd been waiting for this moment. Confident. Purposeful. A congressman who'd built his career on being tough on crime, finally getting to prove it meant something.

I watched him through the window as he coordinated with FBI liaisons, as he took calls and gave orders. He wasn't performing for cameras. Not yet. This was real. Whatever else he was, Michael Carver genuinely believed he was doing important work.

That was the part that made this complicated.

He'd taken cartel money for three years. He'd compromised operations, delayed investigations, created windows for shipments to slip through. People had probably died because of information he'd sold. Not directly, not in ways that would ever be traced to him, but the math was there if you knew how to read it.

And yet.

Here he was at three a.m., running an operation to stop a terrorist attack. Not for the cameras. Not for the political points. Because he'd built a task force that had stumbled onto something real, and he wasn't going to let it slip away.

The raids went down at 3:30. I watched the feeds on my phone as teams hit locations across the city. The warehouse in Hialeah. The storage unit in Opa-locka. The safe house in Little Havana where two of the cell members had been sleeping.

Seven arrests. No casualties. Explosives recovered. A cruise terminal full of people who would never know how close they'd come.

Carver emerged from the federal building around five a.m., already on the phone, already pivoting to the press strategy. The hero of the hour. The man who'd saved thousands of lives.

In three hours, we'd take that away from him.

I finished my coffee and left before the sun came up. Some victories don't feel like victories. They just feel like the least terrible option in a world full of terrible options.

Hour 42

Carver held his press conference at eight a.m.

He stood in front of the Hialeah warehouse, surrounded by FBI agents and local officials, American flags positioned perfectly behind him. The consummate politician, taking credit for work his people had done based on intelligence he knew nothing about.

"This morning, thanks to the dedication and expertise of the South Florida Counter-Terrorism Task Force, we prevented what could have been one of the deadliest attacks on American soil since 9/11." His voice carried across the assembled reporters. "Seven individuals with ties to Hezbollah are now in federal custody. Their plan to attack a cruise ship terminal, potentially killing thousands of innocent people, has been stopped."

The questions came fast. How did they find the cell?

How long had they been tracking them? Was this connected to other threats?

Carver answered them all with practiced ease. A hero at the height of his moment.

Laura watched from my apartment, her expression unreadable. "Enjoying his last few hours of freedom."

"Time to start phase two?"

"Yup."

Feeding evidence to multiple sources simultaneously is harder than it sounds.

You can't just dump documents and hope for the best. Each recipient needs to feel like they discovered something. Like they're breaking the story, not receiving it. The moment anyone suspects they're being handed a narrative, they start asking questions you don't want to answer.

Laura had spent three days building the architecture for this drop.

"Three journalists," she said, pulling up profiles on her laptop. "Heinrich at the *Miami Herald* has been investigating public corruption for six years. Rodriguez at the local NBC affiliate needs a win after getting scooped on the last two major stories. And Chen at ProPublica has been building a database of cartel-connected officials for eighteen months. She's missing the Carver piece."

"They won't coordinate?"

"They won't know about each other. Each one gets a different slice of the evidence. Heinrich gets the offshore accounts. Rodriguez gets the communication logs with cartel intermediaries. Chen gets the pattern of legislative favors." Laura smiled slightly. "They'll all break different angles of the same story within hours of each other. It'll look like the dam burst, not like someone opened the gates."

The federal prosecutors were trickier.

"Sandra Okonkwo in the Southern District has been trying to build a public corruption case for two years. She's got pieces but nothing that ties everything together." Laura pulled up another file. "James Whitmore at Main Justice has oversight on cartel-related cases. He's been suspicious of leaks in the Miami office but can't prove anything."

"So we give them proof."

"We give them breadcrumbs that lead to proof. Different breadcrumbs for each. Okonkwo gets financial records that show the pattern. Whitmore gets communication metadata that suggests the source of the leaks." Laura closed the laptop. "By the time they compare notes, they'll have enough to move. And neither will know the other got a push."

The timing had to be precise. Too early, and the corruption story would overshadow the terrorist takedown. Too late, and Carver would have time to spin his hero narrative into armor.

"Eight hours after the raid," Laura said. "The press conference will be wrapping up. Carver will be at maximum visibility. Maximum height to fall from."

I watched her work, routing documents through anonymous servers, crafting emails that would appear to come from concerned insiders, building a trail that led everywhere except back to us.

This was the part of tradecraft they didn't teach in training manuals. The art of making truth look like accident. Of guiding people toward conclusions they thought they'd reached themselves.

"You've done this before," I said.

"Information warfare is just warfare with different weapons." She didn't look up from her screen. "The target never sees the bullet coming. They just wake up one day and realize they've already lost."

At exactly two p.m., eight hours after the raid, Laura pressed Send.

Three journalists received anonymous tips.

Two prosecutors received evidence packages.

And Michael Carver's career began its final descent.

Hour 46

The first search warrant was executed at six p.m.

FBI agents arrived at Carver's congressional office while he was still inside, still fielding congratulations for the morning's heroics. The look on his face when they handed him the warrant was something I wished I could have seen in person.

By eight p.m., they'd executed warrants on his homes. His bank accounts. His campaign offices.

By ten p.m., he was in federal custody.

By midnight, his attorney was negotiating terms for his resignation.

The news coverage was almost comical in its whiplash. Morning: Congressman Carver, American Hero, Saves Thousands. Evening: Congressman Carver Arrested on Federal Corruption Charges.

The public story was simple. Financial irregularities discovered during routine investigation. Suspicious transactions flagged by automated systems. The hero of the morning revealed as a criminal by nightfall.

The real story was more complicated. But nobody would ever know that.

∽

FBI Miami Field Office, 9:23 a.m.

Marcus Webb stared at the Carver file and tried to understand why it bothered him.

The case was clean. Too clean. A sitting congressman taken down in less than twenty-four hours, the evidence appearing from multiple directions simultaneously, each source apparently independent. Financial records here. Communication logs there. A pattern of legislative favors documented by ProPublica before the FBI had even finished processing the warrants.

Webb had seen coordinated takedowns before. This wasn't coordination. This was choreography.

He pulled up the terrorism case file. The anonymous tip that had triggered the raid on the Hialeah warehouse. Detailed enough to be actionable, vague enough to be plausible. The kind of tip that looked organic if you didn't look too hard.

Webb looked too hard. It was his defining flaw.

The tip had arrived at 10:47 p.m. By 3:30 a.m., raids were underway. By 2:00 p.m. the next day, Carver was in handcuffs. Someone had orchestrated a terrorist takedown and a political assassination in the same news cycle, and made both look like they happened naturally.

That took resources. Access. Tradecraft.

He opened a new file on his computer. Typed a name he'd been circling for months: TYLER, DANIEL.

No evidence. Not yet. Just instinct and a pattern that was starting to look less like coincidence and more like architecture.

Webb closed the file and poured himself another coffee. He could be patient. Patterns always revealed themselves eventually. You just had to keep watching.

"I NEVER TOLD you the full story about Karachi," Laura said. We were sitting in my apartment after the Carver takedown, both of us too wired to sleep. She'd mentioned Hamid once before, in Vienna. The broad strokes. But something about tonight had cracked something open.

"Tell me," I said.

"I ran him for eighteen months. By the book. Every protocol, every precaution. Dead drops, coded messages, irregular meeting schedules. Everything Langley teaches you about keeping an asset alive." Her hands tightened around her glass until her knuckles went white "I was so careful. So goddamn careful."

"What happened?"

"Someone in our station was dirty. We never proved it, but there's no other explanation. Hamid's name ended up on a list. The kind of list that gets people killed in the middle of the night."

I watched her. The tension in her jaw. The way she blinked too often, fighting something she didn't want me to see.

"I got a warning. Six hours before they were going to take him. I had a plan. Extraction route, safe house, new identity. Everything he needed to disappear with his family and start over somewhere safe."

"But?"

"But my station chief said no." Her voice went flat, dead. "He said the intelligence Hamid was providing was too valuable to lose. He said we should wait, see if the threat was credible, avoid burning an asset over unconfirmed rumors."

"He wanted you to leave Hamid in place."

"He wanted to protect the operation." She laughed, but

there was no humor in it. Nothing but broken glass. "That's the calculation, right? One life versus the intelligence that life provides. The trolley problem, except the trolley is real and the people on the tracks have names and families and daughters who call them Baba."

I thought about every operation I'd run for my father. The calculations. The acceptable losses. The people who became numbers in a ledger.

"You followed orders."

"Yes, I did." Laura pulled into a parking lot and stopped the car, but didn't turn off the engine. Her hands were still gripping the wheel. "I told myself my station chief knew things I didn't. That there were factors I couldn't see. That the protocol existed for a reason."

"And Hamid?"

"They took him from his home at two a.m. His wife heard the whole thing. His daughters too." Laura finally looked at me. Her eyes were dry, but something behind them was drowning. "They found his body three days later. What was left of it."

The engine hummed. Neither of us moved.

"That's why I break protocol with you," Laura said quietly. "That's why I told you about my operational directive when I shouldn't have. Why I let this become something more than handler and asset." She reached over and touched my hand. "Because I followed the rules once, and a good man died, and his daughters grew up without a father. Because the protocol didn't save him. It killed him."

"Laura—"

"I'm not asking for absolution." Her fingers tightened around mine. "I'm telling you why I am the way I am. Why I trust my instincts over procedures. Why I'll burn my career to keep you alive if it comes to that."

I understood something then. The way she watched me when she thought I wasn't looking. The fear beneath her competence. She wasn't running me. She was trying to redeem a failure she'd never forgive herself for.

"Hamid made his own choice," I said. "He knew the risks."

"Everyone says that. It doesn't help."

"I know." I squeezed her hand back. "But I'm not Hamid. And you're not the same person you were in Karachi."

Laura looked at me for a long moment. Then she put the car in drive and pulled back onto the road.

She didn't say anything else. But she didn't let go of my hand for a long time.

Hour 48

Adam called exactly at the deadline.

"Impressive," he said without preamble. We were on speaker, Laura and I sitting in my apartment, exhausted but satisfied. "The task force stops a major attack. Then immediately after, we discover the congressman leading that task force is corrupt. Beautiful timing."

"Just worked out that way," Laura said.

"Nothing about this just worked out. You two orchestrated the whole thing. Accelerated the terrorist investigation. Neutralized the threat. Then took down Carver exactly when you'd promised." Adam's voice had something in it I hadn't heard before. Respect, maybe. Or concern. "That was sophisticated work. The kind that requires seeing multiple moves ahead."

"Thank you."

"Don't thank me yet." His tone shifted. "You accomplished both objectives. That's good. But you also operated well outside your authority. You ran an intelligence operation without oversight. You fed information to federal agencies without authorization. You made decisions that should have been made by someone with more experience."

"There wasn't time to ask permission," I said.

"There's always time to ask permission. You just didn't want to hear the answer you'd get." A pause. "I'm not criticizing. I'm observing. You two have developed capabilities I didn't expect this quickly. That's valuable. But it's also dangerous."

"Dangerous how?"

"Dangerous because assets who can operate independently are assets who might decide to operate against their handlers. Dangerous because people who can orchestrate something like this are people who might orchestrate things I won't approve of." His voice hardened slightly. "I'm watching, Danny. I'm always watching. Remember that."

The line went dead.

Laura and I sat in silence for a long moment.

"That didn't sound like praise," I said finally.

"It wasn't. It was a warning." She stood, moved to the window. "We showed him too much. We should have made it look messier. More improvised. Less...competent."

"Too late now."

"Agreed. At least we know where we stand. He's impressed. He's also suspicious. We need to be more careful going forward."

"More careful about being good at our jobs?"

"More careful about looking like we're good at our jobs." She turned to face me. "There's a difference between being valuable and being threatening. We just crossed the line."

. . .

THE NEXT MORNING

Randy called while I was making coffee.

"Saw the news," he said. "The congressman thing. That was you, wasn't it?"

"What makes you think that?"

"Because you've had that look the past few days. The one you get when you're planning something big. And because Laura's been making calls she won't explain." He paused. "I'm not asking for details. I said I wouldn't. But I'm asking if you're okay."

"I'm okay."

"And the operation went well?"

"The operation went well. We stopped a terrorist attack and took down a corrupt congressman. Both objectives achieved."

"Jesus." Randy was quiet for a moment. "A terrorist attack?"

"Cruise terminal. Would have killed thousands of people."

"And you stopped it."

"We helped stop it. Fed information to the people who could act on it."

"Still." I could hear something in his voice. Pride, maybe. Or awe. "That's different from what we used to do, Danny. That's...that's actually good."

The point is that we're trying to build something different. Something that does more good than harm. Laura and I put together a set of rules. Lines we won't cross, no matter what."

"Rules for being criminals." He laughed. "Only you and a CIA officer would think to put guardrails on breaking the law."

"Yeah, our rules."

Randy was quiet again. Then: "You know, when you first told me about this leverage play of yours, I thought you were crazy. Thought you were going to get yourself killed trying to outmaneuver the CIA. But this...this is different. You're not just building power. You're actually using it for something."

"Trying to."

"Succeeding." He let out a breath. "I'm proud of you, little brother. I don't say that enough. But I am."

I didn't know what to say. Randy and I didn't talk like this. We talked about business. About operations. About money. Not about pride. Not about feelings.

"Thanks," I managed.

"Don't thank me. Just keep doing what you're doing. Keep being different from Dad. Keep proving that a Tyler can be something more than just a criminal." He paused. "I'll hold down Florida. You change the world."

He hung up before I could respond.

I stood in my kitchen, phone in hand, trying to process what had just happened.

Randy was proud of me. Not for making money. Not for being smart. For actually doing something good.

Maybe that was the point of all this. Maybe that was what we were really building.

Not just leverage. Not just power.

But a version of this life that someone could be proud of.

LAURA FOUND me in the kitchen that evening, staring at a bourbon I hadn't touched. "Thinking?" she asked.

"Processing."

"The operation?"

"Everything. The operation. Adam's warning. Randy's call." I watched the boats move across the Intracoastal. "We just stopped a terrorist attack. Saved thousands of lives. Took down a corrupt congressman. By any objective measure, we did something good."

"But?"

"But it doesn't feel like a victory. It feels like we just announced ourselves. Showed Adam what we're capable of. Made ourselves a threat instead of just an asset."

"We did," Laura agreed. "That's unavoidable. The more capable we become, the more dangerous we look. That's the paradox of building leverage. You can't be powerful enough to matter without being powerful enough to threaten."

"So what do we do?"

"We keep going. We've come too far to stop now. Adam's suspicious, but he's also impressed. He's not going to move against us while we're still valuable. And we just proved exactly how valuable we can be."

"And the leverage?"

"The leverage keeps building. Every operation like this adds to it. Every relationship we cultivate. Every problem we solve. Eventually, we'll have enough that Adam can't move against us even if he wants to."

"How much is enough?"

"I don't know yet. But we'll know when we get there." She took my hand. "The important thing is we did it right. We didn't choose between lives and objectives. We found a third option. We proved to ourselves that it's possible to do this job without becoming monsters."

"The fifteen rules."

"They're not just ethics. They're survival. Because the moment we become people who let innocents die for convenience, we become people who can justify anything. And then we're no different from Adam. No different from anyone else in this world."

I looked at her. This woman who'd been assigned to seduce me. Who'd broken every rule to be with me. Who was now building something unprecedented with me, brick by brick, operation by operation.

"I love you," I said. It wasn't the first time I'd said it. But it felt different now. More real. Forged in something harder than romance.

"I love you too." She squeezed my hand. "Now get some sleep. We've got more work to do tomorrow."

"The leverage doesn't build itself."

"No," she smiled. "It doesn't."

Building something that might save us.

Or might destroy us.

But either way, building it together.

17

THE TEST

"Nine months into our leverage play, with the Florida heat already creeping back, Adam gave us Phoenix."

"Viktor Markov," he said, sliding a file across the table. We were in his Coral Gables office, the afternoon sun cutting through the blinds. "Goes by Phoenix in certain circles. Arms dealer. Operates out of Miami but supplies clients across three continents."

I opened the file. Mid-forties. Russian-born, naturalized American citizen. The photo showed a man with cold eyes and an expensive suit, the kind of person who'd learned to blend into high society while maintaining connections to people who solved problems with violence.

"What's his value to us?" Laura asked.

"Currently? Intelligence. He supplies weapons to groups we track. Monitoring his sales gives us insight into who's arming up and why." Adam paused. "But he's becoming a problem."

"What kind of problem?"

"The kind that gets people killed. Six months ago, he

started selling to a new client base. Extremist groups. Domestic terrorists. People planning attacks on American soil." Adam's voice was flat. "Last month, weapons he supplied were used in a synagogue shooting in Atlanta. Three dead, including a child."

The room went quiet. I looked at Laura. Her expression had hardened.

"So we shut him down," I said.

"It's not that simple." Adam leaned back in his chair. "Phoenix is connected. Protected. He has relationships with people in our government, in foreign governments, in organizations that would make shutting him down... complicated."

"Complicated how?"

"Complicated in that a standard takedown would expose intelligence sources, compromise ongoing operations, and potentially create a diplomatic incident with at least two countries we're trying not to antagonize." Adam met my eyes. "The clean solution is to remove him permanently. Make it look like a business dispute gone wrong. His world is violent enough that no one would question it."

I understood what he was asking. Kill Phoenix. End the problem. Move on.

"No," I said.

Adam raised an eyebrow. "No?"

"There's another way. There's always another way." I closed the file. "Give us two weeks."

"You don't even know what the other way is yet."

"Then I'll find it."

Adam studied me for a long moment. I couldn't read his expression. Annoyance? Interest? Both?

"You have two weeks," he said finally. "If you can find a

way to neutralize Phoenix without killing him and without compromising our interests, do it. If not, we do it my way."

Danny's Apartment, **That Evening**

We spread Phoenix's file across my kitchen table. Financial records. Known associates. Client lists. Travel patterns. Everything Adam had compiled over years of monitoring.

"The problem isn't finding leverage," Laura said, pacing. "It's finding leverage that doesn't blow back on us."

"Explain."

"Phoenix knows things. About his clients. About his suppliers. About the people who protect him." She stopped pacing, turned to face me. "If we take him down publicly, he talks. If we take him down quietly, his protectors investigate. Either way, we create problems."

"So we need a solution where he can't talk and his protectors don't care."

"Exactly. Which is why Adam's solution is killing him. Dead men don't talk, and his protectors can write it off as occupational hazard."

I stared at the files, looking for the angle we didn't see. There was always an angle. Every problem had a solution that didn't require becoming the people we were trying to stop.

"What if he wasn't dead?" I said slowly. "What if he just...disappeared?"

"Disappeared where?"

"Somewhere he can't do business. Can't communicate with his clients. Can't be a threat to anyone." I pulled up his financial records. "Phoenix has enemies. People he's crossed over the years. What if one of them finally caught up with him?"

Laura considered it. "You're talking about rendition. Grabbing him and handing him over to someone else."

"I'm talking about giving him to people who have legitimate grievances. People who would keep him alive because they want answers, not just revenge."

"That's still pretty dark, Danny."

"It's darker than I'd like. But it's not killing him. And if we choose the right people, people who'll interrogate him rather than execute him, we're giving him a chance to survive. More than he gave that kid in Atlanta."

Laura was quiet for a long moment. I could see her wrestling with it, weighing the ethics against the alternatives.

"Who did you have in mind?" she asked finally.

I pulled up a name from Phoenix's file. "Andrei Reznikov. Russian intelligence. Phoenix sold weapons to Chechen rebels ten years ago, weapons that killed Russian soldiers. Andrei's brother was one of them."

"You want to give Phoenix to the Russians?"

"I want to give Phoenix to someone who'll keep him locked up forever, asking questions he'll never finish answering. Someone who has every reason to make sure he never sees daylight again, but also every reason to keep him alive as a source."

"That's...actually clever." Laura sat down across from me. "His protectors can't object because it looks like old enemies finally settling a score. Russia gets a prize they've wanted for years. Phoenix disappears without anyone connecting it to us."

"And the weapons stop flowing to domestic terrorists."

"That works." She nodded slowly. "It's not clean. It's not pretty. But it's better than the alternative."

"Better is all we can aim for."

. . .

WEEK One

The first step was making contact with Andrei Reznikov.

This was delicate. We couldn't approach Russian intelligence directly without raising flags. We needed a back channel, someone who could make the introduction without either side knowing exactly who was behind it.

Eduardo came through.

"I know a man in Caracas," he told me over an encrypted call. "Former KGB, now private sector. He has relationships with people in Moscow. If you want to reach someone in Russian intelligence without leaving fingerprints, he's your path."

"Can you make the introduction?"

"For you? Yes. But understand, this man doesn't work for free. And he'll want to know why you're reaching out to the Russians."

"Tell him I have a gift for them. Something they've wanted for a long time."

"A gift." Eduardo's voice was skeptical. "They'll want to know what kind."

"Tell them it's a person. Someone who owes them a debt paid in Russian blood. That should get their attention."

Two days later, I had a secure line to a man who called himself Gregor. He didn't give a last name, and I didn't ask.

"You claim to have something Russia wants," Gregor said. His English was clipped and formal, like something learned in a classroom and never softened. "Many people make such claims. Few deliver."

"Viktor Markov. Goes by Phoenix. Ten years ago, he supplied weapons to Chechen rebels. Those weapons killed

Russian soldiers, including the brother of a man named Andrei Reznikov."

Silence on the line. "Continue."

"Phoenix is currently operating in Miami. He's become a liability to certain interests. I can deliver him to you, quietly, without anyone knowing how it happened."

"In exchange for what?"

"Nothing. Consider it a gesture of goodwill. A demonstration that I can be useful to people who might want to be useful to me someday."

Another silence. "You're building relationships."

"I'm building options. There's a difference."

Gregor laughed softly. "I like you, whoever you are. I'll pass your offer to the appropriate people. If they're interested, you'll hear from me within forty-eight hours."

"I'll be waiting."

WHILE I WORKED the Russian angle, Laura worked on Phoenix himself.

We needed to know his routines. His security. His vulnerabilities. The moments when he'd be exposed enough for us to grab him without creating a scene.

The first day, she mapped his world. Home in Coconut Grove, a walled compound with cameras on every corner and guards who rotated in eight-hour shifts. Office in Brickell, twenty-third floor of a building with security checkpoints and visitor logs. Driver who doubled as a bodyguard, a thick-necked man named Sergei who never seemed to blink.

"He's careful," Laura reported that first night. "Moves like someone who knows people want him dead."

The second day, she followed his driver. Sergei had a girlfriend in Hialeah, a woman he visited every Tuesday afternoon while Phoenix was in meetings. That was useful. A driver distracted by a woman was a driver not watching his principal.

The third day, she found the gap.

"Every Thursday night," Laura said, spreading photographs across my table. Phoenix entering a building. Phoenix leaving the same building three hours later. A sign above the door read "Paradise Spa."

"He goes in alone, comes out alone. His security waits in the car. Apparently, even arms dealers need their relaxation time."

"A spa."

"Not just any spa. High-end establishment. Very discreet. The kind of place where wealthy men go to...unwind." Her expression made clear what kind of unwinding. "The security stays outside because what happens inside is the kind of thing Phoenix doesn't want witnesses for."

"How'd you get these?" I studied the photos. Clean angles. Good lighting despite the darkness. Professional work.

"Rented a room in the building across the street. Told the super I was a photographer working on an architecture project." She smiled slightly. "He didn't ask questions. Two hundred dollars tends to have that effect."

"So we grab him on a Thursday."

"He goes in, we go in after him, he comes out with us instead of alone. His security doesn't even know anything's wrong until he doesn't show up."

"And by then, he's already on his way to Moscow."

"Exactly."

I looked at the photographs. Phoenix walking into his

spa, secure in his power, confident that his protectors made him untouchable.

He was about to learn otherwise.

Week Two, Thursday Night

Gregor called back within thirty-six hours. The Russians were interested. Very interested.

"Andrei Reznikov has waited ten years for this," Gregor told me. "He wants Phoenix alive. He has many questions."

"I can guarantee alive. I can't guarantee comfortable."

"Comfortable is not what Andrei has in mind. How do you want to make the transfer?"

We worked out the details. A boat. International waters. A handoff that would leave no trace on American soil. The Russians would handle transport from there.

"One more thing," Gregor said before hanging up. "Andrei wants to know who you are. Not your real name. Just...who you represent."

"Tell him I represent people who solve problems. People who might solve more problems for Russia in the future, if this goes well."

"Ambitious."

"Practical. We all need friends."

"Indeed we do." I could hear the smile in his voice. "Good luck, my friend. I look forward to hearing about your success."

Thursday night, 8:47 p.m.

The spa occupied the top floor of a building in Coral Gables that looked like every other building in Coral Gables. Tasteful. Expensive. Anonymous. The kind of place where wealthy men came to do things they didn't want their wives knowing about.

I parked two blocks away and sat in the car for a full minute, breathing slowly, letting my pulse settle. The hardest part of any operation isn't the action. It's the waiting. The space between deciding and doing, when your mind generates every possible thing that could go wrong.

I got out and walked.

The night was warm and still, the air heavy with jasmine from the hedges that lined every property in this neighborhood. Coral Gables after dark felt like a movie set: perfect lawns, perfect streetlights, perfect silence. The kind of place where ugly things happened behind beautiful doors.

Phoenix's security detail sat in a black SUV fifty feet from the spa's entrance. Two men. I could see the orange glow of a cigarette in the driver's window. Sloppy. A lit cigarette ruins your night vision for twenty minutes. If something happened right now, they'd be half-blind.

I walked past them on the opposite sidewalk, just another man in khakis and a sport coat, heading somewhere that wasn't their concern. Neither of them looked up. They'd been sitting there for almost an hour, watching nothing happen. Boredom was the asset's best friend.

Laura's voice came through my earpiece, calm and steady. "He's inside. Arrived at 8:07. Security hasn't moved."

"I'm approaching the back."

"Three hours. That's his usual window. You've got until eleven."

I checked my watch. 8:52. Plenty of time if everything went smoothly. Not nearly enough if it didn't.

The service entrance was around back, accessible through an alley that ran between the spa's building and a high-end jewelry store. The alley smelled like garbage and old grease, the reality that existed behind Coral Gables' perfect facade. A single light fixture buzzed overhead, casting everything in a sickly yellow glow.

Laura's contact had left the door unlocked, as promised. A maintenance worker who owed her a favor, or owed someone who owed her. I didn't ask. The door opened with a soft click, and I slipped inside.

The corridor was narrow, lit by flickering fluorescent tubes that hummed like dying insects. Staff only. No customers back here. The walls were painted industrial gray, scuffed and stained from years of carts and mops and people who weren't meant to be seen.

I moved slowly, placing each foot deliberately, listening for voices or footsteps. Somewhere ahead, I could hear music. Something with strings. The kind of ambient noise designed to make people feel relaxed and wealthy.

Past a laundry room where steam hissed from industrial machines. Past a supply closet with its door hanging open, revealing shelves of towels and bottles of massage oil. Past a door marked "Employees Must Wash Hands." The layout matched what Laura had described. Third door on the left after the stairs. Private suite. The most expensive room in the establishment.

I stopped outside the door. Listened. Muffled sounds from inside. The string music, louder here. Running water from what might have been a bathroom or a fountain. A voice I didn't recognize, female, asking if he wanted more champagne.

Phoenix's voice answered. Something in Russian I couldn't understand. The woman laughed.

I pressed myself against the wall beside the door and waited. Five minutes. Ten. The muscles in my legs started to ache from standing motionless. A bead of sweat traced down my spine.

The door opened.

A woman in a silk robe stepped out, heading toward what I assumed was a bathroom down the hall. Mid-twenties. Dark hair. She didn't see me pressed into the shadow of a doorway. Her footsteps faded around the corner.

I moved.

The room was dim, lit by candles that cast dancing shadows on walls covered in red velvet. The air was thick with incense and something floral, a cloying sweetness that caught in my throat. Phoenix lay on a massage table, face down, a towel draped across his lower back. His eyes were closed. His breathing was slow and even. Relaxed. Vulnerable.

He didn't hear me enter. Didn't hear me close the door behind me, easing it shut until the latch caught with a barely audible click. Didn't hear me cross the room until I was standing directly over him.

"Viktor Markov," I said quietly.

His eyes snapped open. He tried to push himself up, but I put a hand on his shoulder, firm, keeping him in place.

"Don't," I said. "There's no point."

"Who the fuck are you?" His accent was thicker than I expected. The fear stripping away the American polish he'd cultivated over the years.

"I'm the person who's going to walk you out of here. Quietly. Without a scene. Your security is still sitting in their car, and they're going to stay there because you're going to text them that you're fine and you'll be another hour."

"Like hell I will."

"You will. Because the alternative is much worse." I

pulled the phone from his discarded jacket, held it where he could see it. "Text them. Now."

"My people will find you. They'll find everyone you've ever loved. They'll…"

"Your people are going to be very busy in about seventy-two hours. Federal indictments. Asset seizures. The kind of attention that makes protecting you a liability rather than a priority." I leaned closer. "You're alone, Viktor. You just don't know it yet."

Something shifted in his eyes. The calculation of a man who'd survived decades in a brutal business. He was weighing options. Looking for angles.

"What do you want?" he asked.

"I want you to get dressed. I want you to walk out the back entrance with me. And I want you to do it without making me use the sedative in my pocket."

"And then what?"

"And then you take a boat ride."

"To where?"

"Somewhere you're expected." I handed him his clothes. "Get dressed. You have two minutes."

He dressed slowly, buying time, still looking for an opportunity. But there wasn't one. The woman wouldn't be back for another few minutes. His security thought he was getting a massage. And I was standing between him and every exit.

"The sedative," he said as he buttoned his shirt. "What is it?"

"Something that will make the next six hours very unpleasant. Nausea. Disorientation. Loss of motor control." I paused. "I'd rather not use it. But I will."

"You're not going to kill me."

"No. I'm not." I opened the door, checked the corridor.

Clear. "But the people I'm taking you to might. Eventually. After they've asked all their questions."

Phoenix went pale. He understood now. Or was starting to.

"The Russians," he said. "You're giving me to the Russians."

"I'm giving you to a man named Andrei Reznikov. His brother was a soldier. Died ten years ago because of weapons you sold to Chechen rebels." I gestured toward the door. "Andrei's been waiting a long time for this conversation."

"I'll tell them everything. Every operation. Every client. Every contact in the American government who looked the other way."

"That's between you and Andrei. I'm just the delivery service."

We moved through the service corridor, my hand on his elbow, guiding him forward. He walked stiffly, his body tense with the effort of not running or fighting or screaming. I could feel the tremor in his arm, the fear he was trying to hide.

The laundry room door was open now. A woman in scrubs stood at one of the machines, folding towels. She glanced up as we passed, her eyes registering two men in a staff-only corridor where men in sport coats didn't belong.

"Health inspector," I said without breaking stride. "Routine check. Carry on."

She looked confused but nodded, turning back to her towels. We kept walking. Ten more feet to the exit. Five.

The door opened onto the alley. The same yellow light. The same smell of garbage. Laura's car was waiting twenty feet away, engine running.

Phoenix hesitated at the car door.

"You're making a mistake," he said. "I have information. Valuable information. About things your government would want to know."

"I'm sure you do. And I'm sure Andrei will be very interested in hearing all of it." I opened the door. "Get in."

He got in.

I zip-tied his hands in front of him, tight enough to hold but not tight enough to cut circulation. We had a long drive ahead, and I didn't need him losing feeling in his fingers and making noise about it.

Laura pulled out of the alley, headed south toward US-1. Phoenix sat in the back seat, staring out the window at the darkness. Calculating. Still looking for his angle.

We were three blocks from the spa when Laura's phone buzzed.

She glanced at the screen. Her expression didn't change, but I saw her hands tighten on the wheel.

"What?" I asked.

"Scanner traffic. Someone called in a suspicious person at the spa. Two men, one matching Phoenix's description, leaving through a service entrance."

"The laundry woman."

"Has to be. She mentioned the health inspector to someone. Manager probably called it in."

I checked the mirrors. Nothing behind us yet. But Coral Gables wasn't a big place, and Phoenix's security was sitting fifty feet from the spa's front door.

"How long before they put it together?"

"Depends on how fast his guys are thinking. If they're smart, they're already moving."

Phoenix had been listening. I saw the shift in his posture, the way his shoulders straightened. Hope. The most dangerous thing a captive can feel.

"My people will find you," he said. His voice was different now. Confident. "They're very good at finding people."

"Your people are sitting in a parking lot wondering why you're taking so long."

"Not for much longer." He smiled. "That woman saw you. Saw us. She'll describe you to the police, and the police will describe you to my security, and then..." He shrugged, the gesture awkward with his hands bound. "Then we'll see who's making mistakes."

Laura turned onto US-1, heading south toward the Keys. The Overseas Highway stretched ahead of us, a hundred miles of bridges and islands with nowhere to hide and nowhere to turn off.

"He's not wrong," she said quietly. "If they figure out we're heading south, this road is a trap."

"Then we make sure they don't figure it out."

"How?"

I didn't have an answer. The Overseas Highway was the only route to Key Largo. If Phoenix's people got behind us, there was no alternate path, no side streets to disappear into. Just water on both sides and a single ribbon of asphalt pointing straight to our destination.

We drove in silence for twenty minutes. The lights of Miami faded behind us. The road narrowed, hemmed in by mangroves and darkness. Every few miles, a bridge carried us over black water that reflected nothing.

I kept watching the mirrors.

At mile marker 112, I saw them.

Headlights. Two vehicles, moving fast, gaining on us. They'd been invisible a minute ago, hidden by a curve in the road. Now they were maybe half a mile back and closing.

"Laura."

"I see them."

Phoenix saw them too. He twisted in his seat, craning to look through the rear window. The smile was back, wider now.

"That's Sergei," he said. "My driver. I'd recognize those headlights anywhere." He turned to face me. "Last chance. Pull over. Let me go. I'll tell them it was a misunderstanding. You drive away, nobody gets hurt."

"And then what? You forget this happened? Forgive and forget?"

"Of course not. But I'm a businessman. I understand leverage. You've demonstrated that you can get to me, that my security isn't as good as I thought. That's valuable information." His voice was smooth, reasonable. The voice of a man who'd negotiated his way out of tight spots before. "We can come to an arrangement. You clearly have skills. I can always use skilled people."

"I'm not for sale."

"Everyone's for sale. The only question is price."

The headlights were closer now. A quarter mile. I could make out the shape of the lead vehicle. Big. Black. SUV. Definitely Sergei.

"Laura, how fast can this thing go?"

"Fast enough. But if we run, they'll know for certain it's us. Right now they might just be checking every southbound vehicle."

"And if we don't run?"

"They pull us over. Two of them, two of us, plus a hostage who wants to be rescued." She glanced at me. "Bad odds."

Phoenix leaned forward. "Those men have killed for me. Many times. They won't hesitate."

"Sit back."

"They'll put bullets in both of you and leave your bodies in the mangroves. No one will ever find you. No one will ever know what happened."

"I said sit back."

The headlights were right behind us now. The SUV loomed in the mirror, close enough that I could see the silhouette of the driver. Sergei. Thick neck, shaved head. The passenger was on a phone, gesturing.

They were calling it in. Confirming.

Laura's hands were steady on the wheel. "Decision time."

I looked at Phoenix. At the hope in his eyes. At the certainty that his people were about to save him, that the next few minutes would end with us dead and him free.

"Floor it."

Laura hit the gas. The car surged forward, pressing me back in my seat. Phoenix tumbled sideways, caught off guard.

Behind us, the SUV accelerated to match. The second vehicle, a sedan, swung into the oncoming lane to pull alongside.

"They're trying to box us in," Laura said.

"Don't let them."

She swerved left, cutting off the sedan. It braked hard, falling back. The SUV tried to pull alongside on the right, but there was no room. Water on one side, Laura's car on the other.

We were doing ninety now. The bridges came faster, the islands blurring past. Every few seconds, the road would narrow for a bridge span, and the SUV would have to fall back or risk running off the edge.

"There's a turnoff at mile marker 106," Laura said. "Service road. Leads to a boat ramp."

"They'll follow us."

"They'll try. But the road's not marked. If we kill our lights..."

Risky. Driving dark on an unfamiliar road. But staying on the highway was worse.

"Do it."

The mile markers ticked down. 109. 108. 107. The SUV was fifty feet behind us, the sedan another fifty behind that. They weren't trying to pull alongside anymore. They were following, waiting for us to make a mistake.

Laura killed the headlights. The world went black.

For a horrible second, I couldn't see anything. Then my eyes adjusted, and I could make out the road by starlight, a faint gray ribbon cutting through the darker shapes of the mangroves.

Laura yanked the wheel right. We left the highway doing seventy, tires screaming on gravel. I braced against the door as the car fishtailed, caught, straightened.

Behind us, brake lights flared red as the SUV shot past the turnoff. They hadn't seen us leave.

Laura kept the headlights off. The service road was narrow, barely two lanes, branches scraping against the windows as we pushed through. I couldn't see more than twenty feet ahead, but Laura drove like she'd memorized every curve.

"How do you know this road?"

"I scouted three escape routes before we started the operation. This was number two."

Phoenix had gone quiet. I looked back at him. The hope was fading from his eyes, replaced by something colder. He was recalculating. Accepting that rescue wasn't coming.

"They'll find the turnoff," he said. "They'll double back."

"By the time they do, we'll be gone."

"You think you've won." His voice was flat now. Defeated. "You haven't. My organization will keep looking. Forever. You've made enemies tonight that you can't imagine."

"I've had enemies before."

"Not like these. These are people who measure revenge in generations. Who'll hurt everyone you've ever loved just to send a message." He leaned forward. "Your families. Your friends. Anyone whose name appears next to yours in any database anywhere. They'll find them all."

"Then I'd better make sure they never find me."

The service road ended at a small marina. A dozen boats tied up at wooden docks, most of them dark. Laura pulled the car behind a storage shed, out of sight from the main road.

We sat there in the darkness, engine ticking as it cooled, listening. No headlights on the road behind us. No sound of pursuit.

"We wait five minutes," Laura said. "Make sure they're not coming."

"And if they are?"

"Then we improvise."

Phoenix laughed. Soft, bitter. "You're amateurs. Playing a game you don't understand against people who've been doing this for decades."

"We got you out of a building with two-man security and a spa full of witnesses."

"You got lucky. That woman in the laundry room. If she hadn't believed your lie..."

"She did believe it. That's not luck. That's preparation."

He shook his head. "One day, your preparation won't be enough. One day, you'll walk into a room thinking you have all the angles covered, and someone will be waiting who's

smarter than you. Faster than you. More willing to do whatever it takes."

"Maybe. But not today."

Five minutes later, Laura pulled into a marina south of
the port. No headlights. No sirens. No one had followed
us. A small speedboat was waiting at the end of the last
dock.

We got out of the car. I pulled Phoenix from the back
seat, keeping a grip on his arm as we walked toward the
docks. He didn't resist. The fight had gone out of him somewhere on that dark service road, when he'd realized his
people weren't coming.

The boat was small. Fast. No running lights. Just a dark
shape bobbing on the water.

Phoenix stopped at the edge of the dock. Looked out at
the boat, at the black water, at the stars overhead.

"Fifty million," he said. "I can have it wired anywhere in
the world within twenty-four hours. Untraceable. Tax-free.
You let me go, you never have to work again."

I didn't answer.

"Seventy million. And I'll throw in information. Names
of every corrupt official I've ever dealt with. CIA. FBI.
Pentagon. You could bring down half the intelligence
community."

Laura glanced at me. I shook my head slightly.

"A hundred million." Phoenix's voice was rising now,
desperation creeping in. "That's my final offer. A hundred
million dollars and a new identity. I have people who can
make you disappear. New name, new face, new life. Whatever you want."

"There's no price," I said. "This isn't about money."

"Then what is it about?"

I thought about the synagogue in Atlanta. The three

people who died. The eight-year-old girl whose name I'd memorized because someone should remember it.

"It's about consequences," I said. "Something you've avoided for too long."

He didn't speak again as we boarded the boat.

Laura untied us from the dock while I secured Phoenix to a seat in the cabin.

The ocean was calm as we motored out, the lights of the marina fading behind us until there was nothing but darkness in every direction. Stars overhead, more than you ever saw on the mainland. The Milky Way spilling across the sky like something from a planetarium.

We cut the engine three miles offshore and waited. The boat rocked gently on the swells. Somewhere in the distance, a ship's horn sounded, low and mournful.

"They'll kill me," Phoenix said quietly. "You know that. Maybe not right away. Maybe not for years. But eventually, when they've extracted everything useful, they'll put a bullet in my head and dump me in a hole."

"Maybe."

"And you can live with that?"

I looked at him. This man who'd sold weapons to terrorists. Who'd armed the people who shot up a synagogue. Who'd made a fortune from other people's deaths and slept soundly every night.

"I can live with it better than the alternative."

The Russian boat appeared at 11:47. No running lights. No markings. Just a dark shape materializing out of the darkness like something from a nightmare.

The handoff happened quickly. Three men who moved with military precision. They took Phoenix without a word, transferred him to their vessel with the efficiency of people who'd done this before.

One of them handed me an envelope before they left. Inside was a card with a phone number. Nothing else.

"For future business," the man said. His accent was thick, his meaning clear.

I watched their running lights fade into the darkness, Phoenix's silhouette visible on the deck until even that was gone.

"It's done," Laura said quietly.

"It's done."

We stood on the deck for a long moment, neither of us speaking. The water was calm, the stars bright. A beautiful night for ugly work.

"You okay?" she asked.

"I don't know." I watched the empty horizon. "We didn't kill him. That matters. But we sent him to people who might. Who probably will, eventually."

"He was selling weapons to terrorists. He helped kill a child."

"I know. And if anyone deserves what's coming, it's him." I turned to face her. "But I keep thinking about our rules. About the line between necessary and convenient. Did we find a third option, or did we just find a way to feel better about crossing a line?"

Laura was quiet for a moment. "I think we found a way to stop him without becoming killers ourselves. That's not nothing."

"True," I agreed. "But it's not clean either."

"Nothing in this world is clean." She took my hand. "It isn't about whether we can stay clean. It's whether we can stay human. Whether we can keep making the harder choice instead of the easier one."

"And did we? Tonight?"

"I think so. We could have killed him. Adam wanted us

to kill him. It would have been simpler, cleaner, less complicated. But we didn't. We found another way." She squeezed my hand. "That has to count for something."

I wanted to believe her. Standing on that boat in the darkness, having just handed a man over to what was probably a death sentence, I needed to believe her.

"Let's go home," I said.

Laura started the engine. We turned the boat back toward shore, leaving the empty ocean behind us.

"I HAD A FRIEND ONCE," Laura said. "Before all this."

We were in bed, the operation complete, tomorrow's problems still hours away. I traced lazy circles on her shoulder and waited for her to continue.

"Her name was Michelle. We met at Georgetown. Freshman orientation. She spilled coffee on my laptop and spent the next four years making up for it." Laura smiled at the ceiling, but it was a sad smile. The kind you wear when you're remembering something you've lost. "She was the most genuinely good person I've ever known. Volunteered at homeless shelters. Cried at commercials about hungry children. Believed that people were basically decent if you gave them the chance."

"What happened to her?"

"Nothing. She's fine. Lives in Portland now, works for an environmental nonprofit, married to a guy who builds furniture." The smile faded. "She sends me Christmas cards. I don't open them."

I propped myself up on one elbow, looking down at her. "Why not?"

"Because I can't lie to her." Laura met my eyes, and I

saw something raw there. Something unguarded. "I've lied to assets, targets, colleagues, superiors. I've lied under oath. I've lied to men in bed, just like this. But Michelle..." She shook her head. "She knew me before. The real me. And I can't sit across from her and pretend I'm still that person."

"Maybe you are."

"I'm not." She said it simply, without self-pity. Just a fact. "The person Michelle loved was honest. Idealistic. Believed the world could be fixed if good people tried hard enough." She paused. "I've done things that person couldn't imagine. Justified things she would have called unforgivable."

I thought about Diana. The life I'd tried to build in Maryland. The person I'd wanted to be before my father's phone call pulled me back. The friends I'd stopped calling because explaining my life had become impossible.

"So you let the friendship die."

"I killed it. Deliberately. Stopped returning calls. Made excuses. Let her think I'd become someone too busy and important for old friends." Laura's voice went soft. "It was kinder than the truth. The truth is I became someone who couldn't be close to someone that good. Because she'd see through me eventually, and what she'd see would break her heart."

"That's not kindness. That's protection."

"Protecting who?" Laura asked. "Her or me?"

I didn't have an answer.

"This work takes things from you," Laura said. "Not just time and safety. It takes the version of yourself that could have been normal. Happy. Connected." She turned to look at me. "That's the cost the recruiter didn't mention. Not just what you do. Who you stop being."

I pulled her closer. She let me.

"Maybe," I said into her hair, "you find new people. People who know what you are and choose you anyway."

Laura was quiet for a long moment.

"Maybe," she kissed my cheek. "Maybe you do."

THREE DAYS Later

Adam took the news better than I expected.

"The Russians have him," he said, reading our report. We were in his office again, the same room where he'd given us the assignment two weeks earlier. "Andrei Reznikov specifically."

"That's correct."

"And they gave you a contact number. For future business."

"They did."

Adam set down the report. His expression was unreadable. "You just opened a back channel to Russian intelligence. Without authorization. Without oversight. Without telling me what you were planning."

"You told us to find another option. We found one."

"I told you to neutralize Phoenix. I didn't tell you to start conducting independent diplomacy with hostile foreign intelligence services."

"The channel is an asset. A relationship we can use for future operations. One that wouldn't exist if we'd just killed him like you wanted."

Adam was quiet for a long moment. I couldn't tell if he was angry or impressed or both.

"You're right," he said finally. "The channel is valuable. The outcome is better than what I proposed. Phoenix is neutralized, his weapons stop flowing, and we have a new relationship with Russian intelligence." He paused. "But you also demonstrated that you can operate entirely outside my awareness. That you have relationships and capabilities I didn't know about."

"Is that a problem?"

"It's a concern. The last time we talked, I told you I was watching. Now I'm telling you I'm worried." His eyes met mine. "You're not just exceeding expectations anymore. You're outgrowing the arrangement."

"We're not operating against you, Adam. We're operating for ourselves. There's a difference."

"Is there?" He stood, walked to the window. "You came to me as an asset. A criminal I recruited because you had useful skills. Now you're building relationships with foreign intelligence services. Creating capabilities I don't control. Making decisions without consulting me." He turned back. "That's not an asset. That's something else."

"What would you call it?"

"A partner." The word hung in the air between us. "Someone who operates alongside me, not beneath me. Someone with their own agenda, their own interests, their own power base."

"And is that acceptable?"

Adam studied me for a long moment. Whatever he was calculating, it was beyond my ability to read.

"Ask me again in six months," he said finally. "If you keep delivering results like this, if you keep proving that your independence is an asset rather than a liability...then maybe we'll talk about what partnership really means."

"And until then?"

"Until then, keep doing what you're doing. Keep finding solutions I can't see. Keep building relationships that benefit us both." He smiled slightly. "Just remember that I'm watching. I'm always watching."

It wasn't approval. It wasn't a threat. It was something in between, an acknowledgment that the dynamic between us had shifted in ways neither of us fully understood yet.

"We understand each other," I said.

"I think we're starting to."

He walked us to the door. As we were leaving, he said one more thing.

"The fifteen rules. Laura mentioned them once. The ethical boundaries you've set for yourselves."

I tensed. "What about them?"

"Keep them." His voice was surprisingly earnest. "Whatever else happens, whatever you build, keep those rules. They're the only thing that will keep you from becoming the people you're trying to stop."

I didn't know what to say. Of all the things I'd expected from Adam, that wasn't one of them.

"We intend to," Laura said.

"Good." He opened the door. "Now get out of my office. I have other problems to solve."

We left without another word. But as we walked to the car, I couldn't shake the feeling that something fundamental had changed.

We'd come in as assets. We were leaving as something else.

Partners, Adam had called it. People with their own agenda, their own interests, their own power base.

Maybe that was exactly what we'd been trying to build all along.

18

SUCCESSION

ONE YEAR

I stood on my balcony watching the boats move across the Intracoastal, thinking about everything that had changed since that night in the holding cell. Since Adam appeared with an offer that wasn't really an offer. Since I'd become something I never expected to be.

"One year since my father died. One year since Laura told me who she really was. One year since I'd stopped pretending I could ever be normal. The same time of year. The same Florida sun. Everything different except the weather."

Laura came out to join me, coffee in hand. "Deep thoughts?"

"Anniversary thoughts. One year ago today, Tommy died in that cell."

She was quiet for a moment. "Do you miss him?"

The question caught me off guard. I had to think about it.

"I miss the idea of him," I said finally. "The version of him that existed when I was young, before I understood what he really was. The father who taught me to play chess and read people and survive in a world that doesn't care about survivors." I watched a yacht glide past, all gleaming white in the morning sun. "But the man who died in that cell? The one who chose drugs over his family, who put us all at risk for decades, who couldn't see past his own addictions? I don't miss him. I just wish I'd had a different father to miss."

"That's honest."

"It's all I've got. Honest is the only thing I can be anymore." I turned to face her. "At least with you. At least with the people who matter."

She leaned in and kissed me. Soft. Familiar. The kind of kiss that comes from a year of building something together.

"Speaking of people who matter," she said. "Randy called. He wants to have lunch."

"Just Randy?"

"Just Randy. He said there's something he needs to say. Brother to brother."

I nodded. I'd been waiting for this conversation. The one where we finally settled things between us, one way or another.

"Where?"

"Little Havana. That Cuban place you used to go with Tommy."

Of course. Where else would we have this conversation but in the shadow of our father's ghost?

VERSAILLES RESTAURANT, **Little Havana**

The restaurant was exactly as I remembered it. Mirrors everywhere, reflecting light from chandeliers that had seen better decades. Cuban coffee strong enough to strip paint. The sound of Spanish mixing with English, old men arguing about politics, families celebrating birthdays and anniversaries and ordinary Tuesdays.

Randy was already there when I arrived, sitting in the same booth where Tommy used to hold court. He looked good. Healthy. More relaxed than I'd seen him in months.

"Little brother," he said as I slid into the seat across from him. "Thanks for coming."

"Thanks for asking."

A waitress appeared, took our orders without writing anything down. She'd probably been doing this since before we were born.

Randy waited until she was gone, then leaned back in his seat. "One year."

"One year."

"Lot's changed."

"Truth," I agreed.

He smiled slightly. "You gonna make me do all the talking?"

"You're the one who called this meeting."

"Fair enough." He took a breath. "I've been thinking about us. About how things have been since...since everything. And I realized I've been holding onto something I need to let go of."

"What's that?"

"Resentment. Jealousy. Whatever you want to call it." He met my eyes. "When you came back, when you got pulled into the CIA thing, when it became clear you were turning it into something bigger...I told myself I was happy for you. Told myself I didn't care that you were the golden boy, the one they chose, the one who got the real future while I got Florida."

"Randy..."

"Let me finish." He held up a hand. "I told myself all

that, but it wasn't true. I was jealous. I was hurt. I felt like I'd been passed over, like all those years of holding things together while you were gone didn't count for anything." He paused. "And then you started keeping secrets. Big secrets. And I used that as an excuse to feel even more resentful."

"I should have told you more."

"Maybe. Maybe not." He shrugged. "Looking back, I understand why you didn't. I'm not subtle. I'm not careful. If Adam had looked at me wrong, I would have given every-thing away." A rueful smile. "You were protecting the opera-tion. Protecting me, in your way. I didn't want to see that, but it was true."

The waitress returned with our food. Ropa Vieja for him, Cuban sandwich for me. Comfort food from a child-hood that felt like someone else's life.

"So what changed?" I asked when she left.

"The Carver thing. The terrorist attack you stopped." Randy picked up his fork but didn't eat. "I watched that news coverage. Watched them talk about how close it had come, how many people could have died. And you and Laura were behind stopping it. You'd found a way to stop the attack and take down the corrupt congressman, both at the same time."

"To be fair, Adam handed us the whole picture. Carver, the cell, the timeline. We didn't uncover any of that. What we did was refuse to accept his answer when he said there was no way to save both."

"But it was your plan. Your initiative. Your rules, that made you look for a third option instead of just following orders." He finally took a bite, chewed thoughtfully. "And that's when I realized something."

"What?"

"I couldn't have done it. Not the smarts. I've got those. It's the..." He gestured at his head. "I don't think like that. The connections. The angles." I watched the coverage and I tried to imagine myself in your position, with all that information, all those moving pieces, and I realized...I would have made the obvious play. The simple play. I would have stopped the attack, sure, but I never would have seen the angle with Carver. Never would have connected those dots."

He set down his fork, looked at me directly.

"You remember when we were kids? When Dad would take us to watch him work?"

"I remember."

"I always watched what he was doing. The deal in front of him. The money changing hands. The immediate problem and the immediate solution." Randy's voice was thoughtful, like he was working something out as he spoke. "But you...you watched the people around him. The ones who weren't talking. The ones standing in the corners. You'd come home and ask questions about people Dad hadn't even mentioned."

"I didn't realize you noticed that."

"I noticed. I just didn't understand what it meant until now." He picked up his fork again, pushed food around his plate. "You see systems. Patterns. The whole board. I see what's right in front of me. That's not worse. It's just different."

"Randy, you've built something real in Florida. Something sustainable. That takes a kind of vision too."

"It does. And I'm proud of it." He met my eyes. "That's the other thing I realized. I spent so long being jealous of what you were building that I forgot to be proud of what I was building. TJ's clients. The Wall Street pipeline. The real estate expansion. I'm running an operation that Dad never could have imagined. One that doesn't depend on drugs or violence or constantly looking over your shoulder for the next threat."

"You've taken the family business further than Dad ever could. That's huge."

"It is huge. And it's mine. Not yours, not Dad's, not Tony's. Mine." He smiled, and there was something settled in it. Something resolved. "I wanted to be the biggest criminal in Florida. That was my dream. My ambition. And you know what? I am. I'm doing exactly what I wanted to do. And somewhere along the way, I forgot that was enough. That it was more than enough."

I thought about Randy at nineteen, holding the family together while Tommy spiraled. Randy at twenty-five, building relationships I'd walked away from. Randy for the last four years, keeping everything running while I pretended to be someone else in Maryland.

"I never thanked you," I said. "For those years when I was gone. For holding things together."

"You didn't have to thank me. You're my brother."

"That's why I should've thanked you. Because you did it without expecting anything. Without keeping score." I leaned forward. "I kept score, Randy. When I came back, I looked at what you'd built and I told myself I could do it better. That I saw things you didn't see. That I was the smart one and you were just...holding the fort."

"Danny..."

"Let me finish." I echoed his words from earlier. "I was arrogant. I came back into a situation you'd been managing for years and I immediately started making moves without consulting you. Started building things behind your back. Treated you like a subordinate instead of a partner."

"You had reasons."

"I had excuses. There's a difference." I met his eyes. "You

deserved better. You deserved a brother who trusted you. Who included you. Who recognized that your way of seeing things was just as valuable as mine, even if it was different."

Randy was quiet for a moment. Then he nodded slowly.

"Okay. We both fucked up. We both could have done better." He extended his hand across the table. "Clean slate?"

I took his hand. "Clean slate."

We shook on it, and something that had been knotted in my chest for months finally loosened.

"Now eat your food," Randy said. "It's getting cold and I'm not letting you waste a Cuban sandwich. That's basically a sin in this restaurant."

I laughed and took a bite. For a few minutes, we just ate. Brothers sharing a meal. Simple. Normal. The kind of thing other families took for granted.

"You remember the time Dad took us fishing?" Randy asked suddenly. "Out in the Keys? I must have been twelve, which means you were, what, ten?"

"I remember. You caught a barracuda and it almost took your hand off."

"It did not almost take my hand off. It nicked me. Barely a scratch."

"You screamed like you were dying. Dad had to talk you down for twenty minutes."

"I was twelve. I was allowed to be dramatic." Randy grinned. "But you remember what happened after? When we got back to the dock?"

I thought back. The salt smell of the marina. Tommy counting out cash to the boat captain. Randy with his hand wrapped in a bloody towel, still shaking but trying to hide it.

"Dad bought us ice cream," I said. "And he told us..."

"He told us that brothers look out for each other. That

the world was full of people who'd let you down, but family was forever." Randy's grin faded into something more serious. "I know Dad was a mess. I know he failed us in a hundred different ways. But he got that part right. We're brothers. That means something. That means everything."

"It does."

"That's not the lesson I remember most," I said.

Randy looked up from his plate. "No?"

"No. The lesson I remember is from a couple years later. You were fifteen. I was thirteen."

"Which time? There were a lot of bad years in there."

"The Muñoz meet."

Randy went still. His fork stopped halfway to his mouth.

"You remember," I said.

"I remember." He set the fork down. "How could I forget?"

I pushed my plate aside. This wasn't a story I could tell while eating.

"Tommy was supposed to meet Hector Muñoz on a Tuesday night. Big deal. Muñoz controlled distribution through half of Broward, and he was thinking about going with the Colombians instead. If that meet didn't happen, we lost the whole western corridor."

"Dad knew that. Everyone knew that."

"And Tommy disappeared three days before. Just gone. One of his binges. Uncle Tony was in New York. Jake and Colin were too young. There was nobody."

Randy's jaw tightened. "There was me."

"There was you." I watched his face, saw him going back to that week. "I was in the kitchen when you got the call from Muñoz's guy. Tuesday morning. The meet was that night. And Tommy still wasn't back."

"I remember thinking maybe he'd show up. Maybe he'd

walk through the door with some bullshit excuse and every-thing would be fine."

"But he didn't."

"He didn't." Randy picked up his coffee, looked at it, set it down. "And around four o'clock, I realized nobody was coming. Not Dad. Not Tony. Nobody. The meet was happening in five hours whether we were ready or not."

"So you went."

"So I went." He almost smiled. "Fifteen years old. Borrowed one of Dad's jackets because I didn't own anything that looked serious. Practiced what I was going to say in the mirror for an hour."

"I followed you."

Randy looked up sharply. "What?"

"I followed you. Took my bike, stayed a block back. I knew you were going to do something stupid, and I wanted to see it."

"Danny, if Muñoz's guys had spotted you..."

"They didn't. I was careful." I held his gaze. "I watched the whole thing. Through the window of that warehouse on Sunrise."

Randy was quiet for a moment. Processing. Realizing I'd seen something he probably thought no one had witnessed.

"What did you see?" he asked finally.

"I saw my fifteen-year-old brother walk into a room with six guys who could have killed him without breaking a sweat. I saw you shake Hector Muñoz's hand like you belonged there. Like you'd done it a hundred times."

"I was terrified."

"You didn't look terrified. You looked like Tommy. The good version of Tommy. The one who could walk into any room and own it." I leaned forward. "I couldn't hear what you said. But I watched Muñoz's face. He came in looking annoyed, like he was ready to walk. Twenty minutes later, he was laughing. Clapping you on the shoulder. Shaking your hand again."

"I told him the truth. That Dad was handling something urgent and sent me instead. That I was going to be running things someday, so he might as well get used to dealing with me now."

"And he bought it?"

"He respected it. Said I had bigger balls than half the guys twice my age." Randy's voice was distant. "He kept the deal. Stayed with us for another eight years, until he retired to Costa Rica."

"You saved the western corridor. At fifteen."

"I didn't save anything. I just showed up because someone had to."

"That's exactly the point." I held his gaze. "You were fifteen, Randy. You should have been worrying about homework and girls and whatever else fifteen-year-olds worry about. Instead, you were running meets with distributors because Tommy couldn't be bothered to stay sober for the most important deal of the year."

Randy was quiet for a long moment.

"You know what I remember most about that night?" he said. "Not the meet. Not Muñoz. After."

"What?"

"Driving home. Sitting in Dad's car in the driveway for maybe twenty minutes, just shaking. The adrenaline wearing off. Realizing what could have happened. What I'd risked." He looked at me. "And then realizing something else. Something that changed everything."

"What?"

"That I could do it. That I wasn't just Tommy Tyler's kid, following orders, waiting to be told what to do. I could walk into a room and make things happen. I could hold it together when everything was falling apart." His voice dropped. "That was the first time I understood who I could be. Not who Dad wanted me to be. Who I actually was."

"The guy who shows up."

"The guy who builds something that doesn't fall apart when one person fails. That's what I've been doing ever since. Florida, the real estate, TJ's network, all of it." He met my eyes. "I'm not building an empire, Danny. I'm building something that works. Something that doesn't depend on any one person being sober or present or reliable. Something that keeps running no matter what."

I thought about Randy's operation. The systems. The redundancies. The way everything interlocked so that no single failure could bring it down. I'd always thought it was good business practice. Now I understood it was something else.

"You're building something Tommy never could."

"I'm building something Tommy never would. He liked being essential. Liked knowing everything fell apart without him. That's power, in a way. But it's fragile. It breaks the second you break." Randy shook his head. "I don't want to be essential. I want to build something that outlasts me. Something that keeps my family safe even if I'm not there to protect them."

"That's not a weakness."

"It is when you can't stop. When you don't know who you are if you're not building something." Randy's smile was tired. "I've been doing this for twenty years, Danny. Nonstop. And sometimes I wonder what happens when there's nothing left to build. When the machine runs itself. Who am I then?"

"You're my brother. That's who you are."

"Is that enough?"

"It's everything."

Randy looked at me for a long moment. Something shifted in his expression. Not resolution exactly. More like recognition. Like he was seeing something he'd needed to see for a long time.

"You know what's funny?" he said. "I spent all those years building, and the thing I'm most proud of isn't any of it. It's not the money or the properties or the network."

"What is it?"

"It's that my brothers are okay. All four of us. We survived Tommy. We survived each other. And we're still here, still family, still..." He gestured at the space between us. "Still able to sit in a Cuban restaurant and talk about the shit that matters."

"That's not funny. That's the whole point."

"Maybe it is." He picked up his napkin, wiped his mouth. "Maybe I've been so busy building walls that I forgot what I was protecting in the first place." He set the napkin down. "Which brings me to one more thing I need you to know."

"What's that?"

"Whatever comes next, whatever dangerous game you're playing with Adam and the CIA and whoever else...I'm not on the sidelines anymore. Last time we had this conversation, I was walking out the door. This time I'm walking in." His eyes were serious now, all the humor gone. "You understand what I'm saying?"

"I get it."

"Do you? Because sometimes I wonder if you remember you're not alone in this. You've got Laura, sure. But you've also got me. And Jake. And Colin. A whole family of criminals who would burn down the world for you if you asked."

"I won't ask you to burn down the world."

"Maybe not. But if someone tries to burn down yours, we'll be there. That's what I'm saying." He stood, dropped cash on the table. "That's the Tyler way. We fuck up. We fight. We keep secrets and hold grudges and make stupid decisions. But when it matters, we show up. Every time."

I stood too, and before I could say anything, Randy pulled me into a hug. Tight. Real. The kind of hug we hadn't shared since we were kids.

"Love you, little brother," he said.

"Love you too."

He let go, stepped back. "Now go home to your CIA girlfriend. I've got properties to move."

He walked out of the restaurant without looking back. Classic Randy. Say what needs to be said, then disappear before things get too emotional.

"I sat back down in the booth and let myself feel the weight of the moment. Tommy's booth. Tommy's restaurant. But a different family sitting in it now. Scarred, maybe. Rebuilt from pieces that didn't quite fit the same way. But still here."

Maybe that was the real victory. Not the leverage or the power or the operations we'd run. Just this. Brothers who still loved each other, despite everything.

It wasn't much. But it was ours.

UNCLE TONY'S OFFICE, **Coral Gables**

Uncle Tony called that afternoon.

"Come by the office," he said. "There's something I want to discuss."

I hadn't seen Tony in weeks. He'd been traveling, handling business in Europe and South America, the kind of business that didn't get discussed on phone calls. But his voice had a warmth to it that put me at ease.

Uncle Tony's office was in a building that looked like every other building in Coral Gables. Nothing special from the outside. But inside, behind the reception area and the legitimate business facade, was a room that spoke of decades of accumulated power.

Dark wood. Old leather. Books that had actually been read, not just displayed. The office of a man who'd built an empire and survived long enough to enjoy it.

"Danny." Tony stood when I entered, came around the desk to embrace me. He smelled of cigars and expensive cologne, the same scent I remembered from childhood.

But there was something different now. A slowness in his movements that hadn't been there before. When he released me from the embrace, I noticed his left hand trembled slightly before he steadied it against the desk. Tony had always seemed ageless to me, a constant presence while everyone else changed around him. Now I saw the truth I'd been avoiding: he was seventy-two years old, and the decades were finally catching up.

"Sit. Let me look at you."

I sat. He studied me with those sharp old eyes, seeing things I probably didn't want seen.

"You look good," he said finally. "Tired. But good. The work agrees with you."

"The work is complicated."

"The best work always is." He settled into his chair, the leather creaking comfortably. "I've been following your progress. Adam keeps me informed."

"Does he?"

"We've worked together a long time. Thirty years of shared interests, shared risks. He trusts my judgment. I trust his." Tony paused. "He tells me you're exceeding expectations. Finding solutions he didn't anticipate. Building relationships he didn't authorize. Laura Donovan," Tony added, watching my reaction. "That's an interesting relationship you've built."

I kept my expression neutral, but my pulse quickened. "She's my handler. Adam assigned her."

"She's more than that. Has been for a while." Tony's smile was knowing, almost gentle. "Don't worry. I'm not judging. In this business, you take comfort where you find it. But you should know that nothing about her assignment was accidental. Adam and I discussed her specifically. Her background. Her capabilities. Her...flexibility with protocol."

"You vetted my girlfriend?"

"I vetted a CIA operations officer who was about to become intimately involved with someone I care about. There's a difference." He let that settle. "She's good, Danny. Better than good. But is she good for you, or good for the mission? Ideally both. But if you ever have to choose..." He left the sentence unfinished.

I tensed slightly. "Is that a problem?"

"On the contrary." Tony smiled, and there was something in that smile I couldn't quite read. Pride, maybe. Or satisfaction. Something deeper. "It's exactly what I hoped for."

"What you hoped for?"

"When Adam recruited you, after Tommy's death, I had concerns. You'd been out of the life for four years. Living in Maryland, trying to be normal. I wasn't sure you still had what it took." He leaned back. "But I also saw something in you. Something your father never had. The ability to think beyond the immediate. To play a longer game."

"Tommy taught me chess."

"Tommy taught you the moves. I taught you to see the board." Tony's eyes met mine. "All those conversations when you were young. All those lessons about patience, about strategy, about knowing when to act and when to wait. Did you think they were accidents?"

I didn't answer. Something was shifting in my understanding, pieces moving into positions I hadn't anticipated.

"I remember one game," Tony continued. "You were maybe twelve. We played for three hours in my study while your father was handling business downstairs. You were losing badly, but you wouldn't resign. Most kids would have given up. But you kept looking for angles. Kept trying to find a way out."

"I remember. You beat me in the end."

"I did. But do you remember what I told you afterward?"

I thought back. The smell of cigar smoke. The weight of the chess pieces in my hand. Tony's voice, calm and measured.

"You said that losing wasn't the lesson. The lesson was how long I kept looking for options when most people would have quit."

"Exactly." Tony nodded slowly. "That's what I saw in you then. That's what I see in you now. The refusal to accept that a situation is hopeless. The willingness to find a third option when everyone else only sees two."

"There was another game," Tony said. "Years later. You were twenty-three, maybe twenty-four. Just before you left for Maryland. Do you remember that one?"

I did. The night before I told Tommy I was done with the drug business. Tony had invited me to his study, and we'd played until nearly midnight.

"You won that one too," I said.

"I did. But not the way you think." Tony's eyes were distant, remembering. "Halfway through that game, I realized you were going to beat me. You'd developed a position I couldn't break. So I sacrificed my queen."

"I remember. I thought you'd made a mistake."

"You thought I'd gotten careless. So you took the queen and felt clever about it. But that sacrifice opened a line I needed. Six moves later, you were in checkmate." Tony leaned forward slightly. "The lesson wasn't about the sacrifice. It was about what you didn't see. You were so focused on the piece I'd given you that you missed what I was actually doing."

"You're saying I'm missing something now."

"I'm saying that sometimes the thing someone gives you, the thing that feels like a gift or a victory, is actually positioning you exactly where they want you to be." His eyes held mine. "That's not a warning, Danny. It's just something to remember."

"Is that why you talked Adam into recruiting me?"

Tony's expression didn't change, but something flickered in his eyes. "Adam makes his own decisions. I simply pointed out that you had potential worth developing."

"That's not an answer."

"No. It's not." He stood, walked to the window. "I'm old, Danny. Adam's old. Old men think about things young men don't. We look at what we've built and we wonder what happens to it. Whether it outlasts us. Whether it meant anything at all."

He was quiet for a moment, watching something outside I couldn't see.

"Your father was my partner for twenty years. But Tommy was never going to be the one. Too impulsive. Too addicted. Too incapable of seeing past his own needs. I loved him like a brother, but I never trusted him with anything that mattered more than money."

"And me?"

Tony turned from the window, and his expression was impossible to read. "You I'm still watching. Still curious about."

"Curious about what?"

"About what you're building. About why you're building it." He walked back to his desk but didn't sit, just rested his hands on the leather chair. "Most people in your position would be focused on survival. On getting through each operation, each test. But you're doing something else. You're creating something."

"You've been busy." Tony let the word sit. "And not just with what Adam assigns you." He studied me. "You've even developed what I understand are...ethical guidelines. Rules. Fifteen of them."

I felt exposed. More exposed than I'd felt since Laura first showed me her mission brief.

"How do you know about the rules?"

"I know because it's exactly what I would do in your position. It's what I did do, forty years ago, when I was the young man being watched by older men who thought they controlled me." Tony's expression was unreadable. "You think you're outmaneuvering Adam. Adding some insurance. Creating options he doesn't see."

"And I'm not?"

"You are. You absolutely are. Is that despite the system or because of it?" He held up a hand before I could respond. "I'm not going to answer that for you. Some truths only mean something when you discover them yourself."

"I'm just trying to—"

"Don't." He held up a hand, gentle but firm. "Don't explain it to me. I don't want you to explain it."

"Then what do you want?"

He smiled again, that same unreadable expression. "I want you to keep doing it. Keep building. Keep thinking. Keep those rules of yours." He paused. "And pay attention."

"Pay attention to what?"

"To everything. To what's being offered. To what's being withheld. To the shape of things." He came around the desk to stand in front of me. "You're smart, Danny. Smarter than Tommy ever was. Smart enough to see patterns if you're looking for them."

"You're being cryptic."

"I'm being patient. There's a difference." He put his hand on my shoulder, the gesture familiar from a dozen conversations over a dozen years. "Some things can't be given. They have to be understood. Earned. If I hand you something, it's just a gift. If you figure it out yourself..." He squeezed my shoulder. "Then it's yours. Really yours. No one can take it away."

Tony walked slowly back to his desk, and again I noticed the effort it took. The way he lowered himself into the chair, the slight wince he tried to hide.

"I've built something over fifty years," he said quietly. "Networks across three continents. Relationships that took decades to cultivate. Infrastructure that moves money, information, people, without leaving traces. All of it invisible to anyone who doesn't know where to look."

"I know. I've seen pieces of it."

"You've seen what I've let you see. There's more. Much more." He opened a drawer, pulled out a photograph, slid it across the desk. Anthony Jr., but not the version I'd seen at

Steak 954 eighteen months ago. This was a different man; sharper, harder, photographed against a Singapore skyline.

"He left right after your father died," Tony said. "I sent him to build something in Southeast Asia. His own network. His own relationships."

"He didn't say anything. At the dinner, before everything happened; he acted like nothing was changing."

"Because he didn't know yet. I made the decision that night, after watching how things unfolded." Tony took the photo back, studied it for a moment before returning it to the drawer. "He's coming home soon. There are conversations that need to happen. Decisions about the future."

"What kind of decisions?"

"The kind that determine what happens to everything I've built when I'm gone. Whether it continues. Who it continues with. How the pieces fit together." Tony met my eyes. "You and Anthony grew up together. You were close once. You'll need to be close again."

"Why?"

"Because what comes next is bigger than any one person. Bigger than you. Bigger than him. Bigger than Laura and Adam and all the operations you're running." Tony's voice dropped lower. "What I've built, what Adam's built, what you're building now, they're all pieces of something larger. Something that's been taking shape for a very long time. And soon, very soon, you're going to have to decide what role you want to play in it."

He just smiled. "Go home. I'm sure Laura's waiting. We'll talk again soon."

I stood, knowing I wasn't going to get anything more from him. At the door, I turned back.

"Uncle Tony. Whatever this is, whatever you're trying to

tell me without telling me, I'm grateful. For everything you've done. Everything you taught me."

His expression softened, and for a moment I saw something unguarded in his eyes. Something that looked almost like love.

"Your father had four sons," Tony said quietly. "But only one of them ever sat in my study until midnight, losing at chess and refusing to quit. Only one of them asked questions about the people standing in corners." He went quiet, suddenly looking every one of his seventy-two years. "Tommy never understood what he had. But I've been paying attention for a long time, Danny. A very long time."

I left his office with more questions than answers.

Danny's Apartment, **That Night**

Laura was on the balcony when I got home, watching the sunset paint the water in shades of orange and gold.

"How was Tony?" she asked as I joined her.

"Cryptic. Proud. Planning something I don't fully understand." I leaned against the railing. "He knows what we're building. Maybe not the details, but the shape of it. And he approves."

"That's either good news or very bad news."

"I think it's good. He talked about succession. About legacy. About being ready when he and Adam step back."

Laura turned to look at me. "That's a big conversation to have after one year."

"I don't think it's about timelines. I think it's about... potential. He's seeing what we could become. Making sure we know he's watching."

"And Randy?"

I smiled. "Randy's good. Better than good. We're...we're okay. Finally."

"I'm glad." She took my hand. "Family matters. Even complicated family. Maybe especially complicated family."

We stood together as the sun disappeared below the horizon, watching the sky fade from gold to purple to black. The boats had turned on their running lights, little points of brightness moving across the dark water.

"One year," Laura said. "Can you believe it?"

"No. Sometimes I wake up and forget. Forget that Tommy's dead. Forget that I'm a CIA asset. Forget that we're building...whatever this is." I squeezed her hand. "Then I remember, and it doesn't feel real. Any of it."

"It's real. All of it." She turned to face me fully. "The operations we've run. The lives we've saved. The leverage we've built. The rules we've kept. It's all real, Danny. We made it real."

"And what happens next?"

"Next, we keep building. Keep proving ourselves. Keep finding ways to do this job without losing ourselves in the process." She smiled. "And eventually, when the time is right, we take what we've built and we use it. Not for Adam. Not for Tony. For us. For the version of this world we want to create."

"An ethical criminal empire."

"Something like that. Or at least, as ethical as criminals can be." She laughed softly. "It's insane, isn't it? What we're trying to do?"

"Completely insane."

"And dangerous."

"Incredibly dangerous."

"And probably going to get us killed."

"Almost certainly."

She grinned. "Then it's a good thing we're doing it together."

I kissed her. Long and slow and real. The kind of kiss that says everything words can't.

When we finally pulled apart, she rested her forehead against mine.

"I love you, Danny Tyler."

"I love you too. All three versions of you."

She laughed. "Only three?"

We stood on the balcony as the night settled around us, two people who'd found each other in the strangest possible way, building something that shouldn't exist, following rules that most people would call naive.

Maybe we were crazy. Maybe we were doomed. Maybe everything we'd built would come crashing down around us.

But standing there with Laura, I couldn't bring myself to care about the risks.

We had each other. We had our rules. We had a chance to be something better than what we came from.

And in our world, that was more than most people ever got.

EPILOGUE

Epilogue: The Board

FBI Miami Field Office, 11:47 p.m.

Marcus Webb stood in front of his board.

The office was empty at this hour. Had been for three hours. The cleaning crew had come and gone, vacuuming around his desk without comment, used to finding him here long after everyone else had left. His coffee had gone cold sometime around nine. He hadn't noticed.

The board had grown since he'd first started building it, more than a year ago. What began as a simple investigation into the Tyler family had become something else entirely. An obsession, his supervisor called it. An unhealthy fixation on a case that wasn't going anywhere.

Webb had heard the whispers. Knew what people said when they thought he couldn't hear. That he'd lost perspective. That he was chasing ghosts. That the Tyler case was a dead end and he was too stubborn to admit it.

But Webb knew better. He could feel it, the shape of something massive lurking just beneath the surface. Every time he pulled a thread, he found more threads. Every time he answered a question, three more appeared.

Twenty-three years with the Bureau. He'd worked organized crime in Boston, public corruption in Chicago, counterintelligence in New York. He knew what real investigations looked like. Knew the difference between a case that wasn't going anywhere and a case that was being actively suppressed.

This was the second kind.

The board told the story. Or tried to. The story kept shifting, kept revealing new chapters he hadn't known existed.

Tommy Tyler. Deceased. The patriarch, dead in a holding cell the night he was arrested. Suicide, officially. But Webb had seen the autopsy report, had noticed the small inconsistencies that suggested something less natural. Elevated potassium levels that could indicate induced cardiac arrest. A thirty-minute gap in the holding cell footage that no one could explain. The guard who'd been on duty that night, transferred to a desk job in Alaska two weeks later.

None of it was proof. All of it was wrong.

Rachel Tyler. Missing. Tommy's wife, disappeared two years ago. Webb had tracked her to Argentina, then lost her again. She knew something. Something important enough to run from. Something that connected everything.

He'd spent four months on Rachel alone. Traced her flight from Miami to São Paulo. Found the hotel where she'd stayed for three nights before vanishing. Picked up her trail again in Buenos Aires, then Córdoba, then nothing. She moved like someone who'd been trained to disappear. Or like someone who had help from people who knew how.

Danny Tyler. The golden boy. No criminal record before

last year, tried to go legitimate, got pulled back in. Now running operations across multiple states, protected by something Webb couldn't identify.

This was where it got strange. Where the investigation stopped behaving like an investigation.

Webb pulled a folder from his desk, the same folder he'd reviewed a hundred times. Cases against Danny Tyler that had evaporated. Evidence that disappeared from secure lockups. Witnesses who changed their stories overnight, not gradually, not under pressure, just suddenly and completely, as if someone had flipped a switch.

The Carver case was the most blatant. Congressman Michael Carver, arrested for conspiracy in a domestic terrorism plot. The evidence had been solid. Airtight. And then Danny Tyler's name appeared in the file, listed as a confidential informant, and suddenly half the case was classified. Sealed by agencies Webb couldn't even get meetings with.

CIA. It had to be. Nothing else explained the reach, the coordination, the way doors slammed shut whenever he got close.

Randy, Jake, Colin Tyler. The brothers. All protected by the same invisible force.

And then the newer additions. The ones that kept him here past midnight, staring at photographs and drawing lines between faces.

Adam Freeman. Attorney. Connected to dozens of cases involving organized crime, but never charged. His clients walked free with disturbing regularity. The name appeared in the margins of too many files.

Webb had pulled Freeman's records going back thirty years. Found a pattern that made no sense for a criminal defense attorney. Exposed clients in one country who should have been protected. Protected clients in another who should have been exposed. It wasn't about winning cases. It was about something else. Something Webb couldn't quite see.

Anthony Russo. "Uncle Tony." The connection Webb couldn't quite pin down. Legitimate businesses, no criminal record, but his name kept appearing in places it shouldn't. Board memberships. Charitable foundations. Political fundraisers. The kind of respectable facade that took decades to build and usually hid something rotten underneath.

Laura Donovan. The newest addition. The one that had cost him three weeks of sleep.

Webb walked to her section of the board, studied the photographs he'd assembled. A woman who appeared in Danny Tyler's life eighteen months ago and never left. On paper, she was a bartender, then a girlfriend, then a business partner.

But Webb had dug deeper. Had called in favors from friends in other agencies. Had spent late nights cross-referencing databases that weren't supposed to talk to each other.

Her Social Security number was issued in 2019. Before that, Laura Donovan didn't exist. No high school records. No college transcripts. No driver's license history, no credit history, no employment history. Just a blank space where a person should have been, and then suddenly, fully formed, a woman with an apartment in Miami and a job at a bar where Danny Tyler happened to drink.

The kind of cover identity that smelled like government work.

Webb had seen this before. In New York, working counterintelligence, he'd bumped into CIA operations twice.

Both times, the same pattern. People who appeared from nowhere with perfect documentation and empty pasts. People whose backgrounds dissolved like sugar in water when you looked too closely.

Laura Donovan was one of them. He was certain of it.

Which meant Danny Tyler wasn't just a criminal with protection. He was an asset. Working for someone. Doing something that the United States government considered important enough to shield him from prosecution.

But what? And why? And who was really pulling the strings?

Webb pinned a new photo to the board. A surveillance shot, taken three days ago. Danny and Laura leaving a building in Coral Gables. The same building where Adam Freeman kept an office. The same building where Anthony Russo had been photographed on multiple occasions.

Four people. Four threads. All leading to the same building, the same meetings, the same invisible structure that Webb could sense but couldn't see.

"What are you?" Webb asked the photos. "What are you really?"

His phone buzzed. A text from his contact in Buenos Aires.

FOUND HER. RACHEL TYLER. MONTEVIDEO. CONFIRMATION PENDING.

Webb stared at the message. Montevideo. Uruguay. Rachel had moved again, but this time he'd tracked her. This time he was close.

She was the key. She had to be. The wife who ran. The woman who knew Tommy's secrets. Whatever had gotten him killed, whatever web Danny had gotten himself caught in, Rachel had seen it coming. Had known enough to disappear before it consumed her too.

Once Webb found her, once he convinced her to talk, everything would unravel.

His supervisor thought he was obsessed. Maybe he was. But twenty-three years had taught him to trust his instincts, and his instincts were screaming that this case, this family, this invisible network, was bigger than anything he'd ever touched.

Bigger than organized crime. Bigger than corruption. Something that reached into the intelligence community, into the government, into structures that were supposed to protect the country but were being used for something else entirely.

He looked at his board one more time. All those faces. All those connections. A web of crime and corruption and secrets that stretched back decades.

"I'm coming for you," he said to Danny Tyler's photograph. "All of you. I don't care how protected you are. I don't care who's behind you. I will find the truth. And when I do, everyone goes down."

He turned off the light and left, the board glowing faintly in the darkness.

The investigation continued.

Vienna, Austria

Dimitri Kovalenko walked out of prison into cold winter air.

Eighteen months. Eighteen months in an Austrian cell because of an operation that had never been properly explained. Charges that had appeared out of nowhere, based on evidence that shouldn't have existed.

But the appeals had finally gone through. Procedural errors, his lawyer called them. Key evidence had been excluded, witnesses had recanted, and the case had quietly fallen apart.

Dimitri knew better. Someone had pulled strings. Someone with enough power to make an international case disappear. The same someone who'd put him there in the first place.

A car was waiting. His cousin Alexei behind the wheel, looking older than Dimitri remembered.

"Welcome back," Alexei said as Dimitri got in. "You look like shit."

"Eighteen months will do that." Dimitri lit a cigarette, the first real cigarette he'd had since his arrest. "What do we know?"

Alexei handed him a tablet. Photos. Documents. Names.

"The Antonov network was taken over while you were inside. Restructured. The people we had in place were removed. New management installed." Alexei's voice was tight. "Americans. Working with someone who has government connections."

Dimitri scrolled through the photos. Recognized faces from the operation that had gotten him arrested. And then, a face he knew all too well.

Danny Tyler. The American who'd sat across from him in that Vienna hotel room, pretending to be a buyer. The one who'd smiled while setting the trap. Dimitri remembered those eyes. Calm. Calculating. The eyes of someone who'd already won and was just waiting for everyone else to realize it.

And beside him in the newer photos, a woman. Professional. Hard.

"Laura Donovan," Alexei said. "She was part of the Vienna operation too. They're partners. They're the ones running the network now."

"I know who Danny Tyler is," Dimitri said quietly. "I looked into his eyes while he destroyed everything I'd built." He touched the photo on the screen. "I've had eighteen months to memorize that face. Eighteen months to imagine what I would do when I saw it again."

"They have protection now," Alexei continued. "Serious protection. Government level. American intelligence."

Dimitri stared at Danny Tyler's face. Memorizing it. Burning it into his memory.

"What do we have in Florida?"

"Not enough. Yet. But I've been building while you were inside. Making contacts. Establishing relationships." Alexei started the car. "Give me six months. I'll have everything we need."

"Make it three."

"Three is fast."

"Three is what I'm giving you." Dimitri took a long drag of his cigarette. "These people took eighteen months of my life. They took our network. They took everything we'd built." He blew smoke toward the window. "I want it back. All of it. And I want them to suffer before they die."

"Even with protection?"

"Protection fails. Everyone has vulnerabilities. Everyone has people they care about." Dimitri looked at the photos again. Danny and Laura, walking down a street in Miami. Happy. Confident. Secure in their power.

They wouldn't be secure for long.

"Find their vulnerabilities," Dimitri said. "Find the people they love. The things they care about. The pressure points that will make them break."

"And then?"

"And then we take everything from them. The way they took everything from us."

The car pulled away from the prison, heading toward Vienna. Toward resources. Toward revenge.

Dimitri watched the prison disappear in the rearview mirror and smiled for the first time in eighteen months.

The game wasn't over.

It was just beginning.

Singapore

Anthony Jr. closed his laptop and looked out at the Singapore skyline.

A year of work, of building, cultivating, positioning. And now it was finally ready.

The network he'd created stretched across Southeast Asia. Legitimate businesses that weren't quite legitimate. Relationships with people who operated in the spaces between legal and illegal. Infrastructure that could move money, people, information, anywhere in the region without leaving traces.

Uncle Tony had sent him here with a simple mission: build something useful. Something that could complement what Danny and Laura were building in the Americas. Something that could eventually be connected, merged, unified into a global operation.

Anthony had done more than that. He'd built an empire.

His phone buzzed. A message from his father.

TIME TO COME HOME. DANNY'S READY.

Anthony smiled. He'd been waiting for this. Watching from a distance as Danny proved himself, as Laura earned her place, as the two of them built something remarkable from the ashes of Tommy's failure.

Danny was smart. Strategic. Ethical in ways that would have baffled Tommy. He'd earned his position, not through blood or nepotism, but through capability.

Anthony respected that. Admired it, even.

But he also knew something Danny didn't. Something his father had shared in confidence, years ago, before any of this started.

Danny thought he was building leverage. Thought he was outmaneuvering Adam and Tony. Thought he was playing a game of his own design.

He had no idea that every move he'd made, every relationship he'd cultivated, every "independent" decision…had been anticipated. Encouraged. Guided from a distance by people who understood the board better than Danny could imagine.

Not manipulated. That was the wrong word. Tony didn't manipulate. He positioned. He created conditions. He set up situations and let people reveal themselves through their choices.

Danny had revealed himself beautifully. Had become exactly what Tony hoped he would become. The kind of leader who could take this thing forward. The kind of person who could be trusted with the future.

Did Danny deserve to know the truth? That his "leverage play" had been encouraged from the start? That his feeling of independence was itself a gift from the man he thought he was outmaneuvering?

Probably. Someday. When he was ready to understand.

For now, let him believe he'd won. Let him feel the pride of building something himself. That pride would make him stronger, more committed, more invested in the empire he thought he'd created on his own.

Anthony typed a response to his father.

ON MY WAY. SEE YOU IN TWO WEEKS.

He looked out at the Singapore skyline one more time.

All those lights. All that money. All that power, humming through a city that never slept.

Soon, he'd be part of something even bigger. Standing beside Danny and Laura, building the next generation of whatever this thing was becoming.

He couldn't wait.

Fort Lauderdale, Florida

Danny stood on his balcony, eyes closed, letting the morning settle in. Salt air off the Intracoastal. A boat engine somewhere distant. The first warmth of the sun on his face.

Laura was still asleep inside. They'd been up late, planning, strategizing, dreaming about the future they were building together.

Eighteen months since his father died. Eighteen months since everything changed.

He thought about how far they'd come. The operations they'd run. The lives they'd saved. The leverage they'd built. The fifteen rules they'd kept, even when it would have been easier to break them.

They'd started as assets. Tools to be used by people with more power. But they'd become something else. Partners. Players. People who could shape outcomes instead of just executing orders.

Adam still watched them. Tony still watched from further back. The CIA still thought they were controllable assets.

But Danny knew better. He and Laura had built something real. Something that couldn't be easily taken away. Something that gave them options, leverage, power.

They weren't free. Not yet. Maybe not ever. But they were freer than they'd been. Freer than anyone in their position had a right to be.

And they'd done it without losing themselves. Without becoming the monsters they were fighting against. Without abandoning the principles that made them who they were.

Maybe that was enough. Maybe, in a world that rewarded ruthlessness, simply remaining human was a kind of victory.

Laura appeared behind him, wrapping her arms around his waist.

"Watching the sunrise without me?" she murmured.

"Thinking."

"About?"

"Everything. Nothing." He turned to face her. "About what we've built. About what comes next."

"What does come next?"

"More of the same, I think. More operations. More leverage. More proving ourselves. Until someday, maybe, we're the ones calling the shots instead of just influencing them."

"That's a big someday."

"It is. But we've got time." He smiled. "And we've got each other. That's more than most people in our position can say."

Laura kissed him softly. "Partners."

"Partners."

They'd built something that shouldn't exist. A criminal operation with a conscience. A love story disguised as an intelligence asset. Fifteen rules that most people would call naive and they called survival.

They didn't know about Webb's investigation, getting closer every day.

They didn't know about Dimitri's revenge, being planned in Vienna.

They didn't know about Anthony Jr., coming home with secrets of his own.

They didn't know that somewhere, in an office in Coral Gables, Uncle Tony was watching their progress with a smile, pleased that his chess pieces were moving exactly where he'd always known they would go.

All they knew was this moment. This sunrise. This feeling of having accomplished something real.

The feeling of having survived.

The feeling of being, against all odds, alive.

"Ready?" Laura asked.

"Ready for what?"

"Whatever comes next."

Danny looked at her. At the woman he loved. At his partner in everything.

"Yeah," he said. "I'm ready."

They turned and walked back inside, into the life they'd built together.

Outside, the sun continued to rise.

And somewhere, the game continued.

AUTHOR'S NOTE

I spent three years researching synthetic identity fraud before writing this novel. What started as curiosity about a single case became an obsession with one of the fastest-growing financial crimes in American history.

Synthetic identity fraud is not a fictional concept. It costs U.S. lenders billions of dollars every year. The scheme is deceptively simple: combine a real Social Security number (often belonging to a child, an elderly person, or an immigrant) with fabricated personal details, and you can build a financial identity that passes verification checks and accumulates real credit. The people behind these operations range from small-time hustlers to sophisticated criminal networks with international reach.

In researching this book, I reviewed published FBI case files, federal court documents, and investigative reporting on major synthetic identity cases. I spoke with investigators and financial crime professionals who have spent years trying to stay ahead of these schemes. Their insights shaped the technical foundation of this story.

The characters, cases, and operations in this novel are entirely fictional. But the methods they use, the systems they exploit, and the vulnerabilities they target are grounded in how these crimes actually work. Where I have taken liberties with technical details, it has been in service of the story or to avoid providing a blueprint for real-world fraud.

If this book makes you look twice at the systems we trust with our identities, then it has done its job.

Scott Tisch
    May 2026